# The Four McKeans

# Passport to Courage

## Character-in-Action Adventure #1

## by Elizabeth L. Hamilton

Character-in-Action
An imprint of *Quiet* **Impact** Inc
www.character-in-action.com

Passport to Courage
Character-in-Action Adventure #1

 Printed in the United States of America. For more information, please visit the publisher's web sites:

www.quietimpact.com
or
www.character-in-action.com

ISBN 0 - 9713749 - 3 - 7

First Quiet Impact Edition, 2002

*For David, my husband,*
*who is truly*
*a man of character,*
*a man who has the*
*courage of his convictions*
*and lives accordingly,*

*and for all those who*
*aspire to courage*
*and a life of*
*character-in-action.*

Acknowledgments

In the heat of writing, it often seems I have only my characters to assist me. I am caught in a vacuum with them, and only they can help the work get done. In reality, though, books are never written in a vacuum, and I have both God and a number of people to thank for helping this one come to fruition.

My thanks, first and always, to the Lord God, for giving me creative ideas and the gift to write, as well as health and strength to complete this book. Second, to my husband, David, for his patience, encouragement, and loving support — and for editing the work with clarity and discernment.

To the real Morgan Britton and the real Bartlett family, whom I fictionalized. Morgan, a former exchange student to New Zealand, allowed me to use her name, her journals, and her newsletters. The Bartlett family, who provided support and inspiration when I taught in New Zealand, also allowed me to use their names, and some aspects of their family life. To my daughter, Deborah, for her professional help on music, and to my son, Mark, for teaching me the value of unexplored territory. Thank you all for your inestimable help and thoughtfulness.

Thanks also to Seifried's Vineyard Restaurant and the Oamaru Blue Penguin Colony for permission to feature their establishments.

# Table of Contents

# COURAGE

(opposite = fear; cowardice)

Doing the right thing in the face of difficulty and obstacles; taking the consequences of your actions, no matter how frightening they are.

Being true to what you know to be right, and standing on your convictions; following a good conscience instead of following your peers; speaking up for the right.

Courage is having *knowledge* of and taking *action* on that which is right.

# 1

## Fear and Death

Fear arrived just before Easter of 2001. At the time, Andrew dismissed the presence as a vague uneasiness, a fleeting sense that he might have been smarter to have stayed out of it. Of course, *it* was nothing more than a prank, or so Andrew tried to reason. This foreboding would pass once people forgot — especially the police.

But the police did not forget, nor did anyone else in Wilmington. And Fear did not leave. Not by a long shot. It moved in, bag and baggage, took up residence in his mind, fed on his guilt, and grew strong.

By the time Death knocked, on August 28, Fear was tough, poised to destroy the lives of both Andrew and Penny, his girl.

Not that Andrew knew that on August 30. Andrew had not even met Penny yet, let alone imagine that his fear might destroy her life.

No. Today, August 30, sitting here on the back deck with his two kid sisters and his kid brother, Andrew knew only that Fear had choked off his personal flow of peace, and now it had a partner — Death.

There ought to be some kind of law against a sixteen-year-old finding a dead body, especially in his own home. Not a law that got you into trouble when you found the dead person, but a law that somehow made it impossible for you to find him in the first place. But there was not such a law, and he had found the dead body.

The teen looked down from his perch astride the deck's wide redwood railing, and surveyed the faces of his three younger siblings. They were so innocent. He should appear cool and unconcerned for their sakes, as if that were possible these days.

He shook a lock of coppery red hair out of his eyes and pushed his shoulders downward. "Relax. Relax. Relax," he breathed slowly to his muscles — but stronger orders urged, "Prepare for battle."

His long legs twitched, and he permitted the left one to vibrate rapidly. What if someone found out before the funeral? He scanned the street. It was empty in both directions.

Alicia, his fourteen-year-old sister, was saying something about their grandfather. Her voice registered in his brain, but not her words.

Andrew shuddered and pulled his black suit coat tighter around him. His mind's eye stared in shock again at the sight of the man lying dead on the kitchen floor. Gray. Still. Lifeless. A shard of broken coffee mug was clutched in the man's right hand, and a warm puddle of milk mingled with darkened blood beside the head.

"If only," Andrew bemoaned silently, "I hadn't decided to get a midnight snack."

"If I had stayed in bed, Mom would have discovered him the next morning. Mom would have been the one to take the shock; to scream for Dad; to help tug the heavy body away from the refrigerator; to call an ambulance."

Why did Grandfather have to die now? Why couldn't this heart attack have been mild like the previous ones? The ambulance could have taken him to the hospital for a few hours, the pain would have subsided, he would have been released, and he would have been back in his office the next day.

"Hey, Grandfather," he wanted to shout, "you need to reschedule your death. I'm in big trouble, and you were going to discuss it with me. Remember? You promised."

He let his tall, athletic body slump forward, and rubbed the head of his little gray schnauzer.

"Let's play baseball." Twelve-year-old Cathryn held out a well-oiled brown leather mitt.

He stared blankly at her.

"Come on, Andrew." She bent to peer into his face, and her long hair fell over one shoulder in a tangle of papaya curls. "You boys can bat first."

"Not baseball. You eternally choose baseball." Caleb's young shoulders drooped beneath his navy suit coat. "Andrew, tell her no. She's always so domineering. We should play quietly today."

Andrew shoved his thoughts, and jumped from the rail, reaching for the mitt. "Come on, Caleb. It's not going to kill you." He scooped up a baseball and tossed it into Caleb's hands.

The ball frolicked briefly among the thin, freckled white fingers, bumped most of them, avoided all of their efforts at entrapment, and fell to rest at the toes of the boy's small black shoes.

Andrew laughed shortly and shuffled down the stairs. At the foot of them, he stopped to shove dark sunglasses up across his own freckles, and to order the barking Schnauzie to stay.

Alicia and Cathryn followed Andrew, but Caleb stayed on the deck. "Come on," he called after them. "Let's play checkers or something." Nobody even paused. Caleb watched them run across the yard, and groaned. "Oh, all right. I'll play baseball on the outside, but on the inside I'm practicing Beethoven," he muttered. He picked up the dirty white sphere, and plodded after them.

Andrew was standing at home plate, the bat resting on his right shoulder. His body seemed ready, but his eyes were flitting from shrubs and trees to the fence that surrounded the vacant lot.

"What's wrong with you?" Cathryn called from the mound. "You're as nervous as a long-tailed cat in a room full of rocking chairs."

"Nothing's wrong. Just pitch the ball." He frowned and showed her a vicious practice swing. Then he stepped away from the plate, pounded the bat against his shoe, and squinted his concentration back to the business at hand.

But Fear had no intention of letting him off easy. It filled his mind with dire predictions. It made his nerves twitch, muscles tighten.

"Leave me alone," Andrew hissed inwardly. "You don't let me enjoy anything." He thought about throwing down the bat and leaving, but there's something about baseball, and Andrew felt that something as he stepped back into the batter's box. It sent eager adrenaline coursing through his body. He hoisted the bat into position again. He spread his feet wide, and screwed his right toe firmly into the dirt at the back of the box.

"Play ball," he shouted.

A low, wide pitch whistled past his ankles. He laughed loudly, scooped it up, and tossed it back to Cathryn. "Ball one."

A fast ball slammed past him. "Strike one!"

A curve caught him looking. "Strike two!"

Okay. Cathryn was good, but not that good. Andrew adjusted his position, gave a few more practice swings, then clobbered Cathryn's fast ball.

"Moon shot!" he crowed. He charged away from home plate, snorting against the ball's dust in his nose, pounding down the hard track, and touching first base a mere instant before the dirty orb peaked in its trajectory.

"I've got it!" Alicia shouted into the sun.

"Not a chance!" Andrew hooted as he skimmed the line from first to second. The thud of his shoe on second synchronized with the thump of the ball hitting the ground. Alicia missed it! She was quick, though — and a good thrower.

His eyes fastened on the dilapidated, once-blue pillow that served as third base. His hands eagerly anticipated the grubbiness of it. His legs pumped toward it, and his ears heard the frenzied cries of the other players: "Third! Third!"

Then, inexplicably, time braked to slow motion. He felt each foot rock slowly forward, lift, and float lazily upward from the hard dirt; felt it break the air of late summer, and drift back down to the base line. He saw Caleb's green-bean-skinny body in its navy suit, his head topped with a shock of carrot hair; saw him watching, his pale blue eyes big behind the gold-rimmed glasses; intently watching the arc of the incoming ball. Now Caleb, too, was rising — up, slowly up, awkwardly up into the cool air, his slate blue necktie floating lazily skyward in the breeze. His thin hand reached for the dawdling ball that seemed to hang on some invisible thread.

Andrew shook his head as time accelerated to normalcy. Abruptly, Caleb no longer ascended, but plummeted rapidly to the ground, his mitt empty, his legs buckling under him.

"Hey, Caleb!" Andrew jeered, "What do you have on that glove? Teddy bear grease?"

"Get the ball!" Cathryn screamed.

But Caleb lay still, frighteningly still.

"Get the ball, Caleb," yelled Andrew. He took one mocking giant step, then stopped.

Caleb wasn't pretending. He was in real pain. He sobbed in big gulps of pain.

Andrew flew to his younger brother's side, descending into the thick field dust with not a thread of consideration for his own dark dress suit.

"What happened? Did you wrench your ankle when you landed? Does it hurt terribly?" Andrew knew first aid for sports injuries, but what was injured — a leg — an arm?

"My finger. My finger," Caleb wailed. Tears coursed through the dusty hollows of his cheeks. "My Beethoven finger's broken!" He clenched the throbbing, crucial center finger of the right hand.

Alicia knelt beside him. "Let me see," she coaxed, prying with her own long, delicate fingers. She saw no blood, but neither did she see much of the actual finger. "All right," she conceded. "I won't look, but let's have Mom check it."

Alicia jumped up, holding out graceful, but grimy hands to help Caleb gain his feet. She looked at the woeful condition of his dress suit. Did she look like that? Hastily, she scanned her clothing. The front of her full, black ramie skirt wore twin dusty knee prints. She brushed frantically, then tugged the back of her hemline forward and brushed three splotches of sandy dust from it.

Caleb hadn't risen. "It's broken, I tell you. My right finger's broken," he repeated. He moaned piteously. What would his piano teacher say, with competition only weeks away? He wouldn't be able to practice now.

Andrew jumped up. "Let's hear it for Caleb!" he cheered, and the girls applauded. "You were brave to try for that ball," he added.

But Caleb ignored the charade. He stood, submitted to Andrew's arm around his shoulders, and walked toward home.

Cathryn and Alicia hovered about them, asking repeatedly how Caleb felt, until they reached the edge of the lot. Then, Cathryn broke away and raced ahead, papaya curls bouncing about her shoulders.

"Mom!" she shouted loudly. "Mom, Caleb broke his finger!" She unleashed a shrill whistle.

Upstairs, Mrs. McKean paused before her mirror. "Fiddlesticks!" she fumed. "I never get all four of those redheads ready for more than a minute at a time. I'm in my bedroom," she called. She fumbled with a last pin to secure her rich auburn hair on top of her head, fastened the double strand of creamy pearls around her neck, and smoothed the modest lines of her simple black dress. She paused before the mirror to notice with pleasure the natural rosy flush that highlighted her youthful face. She jumped up as her offspring jostled into the room.

"He was catching Alicia's throw, and he fell and broke his finger," reported Cathryn.

"No, I didn't." Caleb relinquished his hold on the finger long enough to swipe his running nose. "I was *trying* to catch Alicia's throw, but the ball hit my finger, and crooked it backwards, and broke it. Then I tripped and fell. My finger was already broken when I fell. The *ball* broke it. It was the *ball*, not the fall." Understand? The baseball was to blame — the hateful, filthy baseball.

"Patsy Bolivar!" Mom had two near expletives with unknown origins: *Patsy Bolivar* and *Fiddlesticks*. She came no closer to swearing.

"Patsy Bolivar," she said again. "Why were you playing baseball in your best clothes – and today of all days?" Mom surveyed them angrily, giving each the full force of her daunting green-eyed glare before moving to the next. "Andrew, what were you thinking? You should have known better. You are the eldest. I just don't know what has gotten into you lately. You act as though you're off on another planet somewhere."

"What!" Andrew seethed. He couldn't do anything right anymore. Mom found fault with everything. Everything. He opened his mouth to blurt a retort, to tell Mom it had been her precious little daughter's idea to play baseball, not his.

But Mom had turned to scrutinize her daughters. "Cathryn, look at you! Go and scrub, and do it thoroughly. And Alicia." Mom glared at the elder of her two girls. "Go with Cathryn, and see if you can achieve a degree of respectability without further ruining your dresses."

Andrew followed them as far as the door, where he turned. Mom was thrusting tissues at Caleb for his brimming eyes and flowing nose, reaching gently to take the unsightly finger in her hands. Her alto voice assumed a special softness as she told Caleb to bend his finger.

Oh, sure — tenderness for Caleb. Right on, Mom. Caleb can do no wrong.

He watched Caleb try to comply, try to bend the finger as instructed – and it did bend, very well, but Caleb yelled anyway. “Ouch!”

Huh! Pure exaggeration.

Mom placed the hand in Caleb’s lap. “Only a sprain,” she diagnosed. “It needs RICE: rest, ice, compression, and elevation. You will have to keep it in an elastic bandage with ice on it, and hold it up from now through the funeral,” she ordered.

The funeral! Andrew pulled back his dusty sleeve, and looked at his watch. They must leave for Grandfather’s funeral in ten minutes!

Fear jumped up again, and doused his mind in venom. People at the funeral would know all about *it* — the sheriff would be waiting, would wait until after the funeral, and then cuff Andrew. He dared not go. He couldn’t take the risk. “Mom…” he started.

“Whatever it is, no!” she snapped at him, “Not after what you’ve done!”

“After what *I* have done? So now it’s my fault that Caleb can’t catch a dumb baseball!”

“No, Andrew, it is not your fault that Caleb doesn’t play ball well, but it is your fault that he played ball today.” Mom said.

"Oh. Right!" Andrew swore silently. "I'll get my darling brother an ice pack," he snapped. He dashed from the bedroom, down the gray carpeted stairway, and into the kitchen. Mom probably would have Dad ground Andrew. "I'll probably have to serve six months for one stinking turn at bat," he muttered.

He yanked the ice pack from the freezer and heard Fear whisper coldly, "You're going to serve much longer than six months if one of the guys has told. They'll get you at the funeral."

Fear was right. He must not go. There must be some way to avoid going. Fear tormented him further. "You knew it was disrespectful to play baseball just before the funeral — especially when you were dressed for the funeral. You knew also that it was cruel to force your younger brother to play baseball when said brother loathes every sport ever invented, including baseball."

"Most of all," Fear hissed, "you knew that it was cowardly to go along with the guys when they suggested doing something so totally wrong, regardless of your reasons for doing *it* — and that's the coldest truth of all."

Andrew was trembling. He looked for a towel to wrap around the ice pack. "Mom's right to a degree. I should be more responsible, but four times more responsible so that Alicia, Cathryn and Caleb have no responsibility?"

He ignored Fear's final accusation, focusing on the least of the three evils and anticipating the lecture Dad would give when grounding him, which he surely would do. "Andrew, you must form the courage to do what you know is right — no matter what a brother, sister, or anyone else says."

Dad always used the exact same words. They must be written in bold print on page one of How to Raise Andrew McKean.

Andrew threw a hand towel around the ice pack and stomped up the stairs. He watched as Mom placed the ice on the finger, but he avoided her hazel green eyes, knowing the disappointment he would find if he met her full gaze. No, he could not ask Mom for help. He slipped quietly from her sight and went to wait in the downstairs hall.

* * * * *

Andrew was sixteen that Saturday in late August, and normally as prudent a young man as ever would enter the high schools of Wilmington, Delaware. He was the pride of his father and mother, their firstborn son. Ecstatic at the baby's birth, William and Margaret McKean gave the boy two names that defined the kind of man he would one day become, if some divine authority were pleased to grant their desires:

Andrew, which meant *manly courage*
Trevor, which meant *prudence*
He was Andrew Trevor McKean.

The father and mother had watched the boy from the moment of birth on that twenty-seventh day of May, eager for any indication of those two great traits — especially of the manly courage.

They marked each birthday with a framed photo bearing a quote about courage. These they hung on his bedroom walls, hoping that the mere presence of the great words would assist the boy in building manly courage.

The first year's quote was short and, of course, incomprehensible to a one-year-old boy:

> "One man with courage makes a majority."
>
> Andrew Jackson

As their little Andrew grew, however, both the quotes and his comprehension grew with him. On his thirteenth birthday, they presented his favorite — a military scene bearing the words:

> Last, but by no means least, is courage — moral courage, the courage of one's convictions, the courage to see things through. The world is in a constant conspiracy against the brave. It's the age-old struggle — the roar of the crowd on one side and the voice of your conscience on the other.
>
> Douglas MacArthur

Then, on May 27 of this year, Dad and Mom gave him the sixteenth quote, lettered in sweeping calligraphy upon a painting of the American Colonial Congress:

> I love the man that can smile in trouble, that can gather strength from distress, and grow brave by reflection. 'Tis the business of little minds to shrink, but he whose heart is firm, and whose conscience approves his conduct, will pursue his principles unto death.
>
> Thomas Paine

Yes, Mr. and Mrs. McKean wanted their firstborn son to be a man of character, and they believed that the foundation of character is to have courage — the courage of one's convictions.

They saw small glimmers of such courage in Andrew — enough to give them hope that he would someday embody his name. For example, as recently as the now-fading summer, Andrew had gone to a friend's party, only to leave early when the other teen had produced a keg of beer, announcing that all real men drink.

"I'd rather be a legal boy than an illegal real man," Andrew had said, and he had walked out accompanied by the jeers of his friends.

Reports of such incidents sent the parents' hopes soaring, but others, such as today's ball game, triggered a steep dive. It would be a crash dive if they learned about the pre-Easter caper, but of course they must not learn about that.

His siblings would never learn. They learned very little of what their big brother did, or whether he was developing *manly courage*. Who cared? Not Alicia or Cathryn. Not Caleb, who had just turned eleven.

They cared only that Andrew was their CEO — Chief Escapade Officer. Caleb had dubbed him that last year. The whole idea was childish, and he would die if the other guys ever heard it, but it was an honor of sorts — a recognition by the girls and Caleb that he was their leader. True, he led into trouble sometimes, as Mom claimed, but he also had engineered some great escapades.

* * * * *

Even now, while Cathryn scrubbed as if to remove every last freckle, she agonized to her older sister, "What will we do if Mom tells Dad? He's just sure to put Andrew on clampdown, and there's no way any of us can go tonight without our CEO."

"He'll go even if he is on clampdown, but we better get so clean that Dad asks no questions." Alicia fluttered about with washcloth and brush, trying to make both of them presentable. By the time she finished, her strawberry head shone again beside Cathryn's deep papaya — and none too soon!

From the hall, the cuckoo summoned with three melodious calls, and the girls raced down the stairs to join their brothers. They all were ready, just at the hour Dad had appointed.

Mom inspected them, found nothing but a tiny grass stain that hid on the underside of Caleb's cuff, and sent them quickly and quietly to climb into her minivan. Alicia and Andrew took the back seat, Caleb and Cathryn took the middle.

Dad, unobservant as usual, didn't see Caleb's grass stain. He didn't notice the bandaged finger — or the ice pack. Dad just slid quietly into the driver's seat and asked for silence so they would all be in a proper frame for the funeral.

Andrew breathed a noiseless sigh of relief, and the four complied with Dad's wishes. They were silent, completely silent. But the two in back, even in silence, were incredibly communicative.

Andrew always carried the CEOP: the Chief Escapade Officer's Pad, which was very useful for daily plans, and for secretive times such as this. He pulled it from an inner pocket, and wrote in his tiny script, "Dad and Mom will be in bed by eleven o'clock. We leave at eleven-thirty in the minivan. I have the extra keys." He shoved the CEOP at Alicia, and arched a perfect eyebrow.

Alicia read it, glanced nervously at Dad, then mouthed in awe, "You're driving?"

Andrew nodded and winked, temporarily laying aside his trouble. His siblings all were easy to impress, but Alicia required no effort at all. Her wonderment at his decision to drive was proof.

"You don't have a license," she mouthed, wrinkles running across her ivory forehead.

"Dad's fault."

It was, too. He could have gotten his license the moment he was 15 years and 10 months old. All he needed was the certificate proving that he had passed the Delaware Driver Education Course. That he didn't have because Mom was home-schooling them, but he still would have the license if Dad had been willing to sign as sponsor — which he wasn't. But so what? Lots of kids drove without a license. There must be thousands. How difficult could it be to drive? Only stupidity made people take the driver education course just to get a driver's license.

Huh! These were the United States of America, and the *Constitution* surely included the right to drive, didn't it, along with freedom of speech, freedom to assemble, etc.? Nobody would make him get a speech license before allowing him to write in a school paper what he thought about the cafeteria's mystery meat — if he was in school. He didn't have to apply for an assembly license to attend church; nor did he need a trial license to get a fair trial. He cringed at that particular thought, but goaded his mind forward. Why did he need permission to drive? In fact, why was anyone licensed? Wasn't it unconstitutional? Did the writers of the *Constitution* have to get licenses to ride their horses?

"I'm sorry, Paul Revere," he imagined. "You can't ride tonight unless you pass the test for your horseman's license!"

They weren't licensed to drive the horses that pulled their carriages, either, and cars were horseless carriages, so what gave the government a right to make you get a license to drive a car?

He would drive tonight, and it would be easy. He made certain Dad and Mom couldn't see as he clutched an imaginary steering wheel, and looked jauntily down the highway.

Alicia reached for his pen, and sketched a heavy iron gate on the CEOP, scratching a bold question mark after it.

Around a grin, Andrew mouthed, "Opened by rust — or ghosts."

Andrew secreted the CEOP inside his coat, and sat back. The van moved down the expressway, through the city streets, and quietly up to the in-town funeral parlor. Fear re-emerged.

The funeral director had reserved the spot behind the hearse, since Dad was the eldest son of Timothy McKean, and they merged into the morose line of vehicles. Sorrow harnessed even their imaginations now, as they surveyed the large number of mourners' cars. Grandfather McKean had been highly esteemed in the community. There was Senator Curry. He and Grandfather had gone to high school together. The police chief chauffeured the Mayor and Judge Schilling. There were an attorney, three clergymen, bankers from four banks, and even an army general. All were dressed in black. All of their spouses were in black.

It took thirty slow minutes to gain the gates of the old country cemetery, and thirty more for the service, officiated by the three clergymen.

The McKeans remained dry-eyed until the end of the service, until the mahogany casket slid evenly and slowly into the freshly dug hole, and was blanketed with a thin layer of finality.

Grandfather was gone.

Andrew rubbed repeatedly to get the grave dirt out of his eyes, and peered through the sudden fog. Grandfather was gone, and there was no one to discuss the problem with him — unless....

Unless Caleb's plan worked, superstitious and childish though it was. Logic rebuked him, but Fear was stronger than logic. What choice did he have — prison?

He leaned toward the grave. "See you tonight, Grandfather," he promised. Fear choked the whisper within his swelling throat.

# 2

## A Paua Box

There was little time after the funeral for Andrew to think about the promise to his deceased grandfather — little time and little desire.

His first concern was to escape the prying eyes of the law. Judge Schilling, Sheriff Thomson, and the police chief had sat on the opposite side of the grave during the service, and now approached around freshly-mounded dirt to offer condolences to Dad and Mom.

Andrew stood quickly. “I have something in my eye,” he told Mom. “I’m going to the car.”

Mom was preoccupied with a handkerchief that stubbornly refused to discriminate between tears and mascara. She nodded, but then clutched at his arm. “Take time to greet people, Andrew,” she said without looking at him. “It isn’t polite to go running off without speaking when they have come to honor your grandfather.”

"But Mom, I have something in my eye."

"Andrew, we all have something in our eyes. They are called tears, and they're not a thing of shame." She tightened her grasp and looked up at him through her own hazel mist.

"Let go, Mom. People will see." He glanced around furtively. He couldn't spot the judge or the sheriff now. Where were they?

"Promise me you will take time to thank people for coming to the funeral."

"All right, all right already." He pulled his arm from her grasp, turned quickly, and collided head-on with Judge Schilling.

"Oh, I'm terribly sorry, Andrew." The judge steadied him with a large, strong hand on his shoulder. He kept it there as he continued, "We haven't run into each other since last Easter, have we?" He laughed quietly at his own joke.

"No, sir. I guess we haven't."

"Well, I'm so sorry it has to be an occasion such as this. Your grandfather was a great man, Andrew. One of the finest this community has ever known. Please accept my sympathy. He was so proud of you. Many's the time he told me what a fine grandson you were."

Fear chuckled inside Andrew's brain and he ducked his shoulder, but the hand remained.

"Grandfather was prejudiced, sir," Andrew said, "but thank you for the compliment — and thank you for coming to the funeral."

"It was a sorrowful pleasure, Andrew." The judge started to release his grip, but tightened it again as he said, "That was quite a performance you and the other boys put on last Easter."

Andrew's face betrayed him, especially his eyebrows. "Last Easter?" he squawked.

This time Judge Schilling did release the shoulder. He smiled as he clapped Andrew on the back. "Yes, my boy, I don't get to hear the choir sing often, being a Christmas/Easter Christian, but you did a glorious job of that cantata. I look forward to the Christmas program." He stepped back. "I must let you go now, though. Others will want to speak with you. Drop by my office sometime and get acquainted."

Andrew nodded mutely.

Judge Schilling continued to his goal and was soon hugging Mom, shaking hands with Dad.

Andrew fled, and waited for the family in the black van. Dad and Mom seemed to take forever, but at last they came to the van, and Dad started the engine, suddenly eager to leave. "I want to go directly to my dad's house. Now that my parents both have died, and we'll be moving into their home, we need to make a few plans.

There will be no time to settle before school starts on Tuesday, and it's going to make for a rush, but I think we should move on Labor Day."

Dad didn't want to admit that the rush of the move would start tomorrow, Sunday, not on Labor Day — the rush and the mournful task of going through Grandfather's personal effects. But that was tomorrow. This evening they would visit the house just to be sure all was well.

Hushed thoughts pervaded the car as the McKeans left the highway, and pursued a wide boulevard. The silence swelled with tension as Dad left the boulevard, drove between towering wrought iron gates and down a cobblestone drive. The dogwood trees on either side of the drive were turning crimson in the crisp pre-September air, a dramatic contrast to the funereal black that draped the massive oaken door of the mansion.

Grandfather's house itself stood safe in the curve of the circular drive, protected in front by a crescent of box elder, in back by a row of Norway pines. Everything seemed unchanged.

But Grandfather was gone.

Andrew felt it more here than he had at the funeral. They all did. Caleb even closed his book and gazed at the mansion.

Dad parked the black van near the porch, switched off the engine, and cleared his throat.

"Grandfather had a premonition of death a week ago," he said gravely. "He told me he had prepared an envelope for each of us. He sealed them with wax, and left them on the living room mantel. I don't know what's in them, but this is a serious event. We will go in together, and we will open them together." But Dad didn't move.

Andrew watched Dad stare toward the home. He made no move to open his door. Mom, too, looked at the old mansion, and made no move. Nobody moved. They sat very still, very quiet, and gazed at the beautiful old manor house.

It was not foreign to them. They knew it as well as they knew their own home. Even in their sleep, they all could have climbed the fifteen broad gray steps that led from the light brown cobblestones to the wide front porch. They knew the old house — knew it well — knew that not one stone or beam of it had changed.

But Grandfather was gone.

Abruptly, Andrew snapped the silence. "Let's go," he said quietly. He flung open the car door and started for the house. Caleb was close behind, his thin legs half-skipping to keep up to his tall, athletic brother. Andrew waited for him, then slowed to a more respectful pace.

"There's probably a big check for each of us in those envelopes," he whispered, "and I know just what I'll do with mine."

"Buy a batting cage probably."

"No. I would have last summer. I'd have bought one of those aluminum batting cages with green net. But there's something more important now. Something I have to do — something urgent."

"What is it, Andrew? I won't tell."

"I know you won't, because I won't tell you."

"Well, I bet there's no check anyhow. I think each envelope holds a treasure map to the McKean gold, which is probably buried somewhere on the property." Caleb had never heard of any gold, but the idea had merit.

Andrew mounted the smooth-worn steps in silence; then, turning to stare intently at Caleb, broke the sorrowful afternoon air with a spine-chilling rattle. "Yes, yes. A treasure map! Gold! Gold guarded by hideous poltergeists! Gold guarded by Apparitions Anonymous Association!"

Caleb giggled.

"Ghosts-R-Us working 24/7/365 to watch over your gold," elaborated Andrew.

"Security ghosts: carefully selected, highly trained and licensed for professional invisibility!" Caleb collapsed in laughter on the porch floor.

Alicia came up behind them. "You boys are so crass!" she exclaimed. "How can you go on about ghosts at a time like this?"

Andrew sobered. "Aw, we were just talking about what might be in the envelopes."

"Oh? Well I, for one, hope each envelope holds a photo of Grandfather and Grandmother together. I'll put mine in the little silver picture frame I got from Grandfather last Christmas." She sat down on the top step and veiled her face with strawberry hair. Was Grandfather McKean really dead? She shivered and put her head on her knees.

Dad finally had left the car and now arrived to unlock the door. The foursome, impatient to unseal their envelopes, stepped in the minute the door swung open, walked quickly and quietly through the hall, and took seats in the living room.

"Hurry, Mom. Sit here." Cathryn bounced onto an obese sofa.

"Don't bounce, Cathryn. It isn't ladylike." Mom sat, straightening her black skirt and crossing her ankles to one side.

All eyes eagerly urged Dad to action, but that was not Dad's style.

Andrew groaned when he saw the right hand reach to stroke the red pencil moustache above Dad's lip. Never a good sign. The left hand lifted the blue parchment envelopes from the mantel, but the right hand continued to stroke, fastidiously grooming each hair.

"Grandfather McKean said that these are not cash or checks," began Dad.

Andrew slid onto his spine. Oh well. Hope had survived for a moment. Can't win them all.

"But," continued Dad, "he went on to say that the contents of each is a far greater gift than cash — from him to you."

Andrew glanced at Caleb. Maybe they did contain treasure maps.

"I will hand each of you your envelope, but we will wait until everyone has his or hers before anyone breaks the red wax seal," announced Dad.

He solemnly announced each one's name, then, handed out the envelopes one by one, almost as though it were a graduation ceremony, and paused for effect, his own envelope poised in his left hand.

"Now, we will break the seals."

Alicia studied the little bead of red wax, so carefully embedded with the intricate old seal. It was beautiful. She decided to use sealing wax on all of her letters from now on. She slowly and very carefully slid her fingers under the wax, tearing the envelope, but lifting the fragile little wax seal intact from its pale blue bed.

The other three were not so sensitive, and quickly snapped the red wax blobs.

Caleb, seated on the bench of the big grand piano, yanked his letter from the envelope, and began reading. "Dear Caleb," in a stentorian voice, "it's time you learned that you are a descendant of Thomas McKean, one of the men who signed the *United States Declaration of Independence*. What?" He threw the letter on the piano. "That's my great gift?" He banged the heels of both hands on the locked lid of the keyboard. "So what if some old ancestor signed the *Declaration*? How often does that come up in everyday conversation?"

Andrew hardly heard Caleb, so intently did he open his own letter and read silently: "Dear Andrew, it is time I told you that you are one of the descendants of Thomas McKean, who signed the *United States Declaration of Independence*."

Andrew paused to let it sink in. He had an ancestor named Thomas McKean, and that guy had signed the *Declaration of Independence*. He supposed that was important. It wasn't exactly something you said to a girl the first time you met, of course, like: "Hi, I have an ancestor who signed the *Declaration of Independence*." Still, not everyone he knew had descended from one of those men.

He looked over at Dad, standing in front of the big marble fireplace. "Dad, does this mean we're descendants of *the* Thomas McKean? The one after whom they named a Wilmington high school — the school I start attending next week?"

"Hm — yes, that's right."

Andrew read from the beginning again. "You are a descendent of ...." He read the same sentence four times. If what Grandfather wrote were true....

"Wait a minute, Dad. Do you mean you didn't know until today that he was our great, great something?" Andrew's voice cracked, much to his annoyance, but he pursued the question. "How long have you known, Dad?"

"Since I was ten," Dad admitted in his quiet, precise manner. "I told your mother before we got married, but we opted to not tell you until you were adults because we wanted to keep you out of the reach of that limelight. We wanted you to gain notoriety on your own, if you were to be famous, not grow up cloaked in someone else's fame."

Andrew nodded noncommittally. Actually, he might have guessed he was related to Thomas McKean if he gave history the same love he gave Latin and science, but he hated history. "Am I anything like Thomas McKean?"

"Very much like him," Dad answered. "You already have that Irishman's tall, erect build; his firm, intelligent face; and his well-proportioned body." Dad refrained from adding that Andrew also had the McKean temper, quick to resent any slight intrusion upon his territory or his rights.

Dad might as well have mentioned it, though, for as he spoke Andrew was pondering what right Dad had to withhold information about his ancestor. The information belonged to him. It was part of his birthright. Andrew tried to shake off the affront, and went back to reading.

Dad watched him a moment, absently grooming the moustache again. Then he said, "I hope the rest of you aren't too disappointed. Mom and I really did think it was best to wait."

"Oh, Dad!" Alicia jumped up to dance over and lean against her father. "You should have told us, but I forgive you! It's so romantic! Just think! McKean women were part of the high class of their day. They waltzed in the most elite balls, some of them in this very room! I can almost smell their perfume and hear their gowns swishing. We are high society girls! Me and Cathryn and Mom."

She paused, looked at Mom, and modulated her voice. "Oh, I guess you aren't part of those McKeans, are you? Your last name was O'Hearn. I'm sorry." She looked down at her letter and walked quietly back to her chair.

For a few minutes, everyone was quiet.

Caleb, ignoring their general excitement, fingered a left-handed eulogy on the keyboard cover of the big cherry piano. He wished he had brought his book in from the car. Queequeg was far more engrossing than a long-dead ancestor. Even his exotic name was exciting. He pictured Queequeg, covered with tattoos and shaving with the blade of a whaler's harpoon.

"Hey, here's something weird." Andrew was on his feet again. "I am to have Thomas McKean's old *paua* box." He stumbled over the strange word, pronouncing it *paw-oo'-uh.*

"What kind of box?" they all chorused.

"I don't know. I never heard of the word," said Andrew. "What is it, Dad?"

Dad shook his head. "I don't know. I don't recall my father ever speaking of such a box."

"Maybe the P-box is full of gold!" Caleb's dream revived in an instant, and he leaped from the piano bench, grabbing up his own letter with new hope. "Or at least it contains the treasure map to where they buried the McKean gold! That's what it is. All we have to do is find the P-box, follow the map, and we're rich! We're rich!"

"No, it's filled with diamonds." Alicia unleashed her imagination. "The women's jewelry. They packed it away in the P-box."

"Please don't call it that," begged Mom. "It sounds like bathroom talk."

Cathryn giggled. "But P-box is the perfect name for it, Mom. Our P-box is our prize box."

Andrew stretched his sixteen-year-old frame to its full 5' 10" and affected adult dignity. "Children, children, don't get excited. The P-box is not *ours*, but *mine*. Grandfather gave it to me."

The younger McKeans deflated.

"Does Grandfather say anything more — a description of it, maybe — or where he kept it — or who gave it to him — does he say anything else about it?" Alicia asked hesitantly.

"No, he doesn't give any detail. He just writes, 'I want you to have the *p-a-u-a* box,'" he spelled the odd word this time. "Then he says, 'You will be in charge of it and its contents.'"

Andrew handed the letter to Dad. "Sounds like a mystery, Dad. What do you make of it?"

"A mystery!" Caleb was delighted. "We should start hunting right away. Maybe it's in here." He opened the piano bench on which he had been sitting, and rummaged through the music.

"No, Caleb," said Dad. "You will not start hunting now. It's past dinner time already, we're tired, and we have a lot of work tomorrow to get ready for the move. Whatever and wherever that box is, it is bound to turn up as we sort things."

"Oh, listen!" said Alicia. "Here's something else in my letter. The beginning is like the rest, about Thomas McKean and all, but then it says that I am to have a special gift, the details of which are in the p-a-u-a box. Now you have to admit the P-box is ours, and not just yours, Andrew."

Dad smiled tiredly. "I think my father wanted his four adventurers to have another quest, but first we're going to have to find out what p-a-u-a means, and then find the box that fits." He returned Andrew's letter, and gazed off into space, stroking his moustache.

"Hey, maybe there's something in the box for me." Cathryn decided to finish her letter, now that there was more to it than a famous dead man.

"Here's my inheritance!" said Caleb. "The grand piano is mine!" He frowned. "Oh. It's mine after I get its key out of the P-box. Great!" He threw the letter on the piano a second time. "I'll be a concert pianist with my own Bosendorfer by the time we find the dumb P-box." He scowled blackly, muttering a few forbidden words under his breath.

Alicia got up to look over her younger sister's shoulder. "What do you get, Cathryn?"

"I don't know," said Cathryn glumly. "Grandfather just says there's something for me, but he doesn't say what."

"I'm sure you'll be happy with it when you get it," said Dad, "but right now, we need to get to Mario's. I thought it would be all right to go off the heart-healthy diet for one evening."

"Pastabilities!" Cathryn brightened. "We don't get to go to Pastabilities very often. May we order anything we want, 'cause if so, I'm going to order baked Cannelloni! I love that shrimp, and lobster and stuff Mario puts in it. I want a grape smash to drink, and chocolate gelato for dessert."

"It won't take you long to order, will it?" Dad laughed as he motioned toward the door.

Andrew gave a loud "Oink" and made a pig mouth. Mom said Cathryn was chunky — and Dad said she was pleasingly plump, but Andrew called it near-fat. How big would she get before they would make her diet? Alicia was so thin she could slip through a flute without sounding a note, and that was too thin, but Cathryn was getting tubby.

Caleb agreed. "You sure aren't anorexic," he hissed, squeezing into the doorway with her.

Cathryn giggled. "Nope! You're the one who's anorexic!" She shoved her wiry brother out of the way, and bounced through the doorway.

Caleb snorted. "I'd rather be anorexic than plagued with polyphagia." He caught up and pushed past her. "Your P-box gift is probably a pink pig!" Caleb rushed out, and climbed into the van, waiting to slam the door as Cathryn reached for it, and bumping his sore finger in the process.

Actually, this injury was all Andrew's fault, he thought. Andrew was being mean by making

Caleb play ball. Andrew knew Caleb was no good at sports. In the whole family, Caleb was the only one who couldn't play baseball. In the whole McKean family, everybody could play baseball. Cathryn was a girl, and she was in Little League. Even Alicia, who was a ballet-ruffles-and-lace girl could play a decent game. But he, Caleb, a boy, eleven years old going on twelve — he couldn't throw, catch, or hit a baseball. Not only was he not *able* to play baseball, he didn't even have a desire to be able to play baseball. He didn't care that Dad said every red-blooded American boy played baseball. He didn't. He hated the hard feel of the ball on his hand. He was a baseball klutz.

He should have insisted on going in the house and practicing the piano. Andrew should have agreed to checkers or chess, but no. Andrew insisted he go out and toss a stupid, filthy leather sphere around. Now he couldn't practice his Beethoven or play chess or anything.

Caleb kicked the dull gray seat in front of him. The all-county piano teachers' competition was just two months away, and he couldn't even practice — all because of big show-off Andrew.

Caleb pressed his face against the cold window glass, grumpily nursing both his finger and his feelings. Cathryn bumped him as she fastened her seat belt, and he gave her a whack, but she only laughed.

Alicia, sitting in the back with Andrew, didn't notice. "So, what about this P-box?"

"Yeah, Dad. Who do you think gave it to Grandfather?" Andrew asked.

"I think we need to know *what* it is," said Alicia, "more than we need to know who gave it to Grandfather. I mean, you can know who gave it to him and still have no idea what it is. And if you don't know what it is, how can you hunt for it?"

Andrew was impressed by Alicia's logical approach, and told her so.

"Brain storms can blow through airheads, too," she quipped.

"Alicia's right about not hunting for an unknown quantity," said Dad.

"But we do know it's a box, William. Where might your father have stored a box?" Mom was as intrigued as anyone.

"If it's a large box, he probably put it in the workshop or the garage. He could have put a small box inside the house — in the den, in a bedroom, in a cupboard — anywhere. The whole thing is a mystery to me, but a mystery that I definitely am willing to let wait until tomorrow." Dad parked by the curb in front of Mario's restaurant and opened his door. "I'm exhausted this evening, and we all have a tremendous amount of work to do tomorrow. Let's forget about the P-box for now."

Dad got out and went around to open Mom's door, as always. He was fond of quoting John Wanamaker: "Courtesy is the one coin you can never have too much of or be stingy with." Dad always was courteous and, unfortunately, insisted that his sons learn the same courtesy — learn by practicing on their sisters.

Caleb flung himself from the van's back door and went around to open the door for Cathryn. "Come on," he growled.

Andrew crawled over Alicia to the door, stumbled to the ground, turned in mock gallantry, and offered his arm. He begged to differ with Mr. Wanamaker. You definitely could have too much of a good thing — including this kind of courtesy.

Inside the restaurant, Mario personally seated them, and said he would order for them. "Dinner is on me," he said, "out of respect to the grandfather, may he rest in peace."

Dad's protests were weak at best, and soon a waiter produced an amazing array of food. Mario stood by, announcing each dish as it arrived:

*Deep-fried mozzarella sticks.*
*Baked New Zealand green lip mussels.*
*Buffalo chicken salad with ranch dressing.*
*Mario's broccoli rigatoni.*
*Classic spaghetti and meatballs for the kids.*
*Sauteed shrimp and scallops over risotto.*
*Veal spezzato zingara.*

Much to Cathryn's dismay, the food stopped coming then. Mario beamed at her. "Why is your face so long, little Cathryn?"

Cathryn glanced at Mom, and was about to answer when the waiter appeared again.

"Maybe you will like this." Mario plucked the steaming dish from the waiter and set before her a plate of baked Cannelloni, complete with succulent shrimp, and lobster.

Cathryn's grin returned. She had to wait while the waiter served some kind of chicken dish, but at last they were able to begin eating.

Sensitive to Dad's wishes, not one of them mentioned the box. In fact, there was little talk during the meal. The food was delicious, they were weary, and the talk centered on those two facts.

There was one frightening moment, though. Andrew came near choking on a meatball when two uniformed police officers approached the table. Both men offered quickly to perform the Heimlich Maneuver, but Andrew shook his coughing head, and finally was able to gulp a glass of water.

The officers, he learned, were stopping merely to offer their condolences. They did so and went away, but their visit had awakened Fear.

Fear never liked to watch Andrew enjoy his food, and it set about destroying any appetite that the officers had not stolen.

Andrew dawdled over the rigatoni and the veal, and finally put down his fork.

"Are you sick, Andrew?" asked Mom. She reached a hand toward his forehead.

Andrew pushed his chair away from her and slid down into it. "No, I'm not sick, Mom. Can't a guy stop eating when he wants to? Does there always have to be something wrong?"

That wasn't fair, but Fear affected his tongue as well as his appetite. He had been on the verge of swearing at her.

Andrew tried to think about the P-box. They would have to wait until tomorrow to talk about the P-box, to look for the P-box, but he could think about it. He tried desperately, but Fear turned his thoughts into less pleasant channels.

"Your dad and mom noticed how your little choking episode coincided with the arrival of the cops. You have to get control of yourself. Sure, you want to talk to somebody — but your grandfather is gone. Who will you talk to now?"

There was only one possibility. He looked down at his watch. Midnight was not far away. Only three hours. Three brief hours.

# 3

## Full Moon & White Heather

At precisely 11:30 P.M., a chorus of cheery tree frogs jangled the calm of the boys' bedroom. Andrew came to life instantly, and silenced them with a quick jab to the tiny alarm button. A roll to the left released him from his captain's bed. A second twist brought him to his feet and propelled him toward Caleb's side of the room.

"Caleb, it's time," he whispered.

Caleb awakened promptly, tumbling out of bed and banging his finger on the floor. "Ouch!"

"Sh!" Andrew hissed. He turned toward his bed, and added, "Schnauzie, stay!"

Having slept in jeans and sweatshirts, the boys rapidly tied on running shoes and struggled into their heavy forest green windbreakers. It would be cold at the cemetery.

"I have to go to the bathroom."

"Hold it until we get there. And watch that finger as you go out the window. If Mom and Dad hear us, the jig's up."

With baited breath, Andrew slowly eased open the sliding window, and crawled onto the flat patio roof. What kind of insanity was controlling him? This was little kids' stuff! But he kept going.

A late summer breeze was catching tree shadows as fast as the full moon could create them, and tossing them across dark brown shingles. The two boys shuffled quickly through both dancing shadows and falling leaves to the girls' unlocked bedroom window.

"You waken them," whispered Andrew.

Caleb wasted no time arguing. Andrew was more athletic, but Caleb was lighter, and it took no skill to climb over a window sill.

As he pushed the window open, Andrew hissed, "Don't bang the finger again."

Caleb nodded curtly, brushing aside the filmy white curtains as he went over the sill. He hurried on small, hushed toes to the side of Alicia's white iron canopy bed.

"Alicia. Get up." That's all it took.

Alicia flew from her pink comforter and joined him in wakening Cathryn, who was a bit grumpy until she remembered what they were doing. The girls also had slept in jeans and sweatshirts, and took only fifty seconds to add shoes.

"Don't forget your windbreakers," Andrew whispered from the roof. "It's cold out here."

As the girls grabbed them up and followed Caleb through the window, he turned to whisper, "Do you have the white heather, Alicia?"

She nodded, opening her dark green windbreaker to reveal the four sprigs of delicate white flowers, tucked into an inner pocket.

"Good. Let's go."

The heather was Caleb's brainchild, the whole reason for this midnight expedition, and vital to its success. Andrew applauded Alicia for going to such great trouble to find a florist who would get it for them, especially at this time of year. He hoped it would be worth her effort, but any faith he had in the idea was fading rapidly.

They were on the roof now, happy that Dad and Mom slept in a downstairs bedroom, at the other end of the house. Andrew had positioned a ladder at the far end of the roof, and he motioned them toward the spot. The ladder was gone!

Andrew's conscience argued strongly against going through with Caleb's strange plan, but Fear had not left the building, and there was a small chance that ancient wisdom was right.

Andrew signaled them to sit down. "Wait here," he whispered, feigning confidence.

He sucked huge cleansing breaths, balanced his weight carefully, and inched his way on deep tread soles to the edge of the roof. The branch of a tall oak tree hung over the roof here. It would bear his weight if he didn't thrash too greatly. He placed his hand around the branch, judging the mature wood's strength. Yes, it would support him. That was good news. Further good news was that no other boughs intersected this one as it reached from the trunk to his meager perch. He ventured a look toward terra firma, and groaned. At least fifteen feet of air wafted between him and it. A fall onto his trick knees would doom a baseball career. Those knees already were perpetuating his surgeon's pot of gold, and they wouldn't take much more abuse.

Andrew paused, whispering to himself one of the courage quotes from his wall collection:

> *You gain strength, courage, and confidence by every experience in which you really stop to look fear in the face. You must do the thing you think you cannot do.*

"All right, Mrs. Roosevelt," he muttered, "I'm going to do the thing I think I cannot do."

He waved at his siblings, twined both hands securely around the branch, gave a strong spring, and encircled the branch with his legs — it held.

Andrew opted for a sloth-like mode toward the trunk of the big tree, though he would not be able to see the trunk, hanging with the copper red crown of his head toward it that way. He could only concentrate on his hands and feet above him, and hope for a successful journey.

As he inched his way along, the summer-parched leaves rustled loudly in his ears, and fell dryly on his nose, in his eyes, in his mouth. He closed his mouth and eyes tightly, and developed a rhythm for his arms and legs.

He was making excellent progress, and was calculating that there couldn't be more than three feet of distance remaining, when something moved in the shadows above. It descended to his branch, and brushed razor-sharp against his hand.

He stifled a howl, and tried to distinguish what or who was there, but the shadows revealed nothing. A quaking moment stretched taut, then relaxed. Once more the shadows rested.

He ordered his fingers to move forward, but they did not. Terror of that unseen, but clearly felt, razor glued them to the branch.

It's only imagination. Imagination and guilt. Calm down. Maybe it would be best to say something — ask who it was. He opened his mouth to speak, but the other spoke first.

"Purr."

Andrew spluttered relief. "Shoo, Pierrot!" he hissed. A quick pat bought the cat's cooperation, and two more stretches yielded the haven of the oak trunk. He hugged its bark-clothed torso tightly, thankfully, then gave a confident wave to the three on the roof, and slid to solid ground.

A glance at his watch confirmed a loss of time, but he still could reach the cemetery by midnight. He would take a shortcut, but first he had to get the ladder. It was just inside the garage.

"Wonder why Dad forgot to lock the garage. He's been so protective of the red Nissan 300ZX since he had it restored. Mom's black minivan sits outside, graying as it waits for the two-car garage Dad promised, but not the Nissan." He shrugged, and glanced toward the curb to be sure about the Ford minivan. He was relying on that curbside parking space to ease their departure.

Reassured, he lugged the long aluminum extension ladder to the rear of the house for the second time that night, working quickly to get the younger three safely to the ground.

"We'll leave the ladder here so we can get back up when we come home," he whispered.

Andrew led the race to the street. He fished the keys from his pocket, unlocked the van, climbed in, and remembered just in time to hiss, "Don't slam the doors. Hold them shut until we get to the bottom of the hill."

He looked down the steep, well-lit street. What luck to live up here! He wouldn't have to use the engine or the headlights until they were at least four blocks from home.

"Well, here goes." He began the sentence as a baritone, but ended it as a cracked, high tenor. He scowled in annoyance at this turncoat that had taken up residence among his vocal chords, but continued proudly, "My first time at the wheel."

"Your second felony," whispered Fear. "Are you sure you want to add this to your record?"

He ignored that, vehemently released the parking brake, and guided the van into the street.

"The abecedarian has wheels!" Caleb teased. "I thought you'd never get us off that roof!"

"I thought I'd never get past the ogre in the tree," laughed Andrew. "Did you see Pierrot? Someday that cat will send me to my grave." It was good to speak aloud at last.

"You were safe. I had my eyes crossed for good luck," said Cathryn.

The other three snorted, and Alicia said, "You cross your fingers, not your eyes."

"Oh. Well, it worked, didn't it?"

The van slowed as they reached the bottom of the long hill, and Andrew braked to a complete halt before trying to start the engine. Alicia and

Caleb slammed the doors, Andrew turned the key, and all sighed relief as the engine roared to life. It took a few tries before he remembered to shift into drive, but then he was off at top speed.

"Slow down or you'll slaughter us!" screamed Caleb, clinging to the back of the driver's seat with his left hand.

Andrew didn't slow a bit as he shot back, "If we don't hurry, your full moon and white heather will be wasted, you know. It has to be done at the stroke of midnight — at least that's what you told us."

"What will you say if the police stop you, Andrew?" asked Alicia.

Andrew tightened his jaw. "They won't."

"We could say you were taking me to the hospital because our parents were away."

"I don't think your finger qualifies as an emergency, Caleb," said Alicia.

"Besides," added Cathryn, "we're going the opposite direction from the hospital. Maybe he could tell them he left his license at home."

"It's in the safe with my marriage license." Andrew made a wry face. "Hey, don't worry about the cops. They won't stop us."

"But they always cruise the streets at night." Alicia wasn't helping.

"They do — but we don't. We'll take the pine forest road. The police will never be out there at this time of night. I figure we'll cut off ten miles that way, and there shouldn't be any traffic, so I won't have to worry about running into someone."

"All we have to do is get from here to the pine forest road." Alicia still had her doubts.

Andrew's own confidence was less robust than it had been ten minutes ago, but he managed to find the turnoff without mishap.

"Here it is," he said.

He left the main route, trying to steer with his right hand while switching on the lights with his left hand. The steering wheel jerked, sending the van lurching to the shoulder of the narrow road. "Oops." Hastily, he yanked the wheel back, overcompensated, and threw the vehicle across the middle line.

Alicia stretched quickly across the wheel in front of him, and snapped on the lights.

"I'm too young to die!" screamed Cathryn. "I'm only twelve!"

"Twelve? I'm only eleven!" shrilled Caleb, closing his eyes tightly and clinging to the seat.

Andrew, concentrating far too hard to hear or answer them, wrestled the car back and forth across the narrow road's solid yellow center line.

Hey, he could do this. After all, driving was not all that difficult, remember. Anyone could do it. Yeah. Right.

A novice driver like him tempted the fates on this road. There was no sense in trying to stay on the right side of the road. It couldn't be done. The way this road curled up and down over the hills, its curves connected by nothing but hyphens, he would be doing well to stay in the middle of it. Question was, how to do that steadily.

Even a novice increases confidence as he goes, though, and Andrew gradually began to steer down the center with greater consistency. Finally, he accelerated. They must get there by midnight.

"Caleb, explain again what we're supposed to do," said Andrew, able to talk now that he felt more in control of the vehicle.

"Yes, I forget all but the full moon and white heather," said Cathryn. She maintained her death grip on the seat, but had relaxed enough to allow speech instead of screams.

"Ah, full moon and white heather." Caleb glowed, thinking of the time he had learned about them in Grandfather's library. His voracious book appetite took him there every time they visited, and two years ago, he had picked up a Scottish myth that explained, in spellbinding fashion, the magic of moonlight and white heather.

Caleb could resist magic no more than he could resist a great concerto. He had devoured the story. The cracking black and white illustrations portrayed a crumbling cemetery under a full white moon, with tiny ghosts of delicate white heather quavering atop a fresh grave.

Eagerly, he had read the chapter, trying to commit to memory every detail for possible use. They had wanted to try the magic right away, two years ago, but one missing ingredient had stopped them. Now, Grandfather's death provided that last element – fresh grave dirt.

Caleb inhaled deeply, savoring his grand opportunity to conduct at least part of a McKean adventure. He adjusted his oblong gold-rimmed glasses and looked around the van. "What I read," he began in careful diction, "was that this magic has four mysterial requirements:

1. a full moon
2. a sprig of white heather
3. midnight
4. fresh grave dirt

"If you're missing a single ingredient, it won't work. However, if you possess them all and use them properly, you can make a wish, and it will come true within twenty-four hours." He paused to gather the admiration that was his due.

"We remember that part, Silly." Cathryn stingily denied praise. "Just tell us what we have to do, or we'll be there, it'll be past midnight, and none of it will work anyway." She glared at him.

"Yeah, Carrot Cake, cut to the chase." The eldest was the only one who could get away with that nickname.

Caleb impatiently ran his hands through his carrot red shock of hair. "I'm explaining," he snapped angrily.

Alicia turned to give him a calming look, but caught her breath instead. "Andrew, are we being followed?"

"If I try to look, we'll crash," said Andrew. "Does anyone back there see a car? Cathryn or Caleb, do you see anything behind us?" His voice cut the air. This idea definitely was stupid. What was he thinking? Magic? A guy his age had to be totally desperate to believe in magic. He was.

Caleb and Cathryn stared holes into the forest shadows, but couldn't even see the road behind them, let alone a car on that road. They reported this to Andrew, who growled, "Well, look harder." If someone was following them, it could be the police. Worse yet, it could be some escaped criminal.

"You've done it this time," Fear mocked.

"It was probably my imagination," Alicia said. "I didn't see any lights, and the police would switch on lights and sirens to force us to pull off. Go on, Caleb. Finish the explanation. Cathryn and I will watch, just to be sure."

Caleb turned toward the front again. "Okay. When we reach Grandfather's grave, we scoop fresh grave dirt into a mound, and plant a sprig of white heather in it. Then, at midnight — and I set my watch with the Naval Observatory Clock," he assured them, "— at the stroke of midnight, we touch the white heather, gaze at the full moon, and silently make our wishes. That's all there is to it. Then we wait for the wishes to come true. Oh, and we tell no one our wishes," he added, "no matter how they ask."

"Simple." Cathryn turned from watching shadows. "There isn't anyone behind us, Andrew." She looked out the front window just in time to see, in the stark light of the full moon, the heavy wrought iron railings of the cemetery. A gnarled, naked old black walnut tree swayed drunkenly beside the spiked gate, its faded and torn leaf cloak lying at its feet.

They had arrived, and her body responded with a shiver that puffed out every chunky pore as she announced in a whisper, "We're there!"

"I have horripilation!" said Caleb, rubbing both freckled arms.

Alicia giggled nervously.

Andrew disguised an uneasy laugh as a ghostly cackle. "Horripilation — your spelling bee word, Caleb," he acknowledged, "and it's the best word possible. I have goose bumps, too." He struggled to aim the obstinate van between the huge iron gates, which indeed stood open, their hinges frozen in dark flaking rust.

"Look out!" screamed Alicia. "You just about hit that man!"

"Where?" Andrew slammed the brake.

They all whirled, following her gaze to the right of the spiky fence, but there was no one.

"He's gone. He just evaporated." She stared wordlessly at Andrew. Such things didn't happen to sane, normal people. You didn't pick up a tail on a dark forest road, or see men that weren't there. She hadn't bargained for mystery — or for danger. This was to be just one more innocent adventure.

Andrew's voice chose its childhood range as he reassured, "We're spooked, that's all. You can imagine all kinds of things when you are in a graveyard, especially when there's a full moon, and a chilly autumn breeze, and dead leaves, and bare branches. It's probably because of all the ghost stories we read — and because of Grandfather's funeral." He convinced them no more successfully than he convinced himself.

One last curve stood between them and the long straight climb up the hill. He navigated it cautiously, and stopped beside Grandfather's grave. "This is it," he announced, switching off the engine. "What time do you have, Caleb?"

"Exactly three minutes before midnight."

All breathing paused. Three minutes. Three brief minutes.

Only three minutes? They sprang to life and scrambled from the black van, nervously looking into the night shadows, racing pell-mell toward the grave, fighting off niggling little thoughts that threatened from every side. Thoughts that said:

1) someone might have followed them
2) a man might be watching them
3) Grandfather was there beneath the fresh grave dirt

From the matching green windbreakers outward, all four bravely and rapidly pursued their plan, but deep within the navy sweatshirts and blue jeans, hearts quaked and bravery threatened to crumble.

"Make mounds!" ordered Caleb. "Make mounds as fast as you can. Hurry! Make mounds!"

Four pairs of pale freckled hands rapidly scooped up molehills of leaf-moldy grave dirt.

Caleb winced and told his injured finger to

stay out of the way. Alicia cringed as dank dirt crawled under her nails, freshly painted with pink pearl polish. Cathryn screamed when she caught a night crawler in a fistful of dirt. Dampness oozed around them, turning burnished locks to frizz, but nothing stopped the flying hands and pounding hearts.

Caleb glanced at his watch and shouted breathlessly, "Finish! Finish!"

They were done. Four small mounds rose forlornly against the graveyard backdrop. Cathryn gave hers an extra pat as Alicia hurriedly handed out the sprigs of dainty white heather. They punched the heather into the mounds.

Caleb held his watch to the brilliant moonlight. "Twenty seconds and counting." His boyish voice somehow assumed a spine-chilling rasp. "Get ready."

Trembling fingers grasped each sprig of white heather. Feverish eyes gazed toward the full, glistering white moon, and heads nodded mutely.

"Ten, nine, eight, seven, six, five, four, three, two, one, WISH!" Caleb commanded.

The breeze paused to listen, as four hearts earnestly implored some mystical, supernatural life form to please gratify their deepest yearnings.

Then — silence.

One by one, Andrew, Alicia, Caleb, and Cathryn slowly released the tiny stems of fragile white flowers, each stem now bent with the fierce intensity of the grasp. One by one, Caleb, Alicia, Cathryn, and Andrew slowly eased tense-rigid bodies back onto their heels.

Eerie silence.

Somewhere beyond the midnight black van, brown leaves crackled in the dry dust, crackled as though crushed beneath a heavy foot. Neck hairs rose involuntarily and four heads pivoted slowly in the direction of the sound.

Nothing.

The four turned haunted eyes back to gaze at the sullied, disrupted grave site.

Silence still.

Cathryn gently patted the mound around her frail little bit of broken heather.

"Grandfather's in there, you know." Alicia quietly relit sadness in their hearts' innermost chambers —

— and silence returned.

"I guess we should go home." Was it Fear speaking, or the eldest's responsibility?

Nobody moved.

The moonlight was far too luminous now. Such beauty was inappropriate. The new-found gentleness of the breeze also was inappropriate.

Propriety belonged only to the salty rivers that flooded their cheeks and inundated their taste buds. Brackishness seemed right, and each of them welcomed it.

But they sat silent, unmoving.

Eventually, they dug for handkerchiefs to corral the brackish droplets that slipped from the rivers into their nostrils.

"You told Grandfather that we would see him at midnight." Cathryn's tearful statement offered no accusation, only a reminder.

"Was that your wish, Cat," Andrew asked gently, "that Grandfather would come back to life and you would be able to see him again?"

"Stop!" warned Caleb, springing forward and clapping his hand over Cathryn's mouth. "You can't ask her that, Andrew. Remember, we must not tell our wishes, or even answer whether or not this or that is the wish we made. She can't answer a question like that." He cautiously removed his hand from her full pink lips.

The foursome crouched in the midnight cemetery a few chilly moments longer — silent, frightened, thoughtful.

Then, moved by the same unknown power, they looked up at one another. They bent forward submissively and wordlessly, and began to dig.

They leveled the little heather mounds. They stripped away handfuls and fistfuls of dirt. Slowly at first, then more rapidly they worked: hushed, intense, unthinking, flinging the mixture of loam and sand behind their kneeling bodies, and digging their way down, down, down to the hard, polished wooden coffin that had been lowered here less than eight hours ago.

Dirt pushed painfully beneath their nails as they tunneled rhythmically, swiftly into it. Dirt ground between their teeth. Dirt leapt into their eyes — an excuse for the copious tears that washed freckled cheeks.

All four were breathing heavily, rapidly. The sweatshirts inside their windbreakers began to show dark warm dampness beneath the arms. The knees of their jeans darkened with cold, dank dirt from the grave.

Suddenly: "I touched it." Andrew's hands withdrew as though in pain, and hung paralyzed in the cold night air. "We shouldn't do this."

Everyone stared, frozen.

Then, with renewed energy, the foursome dived forward again. They scraped, dug, brushed, and dug again until they exposed the head end of the casket, the middle of the casket, the foot end of the casket. They freed the hinged lid from its desolate burial chamber....

... and stopped abruptly.

Andrew fought with his conscience. This was wrong, so wrong. He knew Grandfather was dead. He had seen him on the floor. Grandfather could not come back to life, no matter how hard they wished. But he needed his grandfather — he desperately needed Grandfather. His wish could never come true with Grandfather still in that coffin, but if they reached out and lifted the heavy lid of the gleaming — wooden — coffin, they would be able to see — Grandfather — one last time. The magic just might work. It just might.

They looked mutely at one another. Who would make the decision? Who could make such a decision? Who had the courage?

The wind whispered an answer, but they sat unspeaking, not understanding the wind.

"Do we want to open it?" murmured Alicia.

"No," came a firm, bloodcurdling answer.

"Run!" shouted Andrew.

# 4

## The Fifth Wish

Running put no distance between them and the voice. It pursued effortlessly. "Now that you've made your four wishes," it intoned, "you'd better consider one more."

Somehow, Andrew accelerated, Caleb close behind — and somehow, Alicia passed them both. Terror deafened them as they raced blindly down the road and through the gruesome gates — none of the three heard Cathryn's piercing panic siren.

Two powerful, hairy hands seized Cathryn; two muscled arms bound tightly around her chunky body, despite her frantic kicking, despite her high, hysterical screams.

The hands and arms inflicted no pain, but Cathryn's senses lied about that, and her mind shrilled with horror that her siblings had escaped without her — that she alone remained in the cold cemetery, in the clutches of a sinister fiend.

"Let me go! Let me go!" The words blubbed in spite of her best efforts. Every ounce of strength lashed out against the man, and her heart pumped spastically.

"Be still," replied a deep, satiny voice.

"Let me go or my dad will get you, villain!" she gasped. "He'll call the police, and they'll put you in jail for the rest of your life! They'll, they'll...." Cathryn's words were swept away by torrents of salty-wet terror.

She focused her full energy on battling him, working her small, chubby right hand free of his grasp, and raking dirty purple fingernails across the cruel stubbly cheek.

The enemy snared the liberated hand and pinned it decisively against her body. "Quiet," he ordered.

Cathryn cried out again, in a voice raw with panic. She pressed her stretched body forward to bite fiercely at his hands. He held them out of range. She thrust her weight backward, trying to bite a chunk from his grizzled chin. Failure. She twisted and kicked at him.

"My brother's calling the police right this second," she sobbed, hoping against hope that it was true. Her voice degenerated to a childish whimper as she felt a cold fist close over her heart.

"Shhhh." The smooth hiss of an asp.

She strained to see the evil face clearly, but too many ghosts wafted between. She saw only that he was a tall man with an untidy moustache above his malicious mouth. She snatched at it.

"Outch! Itsh-mee," he said.

He must be drunk. He was! It came to her in a rush. He was three sheets to the wind. Why else would he be in a cold cemetery at midnight?

The little remaining blood drained from her freckled face, leaving it stark white in the full moonlight. What would he do to her? When he became sober again, would he let her go? Would he hold her for ransom, or did he plan something worse? Something like rape — or murder?

Without warning, her body shook violently. Her teeth chattered wildly. Despite the too-close heat of the big man, her skin grew clammy. She felt strangely disembodied, and gray fog began to swirl around her. The fog grew deeper. She tried to speak, but her voice tangled among her vocal chords and refused to come forth. The moon and the starry sky went whirling, whirling, whirling into the fog — Cathryn blacked out.

An eternity later, the quiet security of Dad's hands and Dad's voice soothed her back to warm, protected consciousness. Where was she? At first, she kept her eyes sealed against the memory of the terrifying graveyard and the kidnapper. She must be in bed at home. It had been no more than a bad dream, a nightmare. So real, but only a nightmare. She still did not open her eyes.

"You're all right, 'Chibichan.'" It was Dad's pet name for her, *chee'-bee-chawn*. He had brought it back from Japan. He soothed again, "Poor little Chibichan."

Cathryn listened and snuggled against him. In a minute, she would open her eyes, but not yet. Her nostrils sucked in air, damp cold air that smelled of dead leaves and mold. Strange. The air in her bedroom smelled of Alicia's rose potpourri.

"Are you awake, Cathryn?"

She allowed blue-green eyes to open slowly, just wide enough to admit a peek of Dad's firm mouth, crowned with the red pencil moustache. Then she closed them again. Dad had the most loving, the most handsome face in the world — in spite of his midnight chin stubble.

"You need to get up, Cathryn. We need to find your brothers and sister before they try to hoof it all the way home."

Home? She opened her eyes wider. They were not at home. They were outside in the cold, but she was warm. She looked down. She was wearing Dad's big black parka. She snuggled into its warmth, and let him guide her across the dead leaves to the red Nissan, which waited near Grandfather's graveside.

The tiniest of thoughts, standing high on tiptoe, tried to ask how Dad knew that Andrew, Alicia, and Caleb were running away and needed to be found. She ignored the thought. Another popped up to ask why Dad was in the cemetery instead of at home asleep. Then a third thought chimed in to remind her that she and her siblings were in bigger-than-life-size trouble with Dad, and that they had a huge amount of explaining to do when they got home. Cathryn squelched them all. She had no desire to think — not yet.

She slid into the front seat of Dad's sports car, fastened the shoulder and lap belts, and nestled into the soft red leather cushion. She was safe and warm now. She just wanted to close her eyes and drift off to sleep. But the terrifying scenes of the night waited just behind her weary eyelids. She jerked them open, and looked at Dad for reassurance.

Dad was staring at the vandalism of his father's burial site. One large tear glistened in the moonlight, and he shook his head sorrowfully. He put the car into gear and started down the loop road away from the grave, but reconsidered.

"I should check your mom's van for keys," he said, "or we're inviting ghosts to take a spin." He shifted into neutral, set the hand brake, and hurried to the van, returning quickly with Mom's keys. He drove away, then, in complete silence.

Cathryn wondered why Dad did not ask about the mess they had made of Grandfather's grave. Then she remembered. Dad had no reason to ask. Dad did not see them at the grave. He did not know that they were the vandals who had wreaked such havoc. He had not been there. She looked at his face. Dad would think that someone else had vandalized Grandfather's grave; that some gang was guilty of this deviltry — or that nasty vile man, the drunk who tried to kidnap her. She wondered where the drunk had gone.

Dad arrived sometime after that man made her faint, but how did Dad know to come? How did Dad know they were here? Had he seen the drunk when he came? She wasn't ready to ask.

"Daddy," she said instead, "Thank you for rescuing me. You were just in time."

Dad was too absorbed to answer. Driving slowly along the pine forest road, he concentrated on every tree and every shadow. Somewhere in the darkening blanket that the setting moon was pulling over the sky, three of his children were lost — lost and without flashlights, he suspected.

He rounded an especially sharp curve and braked abruptly, the car lights shining on three huddled figures. "There they are," he said.

Cathryn opened her window and called, "Come and get in. Dad came for us."

"It's a ruse!" Andrew said, his voice tight. "He made her say that. You two get her out while I distract him, okay? One, two, three."

They stormed the car, Alicia and Caleb yanking fervently at Cathryn's locked door, while Andrew ran courageously to the driver's side. That door, not locked, opened readily, and he reached in to grab — Dad?

"It is Dad!" he exclaimed. "Knock it off, guys. It's Dad. It isn't the fiend."

Dad unlocked all of the doors, and the three piled into the back, relieved to see Dad — and overjoyed that Cathryn was safe.

"We're so glad to see *you*, Dad," chattered Alicia, "after that man in the graveyard...."

Dad dampened their enthusiasm abruptly. "You will have plenty of time to talk later, but I want you silent the rest of the way home."

Andrew, Alicia, and Caleb swallowed their joy and exchanged worried looks.

"I want you to think," continued Dad. "about the foolishness you all exhibited by participating in such an escapade."

Andrew cracked his knuckles.

"Think about your fear when I followed your van through the forest, when you tried to see who was following you, but could not."

Caleb dug his nails into his palms.

"Think about how petrified you were when Alicia saw me at the cemetery gate, how my voice at the graveside spooked you, and my detention of Cathryn terrified you. Yes, it was I, but what if it had been someone intent on evil? Imagine in your mind's eye the conclusion of this escapade if I had been a criminal, and not your father."

Alicia shuddered, imagination painting all of them murdered, laid atop Grandfather's grave.

"Even if wishes made on white heather could come true, you three might not have lived to enjoy them," Dad said. "Andrew, you knew you were breaking the law by driving without a license, at night, without permission, and stealing your mother's van. We will decide later how to deal with that. I may have to involve the police."

Andrew gulped. Now was the time for that fifth wish — that Dad would forget everything. He made the wish, knowing it would not come true.

Following Dad's speech, silence permeated the red car as their snail-slow guilt trip carried them from the ethereal cemetery, through the dark pine forest, to the home in the suburbs.

Andrew, forehead clarifying the window with acne cream, listened to superb afterthought concerning his childish antics. "Really brilliant," his conscience chided, "going along with brainless myths — and we call our self a scientist. Ha! Some scientist. Possibly a mad scientist. Not going to win the Nobel Peace Prize on full moon and white heather, are we? Sound like a project for the local science fair? Ha! I think not. But hey, it might make an endearing sound byte on Major League Baseball news someday: 'ATM once spent a night in a cemetery with his kid brother and sisters, making a wish on moonlight and white heather.'"

His mind reviewed the few pathetic reasons he had agreed to go:

* A chance to drive, which he would long regret
* A chance to seem adult, which had flopped
* A chance to get his wish — ha!

Was he going to confess to Dad that he had thought, even for a split second, that his wish could come true? It wouldn't help if he did, of course. He was going on clampdown, pure and simple. Most kids got grounded for smoking, or for doing drugs. There would be a good one — drugs. He could admit to being on clampdown for doing drugs, but which of the guys in chorale was going to believe he got clampdown for making a wish on posies and a big dead moon?

Andrew turned away from the window. In the darkness, he could just discern the twitching of Dad's right jaw muscle. A wave of acid welled up from his stomach and he pumped his right leg like a piston. Dad was going to give it to him this time. Third degree. He would want every detail, and would be none too placid in the process. Talk about waves of anger emanating from someone. Dad would be generating tidal waves. Andrew cracked his knuckles again. He studied Alicia, huddled beside him. Her slim fingers veiled her face, but he knew she was suffering torture — and she wasn't guilty of anything but following his stupid lead. What a skunk he was! He swore at himself. Beyond Alicia, Caleb cleansed his window with bitter tears, his thoughts hidden in some cave beneath the waterfall. Cathryn was silent, which was highly unusual for her. Perhaps she was asleep. Poor kid. She had been scared half to death back there, and they hadn't even realized it until they got out of the cemetery and down to the pine woods road. What a jolt to look around and see that she wasn't with them.

Andrew returned to the blackness of his own window. He was a fool. A sixteen-year-old fool. How was he going to answer when Dad asked why he had done this? Was he really going to say, "I was afraid, so I went to wish I could undo last April's crime against Mr. Ando — especially my part in the crime?" Hypocrite! If people ever learned the truth about Andrew Trevor McKean, he wouldn't have to worry about Dad's clampdown. He'd be on clampdown in a Delaware prison.

* * * * *

Sunday, August 31 dawned earlier, colder and foggier than usual. The four McKeans awoke with one thought: judgment day. They dressed rapidly, and convened in the boys' bedroom to plan their defense. How were they going to face Mom and Dad — especially Dad?

Caleb began to detail an insanity defense from a book he had read, but was interrupted at once by Dad's voice. "Breakfast in five minutes."

The foursome donned woebegone masks, and went down to breakfast. Not even Cathryn wanted to eat, but they knew what Dad would say about that matter, and he did.

"I want you to do justice to this fine breakfast Mother has cooked. We'll hold family court after I've finished my coffee," Dad ordered.

He gestured for them to sit, bowed his head, and extended one hand to Alicia on his left, the other to Andrew on his right. The others quickly joined hands for recitation of the blessing that Dad required every Sunday morning. They all could repeat it flawlessly, but don't ask them what it meant. Their red heads always rose before the last syllable left their lips, selfishly selecting food while their hands still clasped in a circle of unity.

This morning was different. The heads rose reluctantly today, and only after every syllable, including the "amen," had been fully pronounced.

Dad reached for the silver serving tongs. "I like this tradition, Margaret," he told her for the eight hundred first time in their marriage. It was another thing Dad did on Sunday — thanked Mom for teaching him the custom of the father serving plates for family members.

Normally, Andrew reminded Dad of the custom's old-fashioned status, and the fact that they knew better than he how many waffles they wanted, but not today. Today Andrew observed, "I, too, think it's a fine tradition. It upholds the principle of a man being the head of his home." He reached for his serving, wondering how he would eat the seven-inch golden brown waffle that covered the plate. "Thank you, Father."

Dad said nothing, austere silence worse than wrath. Repeatedly, he ran his right index finger along the pencil moustache, pondering a penalty that would leave a lasting impression. He finished two waffles and a poached egg before speaking across his coffee mug.

"Immediately after church, while Mom and I go to dinner at the Brandywine, you four will have sandwiches here, under Mrs. Matheson's care. You then will write in detail your individual accounts of why you vandalized your grandfather's grave. Mrs. Matheson will see that you do not collaborate. Do you understand?"

The foursome nodded silently.

* * * * *

When they returned from services, Mrs. Matheson was waiting. Being "delighted to help," she gave them peanut butter sandwiches with no jelly, and with nothing to drink, the old Battleaxe!

When Dad and Mom returned home from the restaurant, carrying large foil swans that exuded tantalizing reminders of Lobster De Jonghe and Citrus Cous-cous, every member of the foursome was more than ready to say good-bye to Mrs. Matheson and go to clean their grandfather's mansion — immediately — with no further ado.

But Dad was not ready. He sank into his big recliner and asked for their confessions.

Cathryn came first, murmuring, "I'm sorry. I didn't think we were being disrespectful to Grandfather."

Caleb stepped forward. "None of this would have happened if I hadn't told them about the magic. Of course," he dropped his head, "the magic didn't require digging up the coffin."

Alicia gracefully proffered a page of elegant penmanship, each letter "i" dotted with a tiny plump heart. "Dad," she began, but unexpected tears diluted her voice. "I'm so sorry."

Andrew gently pulled her back and took her place. "We all know I'm the real culprit, Dad, and I apologize," he said.

He handed Dad four pages of neat, small printing. "I'm afraid I did not have the courage of my convictions — again. I will take punishment for us all." Tall and erect, his voice low and steady, he looked straight into Dad's eyes.

"My son, obedience is better than sacrifice. I would rather have you take responsibility than take punishment," Dad told him.

Dad allowed the silence to grow deep and heavy, then spoke their sentence.

"You will not be on clampdown. However, from now through the end of the year, you all will forfeit access to TV, computer, and the telephone, except for valid homework needs. Now, change into your work clothing and get in the car."

It was done. They had confessed, sentence had been passed, and all of their secrets were in the light — all except Andrew's darkest secret.

# 5

## Secrets of Genomes

The moment Dad released them, Andrew hit the stairs. The other three followed, chattering, forcing happiness, but Andrew didn't hear them. Fear had awakened again to taunt him.

"Hello, stupid. Hope you don't have plans for the next hour, because you and I need to talk."

Andrew flung his good trousers on the bed, cracked his knuckles, and dove into the closet for old work jeans. Think about the P-box. It was somewhere in Grandfather's house.

"Ha," scoffed Fear. "What good will it do you? Don't you think Dad heard me when you were confessing to him? He knows you had more to say. Think he will just let that go?"

The P-box. Where would the P-box be? What did the P-word mean? What kind of box was it? What was in it?

"All good questions, coward, but all moot. Deprived of practical significance in jail."

Shut up! He zipped the old jeans too hard, completing their life-span.

"Oh, too bad. But you'll soon be wearing striped ones — or an orange jumpsuit."

Andrew ransacked the top drawer of his captain bed and grabbed the old chocolate brown shorts. He had one leg into them when Alicia and Cathryn came into the room.

"I thought it would be awful, sorting Grandfather's things, but it's going to be cool now that there's a magic box," chattered Alicia.

"Magic," scoffed Cathryn. "You always spice things up. It isn't magic, you know."

"Out!" Andrew's roar made them look at him in his briefs, which they hadn't until now.

"Oops! Sorry!" Alicia giggled as she pulled Cathryn to the door. "It may not be magic, but it's full of magical things for us," she argued. "Maybe there's a tiara, set with diamonds and emeralds."

"It still isn't magic," Cathryn insisted.

"Go!" Andrew sent them hurrying out to the van, and outdistanced them, claiming the back seat for himself and his little dog, as usual. He slithered quickly to the far side before adjusting the brown shorts. They were too short, as were most of his clothes. Not that it mattered. He was glad for the four inches he had grown this summer, and quite willing to wear short clothing for work, as long as he had new clothing for school.

School.

That was another matter. School would begin the day after tomorrow, and....

Oh well. Today was today. Andrew yanked his old blue sweater over his head, and leaned over the middle seat to look in the mirror. He ran his fingers through his coppery short hair and flicked the front into short spikes. Was that a new zit? He leaned closer to inspect his nose.

"Andrew," yelled Caleb, "get back in your own seat. You're messing up my hair."

Cathryn laughed and further tousled Caleb's hair. "You mean your carrot salad?"

"Dad, make them stop it," Caleb yelped.

"All of you settle yourselves," said Dad.

"And be quiet so you can hear," added Mom. "I have something interesting to read on the way."

Andrew twisted his mouth, cracked the knuckles of his right hand, and slid down in his seat. Another of Mom's traveling history lessons. Another joy of home-schooling. Ho-hum. Time for a quick nap. He scooped Schnauzie onto his lap.

"Grandfather wrote this about his house," Mom began. "Your home has been in the McKean family since they built it in the 1700s. Few people realize it belonged to Thomas McKean, because he had other homes, and this was the least of them. This was the one in which he lived with his first wife, from whom you descended. Unfortunately, you are lost relatives, and this is the lost home. In one biography of Thomas McKean, it says simply: 'location of their home in Delaware unknown.' He had a second wife, and those descendents — as well as their houses in Pennsylvania — are much better known. Grandfather says he always tried to keep the house and gardens looking just as they did when they were at their best. He knew we would want to do the same, so he left a separate McKean Manor bank account for upkeep."

Interstate 95's heavier traffic made Mom stop in her reading.

"You know," Dad said, "We need someone who can tell us the meaning of *paw-oo'-uh.*"

Active imaginations awakened.

"The meaning doesn't matter," said Alicia. "If we find a beautiful box, we'll know it's the one."

"It may not be at all beautiful," reflected Mom. "It may be more utilitarian than decorative."

"OK. Here are the facts," said Caleb. He then conjured up a McKean man who, he said, was a wizard. His long wispy beard and rangy tangled hair were black, tinged with red. He wore a tall black hat, with a single silver star on the front. A long black cloak dusted the hearth as he moved, and thick glasses rimmed his flaming eyes in black. He worked at the mansion's big kitchen fireplace, creating evil potions, and putting his recipes in a large, heavy black *paw-oo'-uh* box.

"He called the box *paw-oo'-uh* because the formulae, handled improperly, generated in the meddler a monstrous paw and a wild oooooooo-uh scream." Caleb waved his now-bandaged finger to simulate the monstrous paw.

A concerto of laughter rewarded Caleb's description, but Andrew remained stony.

Alicia laughed, then dissented, "No, no. That isn't it at all." She proposed a lovely, young auburn haired McKean mother, who fashioned the beautiful *paw-oo'-uh* box of soft brown deer leather. She crafted it as a case in which to conceal heirloom jewels from British attackers. She sat at the long kitchen table where they had so often eaten with Grandfather and Grandmother, stitching together the pieces of buttery soft leather while her husband protected their home. Alicia stared out the car window, seeing the handsome young husband, long tawny hair pulled back with a burnt sienna cord, sinewy hands holding his burnished musket at the ready.

When quizzed as to why the young lady called it a *paua* box, Alicia started. "She meant to write *Papua* to fool the British, but misspelled it."

Caleb responded less enthusiastically to her romantic portrayal, and turned expectantly to Cathryn. "What do you think?"

"The box is tiny, not large," Cathryn stated flatly. "It's brass, and holds just two objects — the key to Caleb's piano and the key to a secret castle in Ireland. The McKean family owned the castle before they came to America, and the key has been handed down through the generations. Grandfather thought Andrew would know what to do with it because Andrew was working on the McKean genealogy. He would know where to go in Ireland. When we get to the castle, we will find out what Alicia and I get. Our gifts were too big to fit in the box, so they were left in the castle."

Why did they name it a *paua* box? Cathryn was sure that was because of a ghostly Irish piper named Paua that lives in the castle. He plays pranks on people, once he gets to know them, and can keep your castle for himself unless you find out what his name is — like Rumplestiltzkin. "Paw-oo'-uh looks like this," she said. She pulled her red braids vertical, and sucked goldfish cheeks.

Andrew heaved disgust. Children. Not a realist among them. He could only hope the P-box held something of value to him.

Dad caught his eye in the rearview mirror. "Your turn, Andrew. What is this *paw-oo'-uh* box?"

"You know as much as I know."

"Andrew. Don't be like that," Mom said.

"I don't hear you and Dad coming up with anything. That stuff's for kids." He systematically cracked the left hand's knuckles, one at a time.

"Those knuckles will be arthritic by the time you're thirty," Mom scolded.

"So what? They're my knuckles."

Alicia nudged him in the ribs. "Come on, Andrew. Your idea is probably better than ours."

She was undoubtedly right. Their ideas were so childish. "Well, I guess it is time I told you the truth. The box isn't really a box at all," he hypothesized. "That is, the P-word doesn't really refer to the box per se. It refers to our ancestor, Thomas McKean, who signed the *Declaration of Independence.* He is the *paw-oo'-uh.* He knew there would be terrible consequences if he signed. They all knew that. It was a risk to be one of the men who agreed to oppose Great Britain."

He paused for effect. "What they didn't know was that the British had a mad scientist who, even back then, had unlocked the secrets of genomes. With microbial genome sequencing beyond the double helix, added to a few secrets of his own, this scientist was able to mutate men into strange organisms — *paw-oo'-uh* men. On that fateful day when Thomas McKean signed the *Declaration of Independence*, he showed that he...."

Andrew had to clear his throat before he continued, "He had the courage of his convictions. He was willing to stand for what he believed, and accept whatever the British did to him. Two nights later, the mad British scientist captured Thomas, turned him into a *paw-oo'-uh* man, and put him in a *paw-oo'-uh* box."

"Andrew!" Mom exclaimed laughingly.

"It's true," said Andrew, poker-faced. "Ask any scientist. A *paw-oo'-uh* man is a very strange life form in which the original human genes all have been grossly altered. Haven't you heard what they can do with genomes?"

"So why did Grandfather say you would know what to do with the contents of the P-box?" protested Cathryn, giggling to hide her shivers.

"He knew that only a crack modern-day Irish scientist could counteract the work of the mad British scientist. You know how the British and the Irish have always been at war with one another. When I, eldest of this branch of the Irish McKeans, open the box, the Irish win a round. I will open the box and make old Thomas McKean human again. He will still be dead, but he will be able to rest in peace — finally. Until then, of course, we must be prepared for the fact that his spirit haunts every room in our ancestral home."

Andrew's face remained stony somber as he feigned grotesque body shapes, and wailed in doleful, serious tones, "Andrew, help me. Help me." He leaned forward toward Caleb and Cathryn in the middle seat. "What if two or three McKean poltergeists still inhabit the manor, each one looking for the Irish scientist who can release poor Thomas from being a P-man?" he intoned.

"Ghosts!" concurred Caleb. "I knew it!" His brain welcomed their tantalizing images.

Andrew continued to hover over his younger siblings' seat, testing new facial weirdness on each. "Mischievous spirits; things that go bump in the night; fiends in the closet and under the bed; footsteps in the hallway outside your room; creaking boards; wispy blobs of light floating about."

Cathryn slid forward to melt into Mom.

"Why is your face white, Cat?" Andrew asked innocently. "There are ghosts. Right, Dad?"

As Dad turned up the long drive, he looked meaningfully at Mom. He held his silence until he stopped at the foot of the mansion stairway. Then he replied solemnly, "Grandfather McKean said they all are here, from the first Thomas McKean onward. Could he be right?"

* * * * *

All Sunday afternoon, and far into Sunday night, they sorted Grandfather's belongings, from clothing to dishes, tools to books. They emptied every cupboard, closet, and drawer. They wiped oak shelves and mopped parquet floors; vacuumed heavy draperies and tapestry upholstery.

Andrew found no time for ghosts, but he did think about the paua box. Suppose Cathryn had guessed right. Suppose the box did contain the key to an Irish castle? He would have to make the trip to Ireland; make it immediately; and he would never return. He could escape. It could be his passport to freedom.

Passport to freedom!

The thought galvanized him. Find the box today, apply for his passport tomorrow, and fly to Ireland — how long did it take to get a passport? A week? Two weeks?

"You won't be allowed to skip school," scoffed Fear, "and there will be a renewed search for the third felon. The cops will pounce on every printed homework page to see if it came from *that* printer. No more home-school immunity, Copperhead. We're talking criminal investigation."

He would convince Dad to let him continue his home-school program. He could study Latin on the plane, science on the train....

Passport to freedom!

He was running from room to room now, the little gray dog bouncing along behind him. Push aside Grandfather's clothing and feel for a box at the back of the closet. Run to the kitchen and look behind the woodbox by the cavernous fireplace there. Feel for a secret panel in the wall beside the living room fireplace. Reach beneath overstuffed couches and chairs, sweep aside heavy draperies to examine window frames.

Dad's voice cut through his frenzy. "Caleb, Andrew, Alicia, Cathryn. Come to the kitchen."

Andrew shoved the big green wingback chair into place near the den window and dashed to the kitchen.

He sank into a chair, and crossed his legs under the table. His knee bumped a support. Of course. The paua box was under the table, inches from his knee. His passport to freedom!

"Sit up, Andrew." Dad looked around at his assembled offspring. "We need to get organized, or we'll never be ready for tomorrow's move. Boys, you and I will start with the den. Girls, you and Mom will start here in the kitchen. Let's get busy."

Andrew hesitated, wanting to push his hand under the table and find the box. Dad's eyes fastened on him, and he jumped up instead. He would look later.

Fear stomped back and forth behind his eyes as he shuffled toward Grandfather's den. "You'll never find the box before school starts. No box, no key. No key, no trip to Ireland. Your only trip is going to be Tuesday morning's trip to McKean High School. That and the fabulous trip you'll soon win to the county jail." Fear stabbed sharply behind his left eye. "*Do not pass Go. Do not collect $200.*"

Andrew slouched into the den, and glanced at Grandfather's tall clock sitting between the south windows. Nine hours before time ran out on white heather wishes. He shook his head. What a red blockhead — and look what he had to show for his trouble: a pack of guilt and four months without TV; without computer; without Internet; without a telephone. Why had he listened to Caleb for even a second? Fear. That's why.

He caught his reflection in the clock's glass, and swiped his coppery front spikes upward. Fear yanked them back down into his skull, and he squinted his eyes shut. "I need an aspirin, Dad. I'll be right back." He wandered toward the bathroom, rubbing at his brow to ease the pain. He had to find the paua box — today. He couldn't risk being enrolled in school; being on their record.

The paua box wasn't in the cabinet, but he did find aspirin. He swallowed two with a glass of water, and wandered slowly back to the den.

He paused in the doorway to drink in the essence of Grandfather. He wasn't sure what Grandfather had done, but the den epitomized Grandfather. It had character — Grandfather's character. It was unpretentious — no affectation. What you saw was what you got. Shelves of books whispered of Grandfather's wisdom, the wisdom that might have extricated Andrew had not Death arrived first. Death seemed very near in this room.

"Well, Andrew?" Dad returned with a stack of collapsed boxes.

"I'll clean Grandfather's desk." Andrew straightened and entered the room.

"I want to do the desk," objected Caleb. "Please, Dad." The treasure box surely would be in the desk — and Caleb would be the hero.

"Let Caleb do the desk, Andrew," Dad said. "I need your height to help me get books off the shelves. I have a ton of my own coming."

Andrew shrugged his left shoulder, then his right: a clear warning to all who knew him. "You'd better not find anything important," he hissed as he batted Caleb on the back of the head.

Caleb grinned, and played a tiny air violin at Andrew. Then he faced the immense wooden desk, and rolled up the slatted top, stopping to rub his hand across the warm golden oak that had been touched so often by Grandfather.

"Andrew, start with the top shelves and hand down a few books at a time," said Dad. "I only hope we have enough boxes. I bought every one they had at the moving store."

It took only a few minutes for the father and son to establish a silent, robotic flow to their job, freeing their minds for more demanding tasks.

Dad searched his brain for some record of his father mentioning that paua box, but Andrew ignored the P-box for the moment. Fear had ceased stomping on his brain, but now it was gnawing at his conscience.

"One and a half days until school starts. You have to confess. Think of the poor coach. He lost his job because of you. You can't wait until they catch you. You have to confess now if...."

Dad laid a hand on Andrew's shoulder as he put the last books in a box. "Mom will rub those shelves with polish later," he said, wiping his brow with a white handkerchief. He pushed damp red curls off his brow and replaced the soiled square in tailored gray slacks, themselves now wilted and dirty. "How are you doing, Caleb?" He scanned the contents of Caleb's boxes.

"No P-box. I think Grandfather's desk is ready for furniture polish, too." He closed the roll-top tenderly, watching the wooden slats follow the tracks on each side to form a rounded lid on the old desk. Would Dad let him keep the desk in his room? He rolled up the slatted top again. There was room for his computer if Dad drilled holes for power cords. Would Grandfather mind if he drilled a hole or two?

But Grandfather was gone.

He shut the desk "Dad," he began.

Dad did not hear. "Boys, we've only made a dent. Let's get all these things off the mantel." Then, softly, "Oh, Grandmother's kaleidoscope collection. Remember what she always said about kaleidoscopes, Andrew?"

Andrew smiled abstractedly. "You can see dreams in kaleidoscopes." He picked up a brass scope and turned it in the late afternoon light.

Dad reached for another, a rather crudely fashioned piece. So far as he knew, it was the only kaleidoscope handmade by his mother. He rotated the end through a lifetime of memories. Each twist formed a bouquet of reminiscence. He saw his mother handling them: miniature pink rosebuds that she incubated in the kitchen windowbox; golden-headed, brown-eyed Susans she carried in bundles to the church; tall well-formed gladioli of every hue that she nurtured for prize-winning flower arrangements; they were all there in the handmade kaleidoscope. There, too, were the muted violet pansies she had asked for when she lay in bed with summer pneumonia the year before she died. Dad turned from the images. He would keep this kaleidoscope.

"Dad? Are you all right?"

"What? Oh. Yes, Andrew. They're pretty, but all I see is chips of glass reflected in mirrors," he lied. "Maybe you have to be Alicia to see the dreams. Alicia's very like your grandmother."

The boys began packing them. Caleb found a label on one that invited "Welcome to the Magic of Illusion, a Truly Unique Kaleidoscope." He asked Dad's permission to keep it. Another was in a locked case, which piqued their curiosity, but Dad put it in the box. When the mantel was clear, he ordered everything carried to the garage, a job which fell on Andrew's shoulders — literally.

It was just as Andrew athletically hoisted the last box to his shoulder that it happened. His center of gravity shifted suddenly, and he stumbled forward, landing on his knees with the box balanced precariously on his hand.

"Watch what you're doing, son," cried Dad.

"Well, I didn't TRY to fall, Dad!" Andrew struggled to a sitting position. "I caught my toe."

Dad bent to run his hand over the spot and, feeling a loose slate on the hearth, tried to pry it out. It moved slightly, but did not rise.

"The paua box!" shouted Caleb. He dashed to the door, shouting, "We found the P-box! Hurry! We found the P-box! It's in the den!"

"Caleb. We found nothing but a loose piece of slate. Andrew, go to the car and get my tools."

Andrew was back in a flash, but Cathryn, Alicia, and Mom had gathered already, asking excitedly, "Where's the P-box?"

"It's just a loose slate," said Andrew. But was it? He might get to skip school after all.

Dad reached for his largest screwdriver — the one tool with which he was on speaking terms.

"I'm sure the P-box is in there," said Caleb.

"You *guess* the P-box is in there," corrected Cathryn. She was shrinking a chocolate brownie down to size, carefully picking out the flavorful pecan chips, and saving them to eat last.

"It's coming!" Alicia sucked in her breath.

A circle of expectant faces looped around the loose hearthstone, breathless as Dad slowly and carefully lifted the large flat piece of hard gray slate. A gaping hole appeared.

Twelve eyes peered intently, longing to be first to spot the mystery box.

Dad set the slate aside and reached for a flashlight, aiming it toward the darkness.

As the beam glared into the hole — two tiny orbs of light glared back.

Alicia screamed. Everyone sprang backward, and Cathryn covered her eyes. Andrew and Dad bowed over the hole again. There they were, two intense beads of light. Dad turned off the light.

"Squeee! Squeee!"

"A McKean ghost!" yelped Caleb. "It's guarding the P-box! It'll put a curse on us."

Dad shone the light into the hole again. "Cathryn, give me your pecans." He held out one hand, still watching the tiny glowing eyes.

Cathryn relinquished the pecan chips, and Dad paved a trail from the hole into the room.

As though on cue, a triangular little head, furry-soft, poked up to snatch a pecan — another — and another. Greedily, it emerged: long and lean, vanilla fur from the top of its head to the tip of its thin tail; bright cherries for eyes, and a nose like a pile of rosy-pink sprinkles.

"Augustus, we wondered where you were! Poor little ferret." Alicia scooped him up tenderly. "Poor little Gus. Do you miss Grandfather?"

Gus ran up and down over her shoulders, looking for more treats. Everyone laughed.

"Well, no paua box," said Andrew.

"And no pecans," said Cathryn. "May I ...."

"No!" Mom interjected emphatically. "No more food before dinner. Maybe we should do bedrooms next, William, so we have a place to sleep. It's getting late."

Late? Andrew heard no more. Time was the *sine qua non* if he was going to find the paua box in time.

"Sleeping, Andrew?"

Andrew started. "What,.Dad?"

"I say you and Caleb will be moving into the west wing bedroom, so go and clean it."

Mom was herding the girls from the den. "We are going to keep Gus, aren't we, Mom?" begged Alicia. Her eyes pleaded dramatically.

"For now," Mom answered. She sent the girls to their bedroom, and hurried off to the big master suite she and Dad would share.

Andrew jostled Caleb aside at the doorway. The west wing bedroom. Wasn't that the smaller of the two end rooms?

"Why do girls always get the big room?" asked Caleb, running to keep up to his tall brother. "Let's go and convince Dad that we need the larger room for my piano, and your sports stuff."

"Not going to happen, Carrot Cake. People always spoil girls," Andrew growled.

In falsetto, he continued, "Don't you know that we need space for ballet things, for crafts, for each other, for slumber parties, etc., etc., etc.? We need a big closet, too, to keep our pretty dresses tidy." Andrew pushed open the bedroom door.

"We need space, too, brother dear, but men never get it," he said, shifting back to his tenor voice, "so we'll split the room down the middle. I get the front and you get the back."

"Why do you get all of the windows?"

"Seniority."

Caleb crawled back into his foul mood, ran to the window, and yanked back the green and blue plaid drapes to see the great view he would be losing.

"Not so rough with those! That's the McKean tartan from Ireland!" Andrew straightened *his* drapes, aware that Caleb was playing the air violin again. "Come on, Carrot. We have to find the P-box before we leave tonight."

Too late. Mom called that dinner would be ready in ten minutes. "Wash your hands and faces and come to the kitchen."

# 6

## *P - a - u -*

Andrew took less than a minute to wash but, since Caleb was struggling with his injured finger, the older brother waited, opening drawers of bureaus and night stands in their new room.

He fingered the array of souvenirs on top of a bookcase. There must be one from every trip his grandparents had ever taken. There was that old gray clay pipe. Its bowl was molded in the shape of a man's head, complete with wavy hair, pointed beard, and hat. The left half of the hat's broad brim was missing. He picked it up, his nose reminding him that Grandfather had found it on a Chesapeake Bay beach. The pipe felt worn and smooth in Andrew's fingers.

He put it back on the bookcase and was turning to order Caleb to hurry, when he saw a sizeable collection of tiny boxes. Peculiar. He didn't remember ever seeing these in the house before.

Each box radiated a different color of the rainbow, as well as colors that weren't in the rainbow: red, yellow, blue, turquoise, fuchsia, gold, gray, black, brown, green, teal, aqua, orange, violet, etc. Maybe Grandmother had used them when she studied art.

He looked more closely. Not only were the containers different colors, each had a different shape. Maybe they weren't Grandmother's. Maybe Grandfather used them for a geometry class he taught years ago: squares jagging ellipses, rectangles bumping pyramids. He rubbed his fingers around the eight sides of a shiny silver octagon, and noticed that each was of a different material. Earth science. That was it. Grandfather's earth science class. He stroked the textures: polished wood grain, cold bronze, sea-worn shell, pewter, onyx, and crystal. None of the boxes seemed to open, but miniature locks adorned nine of them.

On impulse, he selected a small oval about three inches long. Blue and green swirls covered every side. He had never seen such a material, but blue and green were his favorite colors.

He slipped the cool oval into his deep right pocket, nestling it into his handkerchief. It would be his secret remembrance of Grandfather. He would mention it to no one — not to be deceitful. There was nothing deceitful about it. He had a right to it. It was compensation for not knowing that his ancestor had signed the *Declaration of Independence*. Fear suggested that Grandfather would choose other than compensation if he knew what Andrew had done to Coach Ando.

Andrew jumped up and started for the door. "Come on, Caleb. I'm not waiting." The boys raced to the kitchen, arriving just ahead of the girls.

Sandwiches, chips, and cider diminished quickly. Mom served bundt cake with milk and coffee, then excused them all to go back to work.

Andrew and Caleb decided to start with the closet on the left side of the room, thinking it would be filled with clothing, but when Caleb tugged open the heavy door, they saw nothing but boxes. Piles and piles of boxes. It was crammed with boxes.

"One is sure to be the P-box, Andrew!"

"Could be. I'll sit, and you hand them out."

"What! I'm the one with the hurt finger. You can get them out, and you can open them, for all I care!" Caleb plopped on the nearby bed, scowling.

"Oh, never mind. You sit, and I'll hand them to you to open. Maybe you'll find the mystery box."

Caleb granted one smile. "Thanks," he said.

The first boxes weren't too bad. There were collections of buttons, old postcards, old papers and documents, photographs so old you could barely see the people in them, and even a box of old money — Indian head pennies and some old Confederate notes. Andrew continued pulling boxes from the closet, and checking their contents, until there was only one box left.

He stared at it and whistled softly. "What a beauty! It's big enough to hold jewelry plus your piano key and a lot of other treasures!"

Caleb dove past Andrew into the closet, and hauled out the big black lacquer box. He blew a typhoon of dust in every direction. "This has got to be it, Andrew. Look. It has a padlock. Come on. Let's take it to Dad and Mom."

The boys scrambled for the door, each trying to cling to his half of the heavy box.

Meanwhile, Alicia and Cathryn were cleaning the larger of the two bedrooms, the one with pale pink cherry blossoms on soft blue wallpaper. The girls had finished cleaning the bureaus in their room, and looked around.

"We'd better clear out the closets next," said Alicia, opening the door of the nearer one. "Oh, wouldn't you just die to know who wore this dress? I must try it on!" She pulled the long satin gown over her white tee shirt and shorts. "What color would you say this is, Cathryn?"

"Puke green! It's the color you barf after you've eaten pea soup. She probably got sick at a banquet and threw up all over her dress."

"Gross! How can you say that?" Alicia slipped out of the dress. "Let's pack these things where we can get them out again later." They packed gowns, dresses, skirts, blouses, and jackets, checking all of the pockets as they worked.

Finally, the closet was cleared and Alicia opened a big cedar chest at the foot of one bed. Blankets. But she had promised to sort everything, so they began hauling out the heavy blankets and piling them in boxes.

Cathryn lifted out the last one. "Oh, Alicia! We found it! We found the P-box!"

Alicia bent to look into the chest. In the very center, alone and unprotected, rested a large, lovely brown leather case.

Cathryn caught it up. "It's just like the one in your story. See. It has that buttery soft deer leather that you described, all hand stitched. And look. Look! It has letters on the top of it!" She held out the leathern box to her sister, who excitedly traced the letters with her long fingers: p-a-u.

Alicia jumped to her feet and reached for the box. "I can't read the last letter, but it must be an "a" – and the box is locked! Let's both hold it, and take it to Dad and Mom together."

It was then that they heard Andrew and Caleb racing down the wide hall, calling out, "We found it! We found the P-box!"

"No, you didn't! We found the P-box!" shrieked Alicia and Cathryn.

Dad and Mom turned in surprise as the foursome burst into their bedroom, all shouting that they had found the P-box.

"Hold on. Two boxes?" said Dad. He set each box on the bed, smoothed his reddish moustache, and said, "Have you seen any keys lying around?"

"There's a colossal bunch on a hook by the back door," said Andrew. "I'll get them." He was gone only 20 seconds. "Here they are."

"Wow! There must be a key for everything in this house and two more houses," said Caleb.

Dad sat down beside the boxes, opened the key ring, and removed every key, methodically sorting them into those that might be right and those that were definitely too large. It was maddening to watch, especially when he took time to admire the more intricate ones.

Finally, they were sorted, and Dad began trying them in the lock of the black lacquer box.

"This will take forever," groaned Caleb.

"Ours has to be the box. See, it said p-a-u-a when first engraved." Alicia ran her hand over it.

Caleb was counting the rejected keys, and arranging them in a neat pile on the nightstand.

"Andrew's birthday is the twenty-seventh of May, so maybe the twenty-seventh key will open it."

Everyone groaned, but counted together as Dad tried more keys: "Twenty-four, twenty-five, twenty-six, and — twenty-seven...."

Andrew turned to laugh at Caleb, but at that moment, the twenty-seventh key grudgingly turned in the lock. The box lid popped open ever so slightly.

Caleb whooped, "It's the P-box!" He reached to open the lid wide, but Andrew shoved him away.

"The P-box was given to me, not you."

"We don't even know if this is the P-box," said Alicia, "so how do we know if you should open it?" She placed her own delicate fingers on the lid.

"Wait!" Dad spread his strong arms wide. "Let's let a neutral party open it — Mom."

"Oh, not me," began Mom. She changed her mind at a wink from Dad, though, and carefully lifted the lid, shielding the contents with her body. "Oh, my. What a treasure! If we follow this map, we're bound to have an adventure."

"Let us see! Let us see!" clambered the four.

Dad gave Mom's shoulders a quick hug, and held out the open box — a large collection of maps, the top one entitled "Map of New Zealand."

Andrew turned to leave. "Grandfather got the advantage of our wishing."

Cathryn jumped up and put the soft brown leather box in Dad's lap. "Now let's open the real paua box," she said. She fetched the pile of keys from the nightstand where Caleb had put them.

"I suppose an elegant box like that would have a delicate key," observed Alicia, hoping Dad would take the hint and try only the daintiest.

"Leather isn't solely a woman's realm, as you would realize if you ever took time to think," squelched Andrew. "The McKean men hunted and fished for their food." He had no basis for this statement. "That came from a deer hide, and it may very well have belonged to the man who shot the deer, say Thomas McKean."

"Number sixteen," Caleb announced.

Mom handed Dad the seventeenth key and he inserted it indifferently. "Click." The tiniest of sounds, but it transported them forward, eyes shining, as Dad turned the minute key again. Gently, he lifted the lid of the leather box, the lid with the etched letters, letters that must say paua.

"Um. It smells like perfume, so I'm sure it's yours, Andrew," said Alicia very sweetly. She leaned closer to see what was inside. "Oh, look. Something wrapped in pink rosebud paper. That must be for Cathryn or me."

"Caleb's key must be underneath and...." Cathryn paused. "Andrew, did Grandfather say there was something in the box for you, or do you just get the empty box after we take our gifts?"

"He didn't say," Andrew hadn't wanted to admit that, and his voice cracked as he hurried to add, "but if he wanted me to have the P-box, there must be a reason — something important in it for me, or the box itself is of great value. He wouldn't give something to you three, and nothing to the oldest one in the family."

Dad closed the leather box and held it out to Andrew. "You should be the one to look, son."

Andrew took the box in his muscular hands. Was there a key to an Irish castle? There had to be. He didn't even care if it was a castle. It could be a shack, but there had to be a key to some house, somewhere outside the United States.

He sat down on the very edge of the bed, the box on his knee. This was it — the promised box — he was about to open it. Carefully, he lifted the soft leather lid, and opened the pink rosebud paper. His hands stopped in midair. There must be a mistake. He closed the lid briefly and looked at the letters: *p-a-u-....*

In a trance, he opened it again. Nestled inside were two equal piles of lavender-fragrant envelopes: yellowed, crackly old envelopes, caught in the everlasting bonds of two pale pink ribbons Andrew untied one fragile ribbon and opened the top envelope, scanning the jaundiced page inside. He whistled, his face flushing from his chin to the roots of his hair. Hastily, he folded the old note back into the box, and closed the lid.

Slowly, his finger traced the letters on the lid, and he spelled aloud, "*P-a-u-l*. All that's in here are old love letters from Paul."

It was so still in the bedroom. Dad, Mom, Alicia, Caleb and Cathryn were so quiet.

Suddenly, Andrew felt a wet drop slip from the corner of one eye. He muttered angrily about dusty letters, and jerked out his handkerchief, forgetting the little blue-green oval that nestled in it. The little case plunked to the floor.

"What's this?" Alicia reached for the oval.

"Nothing," he snapped, retrieving it quickly.

Silence returned.

Nobody wanted to believe, to speak, to move, to accept the awful disappointment. They had been so hopeful, so certain. They stared at Andrew with gentle sympathy, and the minutes tiptoed by until....

Andrew stood, placed the leather box on the bed, and walked away with elaborate nonchalance.

# 7

## *Schoolroom or Courtroom*

"Life has been transmogrified forever." Caleb groaned, squinting at Andrew, or at the wad of blankets that must contain Andrew. He reached for his glasses and pushed them over the freckle-speckled nose. "Are you awake, Andrew?"

Andrew made no reply. He knew life had changed, had known it the instant he awakened, which is why he had burrowed deeper into this cocoon, refusing the metamorphosis. School. *Schola* in Latin, from Greek *scholE.* He grunted disdain into his navy bedsheets, remembering the word derivation Mom had made him memorize:

*leisure, discussion, lecture;*
*perhaps akin to Greek echein to hold*

To hold captive; to hold hostage; to hold prisoner; to hold against his will. How apt! He cracked the cocoon just enough to ask Caleb, "What time is it, Carrothead?"

Caleb peered through the smudged glasses. "Zounds! We only have eighteen minutes until breakfast. I get the shower first."

Andrew submerged again, calculating the minimum time needed to shower and dress.

"Hit the deck, lazy bones," ordered Fear. "I've waited over four months for this day, and you aren't going to steal one minute of it. On the other hand, if you walk in late on the first day, it could make my work easier."

Andrew burst his cocoon and flew to the closet. He snatched navy cargo shorts, a white polo shirt, and sweater. Tossing these on his shoulder, he jerked open the underbed drawer for briefs and socks, dashed to the bathroom door, and began pounding. "Move it, Carrot! I'm gonna be late!"

"You expect me to be late so you aren't?"

"The teddy bear's picnic doesn't start until a half hour after high school. Get out!"

"No, you old grouch."

Andrew rained fist blows on the white door. "Out or your piano books go swimming."

Caleb tore open the door. "You wouldn't."

Andrew laughed as he shoved swiftly past his baby brother and slammed the door. He should have thought of that first.

Seven minutes later, he assessed the damp teen in the mirror — the Junior that would enter McKean High School within the hour — the new guy that all the girls would see. No blackheads today. No zits, pimples, or spots. That was a break. His hair waited to be combed into trendy short copper pipes. It was a good color, not as red as Caleb's, not as pale as Alicia's. Lighter coppery eyebrows arched perfectly over deep blue eyes. Most girls liked blue eyes, didn't they? His nose seemed large. Was his nose too large? He turned for a view of his profile. Face was disgustingly smooth. Too many freckles, too, after a summer in the sun. He faced front again. Girls at church seemed to like tall guys. He had to remember: shoulders straight and walk tall.

"Andrew, it's almost breakfast time." Caleb pounded on the door.

The mirror image started, seized a brush and hair gel, and made short work of his hair. He grabbed his sweater and dashed out. "You have time. Just duck under the water and towel down."

He hurried back to the west wing bedroom, wondering if Grandfather had once gotten ready for school in this room.

"If he did, I'm sure I wasn't there," said Fear. "He was a law-abiding citizen, unlike you. You heard those eulogies at the funeral. Think yours will sound like that?"

Mom interrupted with a call to breakfast, and Fear fell silent as the four assembled in the upstairs hallway.

"I wasted that pretty heather. I should have wished to survive school," moaned Alicia. Her strawberry curls were in a ponytail. "My other wish didn't come true anyway. Did any of yours?"

"Nah. We have to convince Mom to postpone her writing career one more year." Andrew tugged his heather green sweater over his hair.

"Slim hope," Alicia sighed, "but why couldn't she continue to home school us while she writes? You and I practically teach ourselves, and we could help Caleb and Cathryn. We can check answer books as quickly as Mom does." She was trying to float down the stairway, arm and hand curved in a smooth arch, fingertips skimming the surface of the polished antique rail as she descended.

Andrew looked at her. "Seriously, if you come up with a workable idea, I'll push it."

"Back to moonlight wishes," said Cathryn.

"Well, my moonlight wish was that we could continue home school," piped Caleb. "It would have come true, too," he hastened to add, "but I must have forgotten some part of the magic." He stopped at the foot of the stairs and turned to his older brother. "I told my wish. Now it's your turn."

Andrew frowned, and said nothing.

"I wished Grandfather would come back to life, even though I know it's impossible," Alicia confessed. "I miss him so much, it was worth a try. Did you wish something about Grandfather, Andrew?"

"No!" Andrew snapped. "And stop asking what I wished, because I can't ever tell anyone!"

"Petulant old man," giggled Cathryn. "I wished what Alicia did." She bounced down the last step. "Race you to the table!"

As they slid, gasping, into their seats, Dad began serving plates. "Punctuality," he informed them, "is a vital character trait at all times, but especially on the first day of school, when you are just beginning to earn the reputation you will have among your teachers and peers. You never simply get a reputation — you earn it." He handed Caleb a plate of perfectly round poached eggs, five sweet orange slices, and hot cinnamon toast.

"So, eat quickly, and it's off to school with all of you. Andrew will be walking, of course, and Mom will drive the rest of you." He tasted his eggs. "Smile," he said. "You're going to love school."

Dad was wrong about that! Those first three months, they used a lot of words to describe school, but love wasn't among them: *hate*, *dislike*, *abhor*, *detest*, *loathe*, *despise*, *dread*, and even *abominate*. They used them as verbs: "I hate school." They used them as adjectives: "Hateful school."

Caleb began coining words: *maxhate* and *floopoo* were their favorites.

"I maxhate my science class," Caleb would complain, and Alicia quickly made up her mind that, compared to home schooling, "That old floopoo school is a pure waste of time."

Andrew himself said very little at first, but he agreed. He would much rather be studying at home — or hunting the elusive paua box.

Andrew finally became vociferous about school on the ninth day. "I've been assigned to French I instead of Latin IV!" he exploded. "They don't even offer Latin, if you can believe that. It's proof that they can't teach as well as you, Mom; and in home school, I got all my work done in four hours a day. Now I go to the illustrious Thomas McKean High School," he mocked, "spend about eight hours there every day, and accomplish a whole lot less. Can't I go back to home schooling? I can teach myself, and you can still write, Mom."

"You'll adapt." Dad was adamant. "You're just having trouble adjusting to the different type of study. Within a month, you will be on top of it."

"On top of it! Public school kids are on the bottom of it!"

What did Dad know — or Mom? They knew nothing about him anymore. They didn't even suspect his worst nightmare — that someone in school would link him to Ed Tao and Bob Stedman. They had no clue that when Coach Ando's case came to court, probably very soon now, someone would level the finger of guilt at their eldest child.

Daily, as Andrew moved through the labyrinth that was Thomas McKean High School, making new friends, hating French, he listened for the slightest hint of suspicion directed toward him — and there was none.

Fear, however, continued to strum on his nerves, and on Wednesday, October 10, as he was shuffling through books in his locker, hurrying to get ready for English class, he heard a commotion down the hall. Someone yelled "accomplice," and he jerked around to look.

His sweater snagged on the spiral of a thin notebook, and pulled the entire precarious stack out of the locker. His gym bag somehow followed, along with his jacket and his backpack.

"Yeah! Give it up for Andrew, guys!"

The voice was followed by a wave of cheers.

"Hey, McKean. Got a closure prohibitive locker?" called the school's star pitcher. "Me, too."

Andrew's joy did not participate, but his embarrassment did. He scrambled to pick up the mess, but as he stood again, his arms laden with books, a slender olive hand held out his billfold.

"This tumbled, too." She smiled from dark almond-shaped eyes.

Suddenly, Andrew's joy was willing! Not only to participate, but to volunteer for overtime. "Stop staring and speak," he ordered himself.

She helped him. "My name's Penny."

"More a yen than a penny," he heard, and realized the words had come from his own mouth. "I'm sorry." His freckles burst into flame.

Penny bubbled easy laughter. "Either way, it's less than what you probably have in here." She was still holding the wallet.

"Oh." He shifted the books and took the wallet, enraptured by the softness of her hand.

"You're new at McKean, aren't you?" she asked. "I would remember an upper classman."

Andrew's eyes deepened almost to navy. This girl was gorgeous. She was gorgeous, and she was speaking to him. She was moistening her wine red lips with a beautiful tongue, and speaking to him. She was speaking in a voice that sang and whispered and haunted. She was swinging a long veil of straight, ebony black hair away from her face as she waited for him to speak to her.

He took a deep breath and plunged. "I am an upper classman. I'm a junior. We moved into Wilmington on Labor Day."

Mischief tickled the corners of her red wine lips and her eyes crinkled to near oblivion. "Do you have a name? Did they call you Andrew?"

He extended his hand, and clasped her silken one, replying, "We should begin again. Hello. My name is Andrew. Andrew McKean. I transferred into McKean High School this year as a junior."

Lilting laughter sent him airborne as she shook his strong hand and replied, "I'm glad to meet you, Andrew McKean. My name is Penny."

"And do you have a last name, Penny?"

"No. Just Penny."

In his mind, he suggested, "I'd be glad to give you a last name if you have none." Aloud, he agreed to call her "Just Penny."

Penny helped him organize his locker again, staying beyond the tardy bell to do it. Andrew was oblivious to the tardy bell.

Andrew heard nothing — except a voice that flowed like honey; a voice that was melodic as a bamboo flute, as bubbling as a crystal brook in spring. Even her name flowed sweetly — Penny.

Andrew gazed at her candidly. Her movements were as fluid as her voice. She wasted not a calorie of energy, expending each efficiently in the accomplishment of its task.

Penny's face, though round, appeared slender inside its frame of black silk. She was slender throughout. Perfectly slender in just the right places. Nothing was amiss. A tide of joy washed over him, followed by a tsunami of self-doubt. Would she agree to date him?

"I've made you late for class," he said.

"It's the first tardy this year," she replied.

"Let me make it up to you?" He closed the locker door and twisted the lock.

"How would you do that, Andy?"

Andy. Nobody ever called him Andy. It was perfect with Penny. Andy and Penny. He grinned. "Let me take you to the Halloween Dance. We can stop for pizza before we go."

Penny's coral pink sweater seemed almost to skip a beat. "I think I'd like that, Andy," she said. "Do you have a car?"

His eyes dropped to his shoes.

"Because I prefer walking," she said. "I can meet you at the pizza shop and we can walk to the dance from there."

Andrew couldn't believe it. It was settled. He offered to walk her to class. She declined, since their classes were in opposite directions, and they parted. He turned several times to watch her hurry away. Penny. He had a girl named Penny.

School improved greatly over the next weeks, but Fear prohibited total happiness. Fortunately, it slept through the Halloween Dance Wednesday evening, but it awakened the next morning and returned to work.

Penny was absent, and he found himself listening again for evidence that someone had become suspicious of him. There was none. Until....

... early on Monday, November 5, when he was leaning into his locker among the now neatly organized books and gym gear. Then it came.

"Hey, did you hear? Ed and Bob's trial starts today." The sophomore, speaking loudly to the hallway in general, glanced toward Andrew's locker. "Are you going, man?"

Andrew's head remained securely hidden in the locker as his muffled voice responded, "Who are Ed and Bob?"

"You mean you haven't heard what old Tao and Stedman did to Coach Ando?" the sophomore continued. "Come on. Everybody in Wilmington knows the guys framed him; concocting that big fib about how he sexually molested a girl after gym class last spring. Coach swears on the Bible that he did nothing of the sort, but every newscast in the area carried it. You must have heard."

Andrew emerged, and closed the locker door quickly.

"Some people say there was a third person involved, and that Bob and Ed are covering for him," the sophomore persisted.

Andrew slipped into a cavalier attitude as he smiled and said, "I don't believe we've met. My name is Andrew McKean. I'm new here."

"Oh. I'm Fred Beers. Sorry. McKean. Any relationship to Thomas McKean?"

"Thomas McKean was my ancestor," replied Andrew, shrink-wrapping the sophomore. The group murmured approvingly, and dispersed to their classes as the bell rang.

The moment had passed.

But the day had not passed. Several times more Andrew heard people discussing the trial that would take place at 4:00 P.M. that day. Would Bob and Ed reveal the alleged accomplice?

Fear danced, drumming on his temples and chanting to the rhythm, "Four P.M., Four P.M., Four P.M., Four P.M." When it did silence the chant for a moment, it was only to tighten the steel band it had affixed around his skull. Then it returned to dancing, drumming and chanting.

If only he could go home early. He could say he was nauseated, which was no lie. Fear's dancing feet had sloshed the fermenting contents of his stomach into his throat. He was nauseous.

But if anyone suspected him, an early exit would attract attention. Mom certainly would have questions. Better to remain inconspicuous and try to endure. He had to escape detection.

Not that Ed and Bob would squeal on him. They were his best friends in boys' chorale — or had been for seven years — until last spring, when they were forced to drop all activities, pending today's trial. They were being tutored this fall, just so they would not be in the high school.

At 1:30 P.M., in chemistry class, Fear made a new, tighter adjustment on the steel band and suggested, "Ed and Bob will crumble. Coach has a killer defense attorney. You know he does. It would be stupid for him to hire some lame brain. He will trick them into a confession. Of course, you won't know until it's too late to do anything. You won't attend the trial. Or will you? Ha-ha. I dare you. I dare you to attend the trial. You think you can wait to hear the details on the news? I don't think so. You can't wait that long. The trial could take days, weeks, even months, and that...."

"Andrew McKean. I asked you what you chose for your science project." Mrs. Washington had little patience with daydreamers.

Andrew lifted his head quickly. "Excuse me, please, Mrs. Washington. I've decided to explore the subject of ethanol and how it makes a car run. In connection with that, I plan to test a variety of renewable energy food resources to determine how they ferment and whether they could be used for fuel. I also plan to research the fuel consumption figures for our school buses, and show how the use of ethanol might or might not improve those figures for the district."

"Excellent choice, Mr. McKean." Mrs. Washington moved to the next desk and Andrew made rapid notes of what he had just said. It was decent — for an instant project — but he would rather have worked on a test of whether paper chromotography would allow forensic experts to identify which inkjet had printed a given paper.

Fear captured his mind again, but quickly released it when the word *paua* appeared behind his doodling pen. They still hadn't found the paua box. They still didn't know what the word meant. Caleb had pled for one exception to their punishment, just long enough to look up the word on the Internet, but Dad had refused. No computer use until January 1 except for a proven homework need, and then Dad or Mom sat in the same room until the computer was unplugged. Oh well — only two more months.

Fear took him hostage again. "The time at the tone will be 2:15 P.M. Bong. Your trial begins in exactly one hour and forty-five minutes. Do you know where your lawyer is? Oh, you don't have one? What a pity. You really should, you know.

You have no excuse for missing the trial. Every other guy in school will be there, and guess who will be conspicuous by his absence? Why don't you just go to the trial, walk up to the judge and say, 'Your Honor, I am the missing accomplice. I helped spread the rumor that Coach Ando molested that girl. I helped destroy his reputation.' You aren't chicken, are you, Copperhead?"

* * * * *

His last class of the day was French I:

*Parlez-vous francais?*
*J'ai un probleme.*
*Que veut-dire policier?*

Just before the bell, the PA system clicked, and Principal Brobdingnagian ordered, "Andrew McKean, please report to my office immediately."

"Yeh, Andrew. Mandatory field trip to Chief Hog's den," yelled a husky male voice. The class tittered, and Andrew's cheeks flamed.

"Hey," called a female voice, "he doesn't have detention. He's just exit delayed."

"Tell him you certainly were not passing notes in class. You were engaging in the discreet exchange of quilled ruminations."

Andrew scooped up his books and fled.

The principal was waiting at his door, and asked his secretary to hold all calls as he ushered

Andrew into the inner sanctum. He motioned to a straight wooden chair across the desk from his own commodious leather one, and Andrew sat at starched attention, awaiting his doom.

This was it. This moment, sitting in a hard chair across from a singularly obese principal was his last moment of freedom. He fixed a blue-eyed stare on the principal's fat teak wood pencil cup, stuffed with plump rubber pens.

"I believe this is the first time we've met, Mr. McKean, isn't it? It seems strange to use the school's name as a student's name." He chuckled, but Andrew remained mute. "I should have sent you my message last week when I first learned of it, but I wanted to convey it in person. Now I've procrastinated far too long, and it may interfere with other plans you have for four o'clock today, but it is very important that you go."

Andrew's eyes never left the potbellied teak cup, but he compulsively cracked his knuckles.

"This is good news, Andrew," continued Mr. Brobdingnagian. "You aren't in trouble."

Good? At four o'clock? Andrew's gaze shifted to a point halfway between the pencil cup and the principal's eyes in their bowls of flabby skin.

"You have received an urgent invitation to attend a four o'clock meeting of the Wilmington Rotary Club today. As I say, I should have told you long ago, but I'm the great procrastinator." The principal showed no remorse for this lack of character on his part.

Andrew made tentative eye contact with the enormous man, noting the clump of greasy gray hair hanging over the left eye. "Thank you, Mr. Brobdingnagian. I'll have to call my parents, but I'm sure they will let me go."

What a godsend! He had no interest in the Rotary, but what a perfect excuse for not going to the trial!

He must have made appropriate remarks as he left the principal's office; must have given Mom enough detail on the phone; but all he could remember later was walking alone the few blocks to the Hilton Hotel meeting room, his conscience seeking a plausible reason for this invitation.

He entered the meeting place just at four, and took refuge in a back row seat, from which he studied the room and its occupants.

On the wall behind the platform table, a large poster boldly offered *The 4-Way Test*, which asked, *"Of the things we think, say or do:*

1. Is it the Truth?
2. Is it Fair to all concerned?
3. Will it build goodwill and better friendships?
4. Will it be beneficial to all concerned?"

Okay, I'll just crawl down the blue steel leg of this folding chair, scurry over the plush carpet, and escape under the swinging door, thank you. No need to pursue me. I get the message. I failed the test. Failed every point. Every last one. Couldn't say yes to one of them. I'm going.

Andrew jumped up — and was ushered to the refreshment table for a glass of water. One was not enough. He drank a second, and a third before his face paled to natural beige. Then he couldn't leave. Not after drinking their water. He slinked back to his seat as the leader lightly pounded his gavel and began the meeting.

"This meeting will come to order. We're very honored to have as today's guest Mr. Andrew McKean, grandson of the late Timothy McKean." Brief applause and warm smiles agreed. "I'm sure we all join in hoping you will be pleased by the part you have to play in our meeting today."

Part? What part? Andrew smiled meekly and nodded, embarrassed by the red tide that ebbed and flowed in his cheeks.

There was nothing required of Andrew for the next half hour — so he worried about the trial. He was noting that Ed and Bob had been in court for exactly forty-seven minutes, when he sensed a change in the meeting and heard the chairman call out, "Andrew McKean, will you please come to the platform?"

Andrew stood up, half thinking he was in court, and made his way to the front of the room.

"They know, Andrew," tormented Fear. "They're going to take you bodily to the courthouse and have you indicted for your part in the crime."

But they didn't. The leaders beamed at him, and each shook his hand as he stepped up. "Mr. Andrew McKean," announced the chairman, and the attendees applauded. "Andrew, as you may have guessed, the Wilmington branch of Rotary International has selected you to be our exchange student for a semester of study in New Zealand."

"To be wha...?" Andrew gasped. "But I haven't applied," he protested.

"We have your application here." The leader held out the document. "I can understand how you would forget, though, with the family's mourning."

This was surreal. Where did they get that application? He couldn't be an exchange student. Mom wouldn't let him go, especially not to New Zealand. And why would he think of crossing the ocean to attend school when he didn't like it here?

Wait a minute! This was too good to be true! Going abroad would effectively remove him from the scene of the trial as well as the scene of the crime! He wasn't sure exactly where New Zealand was, but it wasn't near Wilmington, wasn't in the U.S.A., and that's all he needed!

The chairman continued the formalities. "You are in the upper third of your present class, even though you were home-schooled."

Andrew amended that to *because* you were home-schooled, and half listened to the rest.

— well-rounded personality; blah, blah — ambassador for Rotary International, Wilmington, and the U.S.A. — New Zealand school year late January — leave January 15 to get settled — give round-trip air fare — family with whom to live.

"You will find everything explained in here." He handed Andrew a booklet.

Andrew took the information, pulled back his shoulders, and smiled as a club member loomed before him with a camera. Then, he stumbled off the platform, quickly recaptured his composure, strode across the room, and out into the hall.

"New Zealand." He tried the word aloud when he was outside the hotel. "New Zealand. Where is New Zealand?" There was something odd about this — suddenly, he remembered. The map of New Zealand in the black lacquer box — right on top. He sprinted for home.

Reaching home, he bounded up the steps, opened the door, and raced through the hallway calling, "Mom! Dad! Where's that big lacquer box full of maps?"

# 8

## New Zealand

The box was in the den, in the bottom drawer of Dad's enormous mahogany desk. Andrew raced ahead of Dad and Mom, babbling something about an exchange student program.

"Son, we never discussed the possibility of you being an exchange student," protested Mom.

"That's just the thing!" exploded Andrew. "Somebody submitted an application for me, but it wasn't you, and it wasn't me, so who was it?" He held the den door open for them, impatiently conscious that adult behavior would stand him in good stead.

He strode to Dad's big black desk, and jerked open the bottom drawer. The lacquer box was there, no longer locked, but still heavy with maps. Eagerly, he lifted it out and set it on the desk, opening the lid to reveal the map of New Zealand.

He spread the map across the expanse of shiny desk, studying the foreign names on the two main islands: Rotorua, Auckland, Wanganui, Taupo, and Harihari. Other names were easier on the tongue: Hamilton, Wellington, Nelson, Gisbon, and Christchurch. The largest city seemed to be Auckland, on the North Island. That must be the capital.

Andrew flipped the map over. There was a list of facts, but nothing to show where New Zealand was in the world — where it was relative to Wilmington, Delaware, U.S.A.

"Do we still have Grandfather's old globe?" he asked, glancing around the den. "Oh, good. You kept it." He hurried to the heavy wooden stand, and twirled the sepia colored globe to Europe.

"New Zealand, New Zealand," he muttered. "It's got to be here somewhere. Spain. France. Italy. Isn't it near Scotland or Ireland? Oh, near the Netherlands." His index finger traced a crack in the ancient orb, and he gazed intently to see if New Zealand was in the crack.

Dad walked over quietly, rotated the globe slowly from west to east across Europe, Russia, India, China, and tilted it upward to expose the lower hemispheres. "There," he said, a hitch in his low baritone. He placed his finger on a small island nation, shaped like an upside-down boot. It was near the bottom of the globe.

"That's New Zealand?" croaked Andrew. He gawked in disbelief. "That's on the other side of the world — next to Australia and Antarctica." Misgivings began to chip vigorously at his heart.

"It is down under," admitted Dad, "but as Ovid said, 'Let your hook be always cast; in the pool where you least expect it, there will be a fish.' New Zealand is the pool, the place you would least expect it, but an opportunity may be waiting there. Somebody thought it was important for you to go, so maybe you should give it serious consideration."

"I don't know, Dad. That must be 10,000 miles away!"

"Close. One of my clients went there last year and I seem to remember him saying it was a bit under 9,000 miles as the crow flies. Of course, as the plane flies, it may well be 10,000 miles."

Andrew went back to the desk, where Mom still studied the flat map, Schnauzie dancing around her feet. "Look, William," she said, "this town of Nelson is circled — here on the bay at the north end of the South Island. I wonder why that is. Did your parents ever travel to New Zealand?"

"As far as I know, none of our family ever visited New Zealand. Maybe my dad knew somebody there, but I don't recall any mention being made of it." Dad looked more closely at the map. "I would choose Wellington," he said. "According to the key, that's the governmental capital."

Andrew wondered if he would be given a choice, or if the Rotary would decide for him. Maybe they would send him to Rotorua. Its name looked kind of like Rotary. Rotorua — Rotary. Of course, they might deposit him on that lonely little island at the southern tip of the nation: Stewart Island. That really was close to Antarctica. What if New Zealand was frigid and he froze to death on an iceberg? His funeral would be well-attended by penguins in their best tuxedos. New Zealand was close to Australia, too, though. Was that the continent that was plagued with nasty reptiles? New Zealand probably was Australia without Crocodile Dundee, and he would die at the teeth of some huge crocodile or rattlesnake.

Some bit of trivia slipped forward from the back of his brain — the fact that New Zealand was the land of the Maori tribes. The trouble was, he couldn't remember for sure if the Maori people were cannibals. Did cannibals still exist?

He flicked the map to the back side again to read some of the facts about this strange land. Well, look at that. It wasn't frigid after all.

> *New Zealand enjoys a maritime-temperate climate, characterized by rapid weather changes, frequent though not excessive rain and a small range of temperature from winter to summer.*

The map pegged average temperatures around twenty degrees Centigrade for the month of January. What was the formula for converting Centigrade to Fahrenheit?

There were high mountains, which were snow-covered in winter, but there also were places as warm as Hawaii. Between the North and South Islands was Cook Strait. Wellington was on the north side of the strait, and Nelson, that small, mysteriously circled town, was on the south side.

Nelson must be a beautiful place to live, unless this description was a total prevarication. It seemed to have everything nearby: excellent trout fishing in the mountains to ocean fishing in the bay; wide beaches; sports; a university; art; music; it seemed to be *the center* for a lot of things. In fact, the map's author promised that

> *a short hike from Nelson will take you directly to the geographical center of the entire nation, situated on top of a hill overlooking the bay.*

Suddenly, Andrew saw something else — the trembling fine writing of his Grandfather tucked in a small space just after the description of the Nelson area. He read it silently.

"Andrew, I hope you will go to New Zealand as a Rotary exchange student and learn the secret of the paua box. The Bartlett family agreed to let you live with them in Nelson."

"Look, Dad." A spasm crossed Andrew's face, and he pointed a trembling finger, his body frozen over the desk. "Read that."

Schnauzie barked in response to his master's tension, and Andrew acknowledged him with a brief pat.

Dad and Mom both leaned over the map to read. When they straightened, each face somberly acknowledged the same thing: Grandfather was the one who had sent Andrew's exchange student application to the Rotary.

"Margaret," Dad said softly, "We cannot stand in the way of a dying man's wish." He turned and put his right hand on Andrew's left shoulder. "Son, you will go to Nelson."

Just like that? Without asking if he wanted to go? It was settled? His life was decided for him, and he had nothing to say about it?

He knew the answers without asking. He would go to New Zealand in mid-January.

"We must wait until after Caleb's piano competition on Saturday to tell the others," Dad decided. "It wouldn't be fair to take his mind off such an important event. We must give him time to enjoy both the competition and the results of the competition. That means that, since it ends at noon, we won't speak about New Zealand until after our Saturday evening meal."

"Passport! I have to get a passport, Dad!" The passport to freedom! His heart leapt as he realized that it was suddenly a reality. "Where do I get my passport? Can we go today?" He checked the time.

"It's Monday, and past closing time. Are you in such a rush to leave us?" Mom smiled at him, and then — then she kissed him. Mom hadn't tried to kiss him since he was Caleb's age. But now, she kissed him, and with the kiss, she transferred a single damp tear from her cheek to his.

Awkwardly, Andrew pulled his flushed face away. "I'll set the table tonight," he sputtered, and he fled to the dining room. As he spread the cloth to protect the wood's glowing finish, he became aware of Caleb's sonata leaping from the confines of the old upright piano in the family room. He had to admit that Caleb was talented. There was no doubt about it. Andrew himself didn't play the piano, but he had learned a lot about music in his voice lessons, and he could recognize talent when he heard it.

He stopped and listened. He could tell that Caleb's playing was not only mechanically good, it was musically good as well. That must be much more difficult to achieve. Yeah, Dad and Mom were right. It wouldn't be fair to detract from Caleb's hour of glory on Saturday. Difficult or not, he would keep his own news quiet for five days.

He glanced at his watch. It was 5:40 P.M. "Dinner in exactly eleven minutes," he mused. You actually could set your watch by Dad's lifting of the first plate at 5:51 P.M.. It had been that way as long as Andrew could remember. Dad arrived home from work at 5:46 P.M.; he used exactly five minutes to greet Mom, wash up, and comb his hair; he began serving at precisely 5:51 P.M. Somehow, Mom always had dinner prepared and ready to serve at exactly nine minutes before six o'clock. Of course, since they had moved into the McKean ancestral home, and Dad no longer had to drive out of Wilmington to the suburbs, he got home earlier, but Mom still had dinner ready at exactly 5:51 P.M. Andrew knew she always would.

He placed a stack of soup dishes in front of Dad's place, just to the left of the blue and white tureen. He might soon be setting the table for a Mrs. Bartlett. He wondered what time they ate, and what they ate for dinner. Another misgiving hacked out space for itself in his heart.

"Hi, Andrew. When did you get home?" Caleb had finished his practice. "Did you go to that trial thing?"

"No, I had to go to a Rotary meeting." He shifted to a safer topic. "I heard you practicing just now, Carrot Cake, and you're really getting good," he complimented. "It sounds as though you'll win that competition."

Caleb grinned broadly. "I didn't expect you to remember," he confessed. "I didn't think you cared about anything but baseball — and girls. Are you going Saturday?"

"Of course, I'm going," said Andrew. "I want to see that sprained finger tickle the ivories."

"Oh, it's healed," said Caleb. "Just don't expect me to play baseball Saturday morning." He laughed good-naturedly.

Andrew had not once asked him to play since the day of Grandfather's funeral, and he was very thankful. Almost every day, Andrew and Cathryn went out to the reflecting pool garden to practice with the new batting cage, which Dad had given Cathryn for her September birthday. Sometimes Alicia joined them, but they never asked Caleb to come, and he never complained.

Andrew was just placing the butter dish on the table when Dad arrived, Alicia and Cathryn hurried into the room, and everybody settled into their seats.

"Vichyssoise," Dad said, ladling cold potato and leek soup into a shallow bowl and passing it down the table to Caleb. "Your faces look rather peaceful, so I conclude that the school day was not overly troublesome, and that Mr. Beethoven's Sonata is close to satisfactory. Would that be a fair assessment, Caleb?"

"It's never satisfactory, Dad," replied Caleb, "and thank you for the potato soup." He was quite opposed to French words like vichyssoise, despite his love of unusual English words.

"I just thought of a good idea," said Andrew. "Let's take Caleb out for a special brunch before his competition on Saturday."

"Oh, sure," said Caleb. "Stuff me so I can't play. Ms. Kolinsky would kill me — after I killed myself. You have to eat light before concerts, not big brunches. You can't have your heart so busy digesting food that it can't send blood to your arms, hands, and fingers."

"Andrew's idea was thoughtful," said Mom, "but we will honor Caleb's wishes. Now. Let's hear about everyone's day."

Alicia's ballet class was preparing for the holiday performance of the Nutcracker Suite, and Alicia hoped to be a snowflake this year. "Did you know that before Peter Tchaikovsky wrote the Nutcracker Suite, he was just a government clerk? Nobody knows what his exact assignments were, though, because he was so not in love with his job that he later forgot exactly what it was that he had done. My ballet teacher told us that Tchaikovsky thought he wasn't good in music, and that at the age of 21 he said, 'even if I actually had any talent, it can hardly be developed now.'" Alicia shook her head. "Can you believe it?"

Everyone expressed amazement.

"Your turn, Cathryn," said Mom.

"My gymnastics class is going to put on a winter holiday exhibition in the mall, and teacher said I'm ready to do my balance beam exercise this year. I have to practice a lot, though, 'cause I'm still having trouble sticking the landing. I keep falling backwards on my you-know-what." Cathryn giggled and pushed red curls off her face.

Andrew shared a snort with Caleb.

"Caleb, what did you do in school today?" Dad interrupted them. "We know what you're doing in piano lessons, but we don't hear much about school."

Caleb rolled his blue eyes elaborately, and pushed his gold-rimmed glasses tight against his carrot eyebrows. "You mean floopoo school?"

"I thought you were learning to like school," said Mom. Her dismay was obvious as she put a hand on the shoulder of her youngest.

"I guess I don't hate it so much anymore, but there's this boy named Rodney who always pushes me in my locker."

Andrew had a few quick words about Rodney, and promised to show his little brother some guaranteed surprise moves for Tuesday.

Then he reported what he could of his day. His science project was to center on ethanol and renewable energy sources, he told them. Mrs. Washington thought it was a good project, but it wasn't due until sometime in February, so he wasn't going to begin yet. He gave Dad and Mom a quick, knowing look.

Alicia and Cathryn cleared the main course dishes, and Mom produced sherbet glasses piled with Cherry Garcia frozen yogurt. They ate the dessert in appreciative silence until, as they finished, Andrew's eager lips almost told his secret.

"Dad, when I...." He gulped. "Would you let me teach myself just from now through the end of the year?" he finished.

Dad pushed aside his empty yogurt dish and took a long drink of vanilla coffee. "Well, I doubt it, Andrew, but I'd be willing to discuss it if you come to the den. I have a big spreadsheet to do, and we can talk while I work.

In the den, Dad explained that Andrew must be in Thomas McKean High School to qualify as an exchange student. Home schooling simply was not an option this year. "Besides," Dad said, "the teaching at your school is not as lacking as you think. You grew up with the ideal — studying one-on-one with a gifted tutor, so you've been able to move quickly through the curriculum. Now, you are experiencing a less ideal method in which a teacher must instruct a large group of students, among whom are varying abilities. It's up to you to discipline yourself to achieve your utmost. I believe that you will eventually find students in your school who are at or above your level. Next year." He winked, and focused on his computer monitor, scrolling to the bottom of his spreadsheet.

"Do you know anything about New Zealand schools, Dad?"

"Not really." Dad's eyes remained on his work as he entered a formula. "My client was told before he went that New Zealand is twenty-five years behind the United States, but when he came back, he said they are very up-to-date. The twenty-five year myth seems to relate to their relaxed life style. Of course, that's all hearsay on my part. I guess you'll have to find out for yourself." Dad began entering figures with nimble fingers.

It was amazing how rapidly Dad could work the ten-key pad. No wonder they all called him Mr. Whiz-fingers. Andrew waited for a break, but the fingers kept flying.

"May I go on the Internet to find out?"

Dad raised his red-brown eyebrows and looked over his computer glasses, his right hand frozen in midair. "To find out what?"

"To find out the rating of New Zealand's schools. It would be good to know how they stand in the world. I'm going to spend a whole semester there, and I'd like to know if I'll be behind when I get back. So what do you say, Dad? May I go on the Internet and check it out?"

Dad began to stroke his moustache, and Andrew automatically cracked the knuckles of both hands. "Didn't we have an understanding that the computer was off-bounds until January?"

"This could be classified as homework. It has a lot to do with next semester's schoolwork."

"Next semester, you will have completed your punishment." Dad pushed the half glasses back into place and looked at the monitor. Dad would not relent.

"Did your client know anything at all about the schools there, Dad?"

Dad's swift data entry paused again. He brushed an invisible speck from his long white sleeve and swiveled to face his eldest.

"He didn't take his family with him, so he had little experience with the schools. All he knew was that most students were required to wear a school uniform. He said the uniforms were almost always immaculate. It seems the schools are very strict about how students look when off the school grounds, since they are representing the school. Most of the uniforms he saw were plaid. Maybe your school will wear the McKean tartan."

"Right!" Andrew thanked Dad for taking time to talk, and went up to his bedroom, Caleb's sonata resonating in his ears.

What a day. He needed exercise — jogging, or swinging a bat full force. Too late to be out on Wilmington's streets, though. He dropped to the floor and did three minutes of push-ups. He did another three minutes of mule kicks, and flipped on his back for two minutes of sit-ups. Sweat began to trickle from his armpits, but his stomach still felt tight as a fist. He dashed from his room and ran down the broad, carpeted stairway, turned and ran up, then ran down again. As his big shoe reached the bottom step for another upward dash, Dad called from the den.

"Whoever's racing on the stairs, please stop immediately. This is not a gym club."

Andrew braked, and walked up the steps softly. When he reached his room, his flitting eyes found the big king size pillow. He yanked it from its navy cover and began beating it. He walloped it with both fists. He threw it on the bed and clapped it between strong hands. He thumped it. He crushed it. He flung it on the floor and stomped on it. He put it back on the bed and wrestled it. He hurled it against the high ceiling and caught it on his feet. Finally, he threw it back on the bed and fell on it. His stomach unclenched at last. He lay there for five minutes, panting and resting.

Then, he got up and went to his desk. He picked up the photo of Penny eating pizza, stretching her chin upward and dangling a long string of mozzarella onto her lips from a big drooping slice. Was that only five days ago? He still didn't know if she had enjoyed their date. She wouldn't let him walk her home. She said she would catch the bus by the pizza shop. Funny, she still hadn't told him her last name. And he hadn't seen her since the dance. Was she sick? Maybe she was avoiding him. Maybe the truth was that she had a rotten evening with him, and didn't want to see him again. He wanted to see her, though. Even if she told him to get lost. At least, he would be breaking up with the greatest girl in the junior class.

He sighed. Homework would not get done this way. A new thought struck. How would he tell Penny he was going away for six months, and would she please not date while he was gone? He would write to her every day. He could promise that. But did he expect those flying feet to skip the Valentine Dance? Was that fair? Could he ask a cheerleader to sit on the sidelines of basketball season, and not attend its parties? He hadn't seen her cheer yet, but he could imagine it — could dream it. Unfortunately, he could not imagine or dream that she would wait for him to return.

He reached for his hard trigonometry book. As he turned the pages, Penny faded and every circle, every angle, every triangle became a map of New Zealand. Sine, cosine, radian, tangent, arc — every word seemed to mutate into *Nelson* or *Bartletts*. Shaking his head to scatter the thoughts, he focused on the first problem:

*Express the following angles in radians.*

*(a.) 12 degrees, 28 minutes*
*(b.) 36 degrees, 12 minutes*

Simple. He could do that. 12 + 28/60 = 12.467 degrees. Multiply by pi = ....

Caleb came in and started getting ready for bed. "Will you have the light on long? I'm tired."

"Turn toward the wall, Carrot. I just got started." Let's see. Multiply by pi = ....

Caleb snapped off the overhead light and said, "I'm glad you're going to my competition on Saturday. Good-night."

Andrew murmured in return and hit the calculator keys. Divide that product by 180 and part (a.) was done. He completed the second part of the question and turned the page.

*The lengths of the three sides of a triangle could be only which of the following?*

*A. 0, 1, 2*
*B. 1, 2, 3*
*C. 2, 3, 4*
*D. 2, 4, 6*

Good question. Andrew attacked it, and managed to stay focused until he finished.

As he closed the book and got ready for bed, though, he granted his thoughts free mileage to New Zealand. They quickly appropriated them, and remained there as he fell into bed.

Slave to a new routine, Andrew shook the little blue-green oval box, and placed it on the nightstand. It made no sound, this empty blue-green casket. But how could it? Its master was gone, his voice silenced — silenced except for the shakily written words of the old map.

Andrew whispered Grandfather's message to Schnauzie, who was snuggled tight beside his pillow: "I hope you will go to New Zealand and learn the secret of the paua box."

Gradually, the words and Schnauzie's snores harmonized into a lullaby, and the teen descended into troubled dreams of Nelson, of the Bartletts, of Penny — and of Coach Ando's defense.

The trial would continue tomorrow.

# 9

## On Trial

The trial did continue —in more ways than one. Andrew's awakening was only a recess in it.

First light had not found his window, but he had to get up, to distance himself from the nightmare. His ears rang with the voice of the black-robed judge pronouncing sentence on Ed, Bob, and him. He turned off the alarm, reached for the glimmering blue-green oval, and slid his legs off the bed. The floors were cold at five o'clock in the morning. He looked across to the other bed.

Caleb slept peacefully, his lips slightly parted, the slim crack between his two front teeth producing a rhythmical whistle. Musical, even in his sleep.

Andrew crept to the huge closet and stepped inside, closing the door before turning on a light. He shook his head and adjusted his shoulders. How could dreams seem so real, even after you were awake? The judge's voice still resonated. "I do hereby sentence each of you to one year in prison and ten months of community service in addition to a fine of seven hundred fifty dollars."

He bent to find his tan cross-trainer shoes, and had trouble straightening again. His knees were stiffer than usual, tight, as though he had been standing at attention all night. He sat on the floor and massaged them, wondering when his surgeon would order the next new procedure.

A toilet flushed downstairs. Dad was up. He never slept long, it seemed. He was a morning person — early morning. He would be going to the kitchen now and starting the coffee. Mom said she never awakened until after her second cup of coffee, or at nine o'clock, whichever came first.

Andrew stopped massaging and leaned back to choose today's clothing. If the trial was on his agenda, he should wear the light gray pants, a white shirt, and the pale pink sweater. That would make him look sickly enough for the judge to take pity. If he was going to see Penny today, the camel colored khakis with the pale green shirt and the gold sweater were best.

Some jock! Choosing an "outfit" instead of throwing on old jeans and a sweatshirt. That was Alicia and Mom's fault — always drilling into him which colors were best with his coppery hair and which colors made him look sick. They didn't think he listened, but he did — especially since meeting Penny. Tomorrow would be exactly four weeks since she had rescued his wallet, and he still didn't know her last name. He would ask today. He would tease her — if she was back in school, and if she wasn't avoiding him.

Andrew surveyed his clothes again. This was Tuesday, second day of the trial, but since no one seemed to suspect him yesterday....

He got to his feet and reached for the camel khakis, green shirt, and gold sweater.

He slipped the smooth oval into a pocket of the khakis, thinking for the first time that it might possibly be a good luck charm, which would be very welcome today. He rubbed its smooth lid, just in case. Then he turned off the light and crept softly through the bedroom to the bathroom.

The hot shower soothed his aching knees. He stood still and let it cascade over him. The judge's voice was gone now, but when he closed his eyes, the black robe still sat within his blue pupils. He hummed to change the mental scenery while he scrubbed.

*Find a penny, shiny new.*
*Find a penny, shiny new.*
*Find a penny, shiny new.*
*That's what love is like with you.*

He stepped out of the shower and stared

into the mirror. A grin played across his thin lips. He hadn't realized he had memorized that song. It was just a few weeks old, but it was good!

He toweled dry and dressed, still humming. Today's schedule was? He ran through it as he combed his hair. First hour, homeroom study hall; second hour, English grammar; third hour, trig; fourth hour, French I; fifth hour, lunch. He squirted purple gel on the front of his hair and carefully brushed it until it stood straight.

Copper hair. Maybe he should dye it black like Penny's. Penny. Penny. Pennies are made of copper. What was that kids' song Mom taught him when he was about three?

*Look what I found.*
*A penny, a penny,*
*A little copper penny.*

Maybe it was Penny who should dye her hair — to match his.

A final check of the old profile and he was ready, but breakfast wouldn't be ready for another twenty minutes. He decided to skip breakfast and go to school early. Maybe he could find Penny before classes began.

Dad stopped him as he reached the front door. "What's the rush, Andrew?"

"I have to meet someone before class." It was close to the truth.

"At least, go and get a couple of breakfast bars — and tell your mother good-bye."

Andrew complied, and was soon sprinting down the street. He paused at the park to gulp down both bars, then set a slower pace for the last few blocks. Arriving well before the first bell, he wandered the halls, but nowhere did he see Penny. The entire baseball team stood near his locker discussing the trial, and several called to him.

"Hey, Tall Unit! Didn't see you at the trial yesterday. You should have gone."

"You should not have gone! It was brutal. If Stedman and Tao don't have someone warming up in the bullpen, they're history. Their attorney's throwing nothing but junk."

"But that's good for Coach."

"You going today, ATM?"

"I had an appointment yesterday, and today's locker room cleanout, isn't it?" He certainly hoped it was.

"What is this? Tuesday? You're right." The big catcher scowled. "We need Coach back here. I want to be there when he's acquitted."

"You will be. This should go on for weeks." Andrew maneuvered around them to his locker.

Despite his early start, the final bell was ringing as Andrew reached homeroom. He slid his knees under the graffiti-carved desk, and glanced across the aisle. Penny? She had never been in his homeroom before.

"What are you doing here?" he whispered.

"I'm glad to see you, too," she retorted.

Andrew smiled warmly and she received the smile with clear-enameled fingertips. Then she blew a soft, glistening wine kiss back to him. She apparently did not want him to get lost! Andrew shuffled his books, and dared to look at her again.

Penny was opening a yellow notebook. Her eyes were different, as though she had left hazy shells around the little almonds. He liked the effect. He liked her soft crimson sweater, too.

Morning announcements garbled from the wall speaker, and Andrew began making absent-minded marks on his notebook while he listened. An upside down boot gradually emerged, its foot detached slightly from the leg and lying a half inch to the right of it. He circled a spot on the lower portion, just where the boot broke at the ankle, and involuntarily sketched the word *Nelson*.

Penny sailed a note across the polished wooden floor, and he pulled it to safety. "Looks like a dead cowboy boot."

He grinned, and wrote beneath her modest script the first words that came to his mind:

"Hangman's boot." He launched it with his toe and watched it cross the wooden strait.

It found safe harbor beneath the sole of her black boot, just as Andrew realized what he had done. Fear stood up and applauded within his brain. "Excellent! That practically screams that you are worried about the trial, which implicates you beyond any reasonable doubt. Well done."

From the corner of his deep blue eyes, he saw Penny writing. The note arrived back in his port, and he quickly retrieved it.

"Brainy Award!" commended a little heart medal, and beneath it, "Order a pair each for Ed Tao and Bob Stedman."

"And a pair for Andrew McKean," said Fear.

Andrew had to acknowledge the note. He turned with a half-smile, and she returned a full one. Then she pushed her long jet-black hair back over her shoulder, releasing fragrant perfume. His nose captured it and sent it flowing toward his heart, but Fear intercepted.

"You have no right to encourage her. You'll only break her heart when you go to jail."

Painful truth. Andrew gave Penny one more smile, and spread the shield of his grammar book in front of his face. Study period would end in about twenty minutes. Until then, he would have to keep his nose buried and look industrious.

When the bell rang, Andrew risked Penny's misunderstanding, jogged to English class, chose a front seat, and pretended deep concentration.

The rest of the class entered in a clatter of pandemonium, paper weapons flying as fast as the gossip. The hot topic was, of course, Coach Ando's trial, with an almost even split between those who thought him guilty and those who thought him innocent. Jocks and cheerleaders sided with the coach. Geeks and freaks sided with the two boys and the poor girls, whoever they were. Wasn't it odd that the boys would not tell who they were?

A short plump blonde stated loudly that her sources told her one girl had long black hair.

The class clown leapt to the teacher's desk and shouted that the molestee not only had black hair, she was Asian-American.

Asian-American? Long black hair? Andrew cringed. They never had identified their fictitious girl in any way — Ed, Bob and he.

"Be sure your sins will find you out," hissed Fear, "and ruin every life about."

The wall speaker crackled, and silence rushed to listen as the principal said, "Andrew McKean, please report to my office."

"Lub-dub. Lub-dub! Lub-dub!!" Andrew's heart nearly pulverized his sternum. He stepped up to Miss Hogue's desk. "May I have a hall pass, please?" he croaked. Crumpling the pink slip into a cold, sweaty palm, he hurried from the room, desperate for a fountain, desperate for a bathroom, desperate for air. He used both fountain and bathroom briefly before reaching his destination. Then, with a huge, arid gulp, he presented himself to the principal's secretary.

"Lub-dub. Lub-dub! Lub-dub!!" Were all secretaries hard of hearing? His heart hammered against its rib-barred cage, but she was oblivious.

"Too bad you don't have a valid alibi," said Fear. "Brobdingnagian is waiting in there with two of Wilmington's finest, and you're going down."

"Mr. McKean? You may go in now."

Andrew tried to walk tall. He had done wrong, but he still was a McKean.

"Ah, yes," agreed Fear. "A McKean. How proud Thomas McKean would be to know that his young descendent is about to be expelled from the school that bears his name."

That was true. They would expel him. If only he had gotten away to New Zealand. He had been so sure Ed and Bob wouldn't crack. They must have told immediately. Maybe the police got a confession out of them before the trial. Maybe that's when he had been implicated. But if so, why hadn't they come after him sooner?

"Good morning, Andrew." Brobdingnagian seemed in terribly good spirits. "Please sit down."

Andrew slipped his sweaty right hand into his pocket as he sat, frantically rubbing good luck out of the little oval box.

"I'm sure you must be wondering why I called you out of class again, Andrew. I normally wouldn't see you twice in a year, let alone twice in as many days." The extra-portly man leaned back in his leather swivel chair.

"It's coming." Fear jumped up and down in Andrew's head. "Judgment is coming."

Mr. Brobdingnagian looked at him purposefully and said, "I got word today...."

Here it came.

"... that the Rotary selected you as their exchange student."

It wasn't expulsion! At least, probably not.

"Hold on," warned Fear. "This could be a curve ball. Don't run the bases before you hit."

Mr. Brobdingnagian looked closely at the pale freckled face. "We're all very proud of you, even though we've known you such a short time. I did know your grandfather well, and he always spoke highly of you. I see that your reputation is well earned, and I'm delighted to have you as a representative of Thomas McKean High School. I would very much like to announce this before the student body at this afternoon's football pep rally, if that's all right with you." The principal was standing now, extending his hand.

Andrew jumped to his feet, and felt the blood drain from his head. He was about to go out like a light. Sternly, he willed the blood upward, and took the extended hand. He shook it firmly, as his grandfather had taught him, and replied, "Would it be possible to wait until next week for the announcement, sir? You see, I promised that I wouldn't tell anyone until after my younger brother's piano competition. It's important for him to have the spotlight this Saturday."

"Of course," said the principal, still holding his hand and pumping it up and down. "We will save the announcement for Monday morning's student assembly, and you will sit next to me on the platform. I'm glad you are one of our students, Andrew, and glad you were selected. Congratulations! The Rotary has made a good choice. From what I have heard, you are a man of character."

Andrew's face flushed, and he looked down at the plump hand that still enveloped his own. Mr. Brobdingnagian laughed loudly and released the handshake. "Thank you for coming, Andrew. You may go back to class now."

Andrew fled. He didn't ask the secretary to initial his hall pass, but he didn't care.

He simply fled.

He had to be alone. He had to think. He hurtled down the stairway to the subterranean privacy of the locker room.

Man of character? Hypocritical worm. Spineless slime of a worm. A man of character would confess and take the full consequences of his actions. His conscience tormented him as he stood in the doorway.

Why not do it? Thomas McKean would have confessed — pretty sure about that. He risked his life to sign the *Declaration of Independence.* So, why not be like him? It was only printing flyers. Nobody was killed. Confess and be done with it. A few months in jail is a few months in jail. At least the man-of-character pretense will end.

Andrew found his way to a washroom sink. He scrubbed his hands and returned to the locker room where he slumped onto a corner bench: a bench against the innermost wall, against the end of a bank of steel gray lockers. The little oval box in his pocket dug into his thigh, but he let it dig. He deserved far worse pain than that.

"Man of character. Man of character." The words echoed within, accompanied by the heavy thumping of his heart. He banged his head repeatedly against the hard, cold locker.

What was character, anyway?

Andrew's heart, refusing its normal beat, was making him dizzy. He leaned his head back against the cold concrete wall. "I know I'm a coward, but I can't do it. I can't. I can't." He breathed the words into the locker room air, and they returned more foul than when they left.

Abruptly, he leapt to his feet and staggered to the bathroom, but not in time for the transition of his stomach's contents, which gushed onto the floor. He stumbled to the sink, rinsed his mouth, then applied a fistful of paper towels to the putrid puddle. Was that only two breakfast bars?

As he went back to the sink to wash his hands and face, he looked in the mirror. He could almost see and hear the cliché angel on his right shoulder, "Go back to the principal and confess, Andrew. That's what real men of character would do — men of courage. You'll feel better if you do."

The cliché devil on his left shoulder smirked, and retorted, "Sure. You destroyed one man's name and reputation, why not another? Of course, you didn't even know Coach Ando, so that didn't matter. You do know your dad, though. Go and tell the principal, man of character. You'll destroy the entire McKean family."

Andrew scrubbed his hands again, harder. He rubbed a wad of paper towel over them, and tossed it in the waste can. He couldn't tell. Dad would be livid. Mom would be crushed. Andrew himself would land in jail. Alicia, Cathryn, and Caleb would all be marked by it, too.

The bell over the mirror derailed his train of thought with a harsh clang, and he dashed to the door. Warning bell. Classes would change in three minutes. He mustn't be caught down here.

"A bit early for cleanout, Andrew," called a voice. It was the new coach.

Andrew turned and frantically summoned an alibi. "I had to get something out of my locker," he lied – and immediately wished he hadn't. "I have to wash my hands, and get up to class now." He ducked into the washroom and scrubbed again. The hands still felt filthy.

"See you at three o'clock, Coach," he called. He raced pell-mell up the stairs, gasping to a halt before his locker just as the first students spilled into the hall. He stuck his head in the locker and exhaled deeply. Then he sucked in a big breath of locker-stale air, and stepped back, inappropriately serene. He gazed nonchalantly into his small locker mirror and whisked his copper spikes to attention. Then, his filthy, trembling hands calmly selected books for his trigonometry class.

"Hey, didn't see you at the trial yesterday, Andrew," called Jim.

"Previous appointment," Andrew replied. Had everything in the world given way to the trial?

"They didn't do much. The judge told Ed and Bob he was trying them for the defamation of Coach Ando's character. Then the lawyers told everybody what they were going to prove. Except Ed and Bob's lawyer is such a wimp, you could hardly tell what he hopes to prove." Jim slugged Andrew on the upper arm and fell into step beside him saying, "Hey, can you help me with my science project? I want to make a live volcano, and I'm not sure what to use for lava."

"Sure." They turned the corner, and there was Penny, waiting by the classroom door.

"Hi, Jim. Do you mind if I steal Andy a minute?" she said sweetly.

Jim winked at her, raised his eyebrows knowingly at Andrew, and went into the classroom.

"What happened to you?" Penny showed real concern as Jim left.

"I was called to the principal's office."

"I mean first hour — in homeroom."

"Oh, I had to leave early to get a front seat in English class." He averted his gaze. Her eyes were too demanding.

"Back up the turnip truck, Andy. One minute, you were hilarious with your hangman's boot. The next minute, you plunged into some kind of mood. I hope you aren't a melancholic who's always going into a mood. I once dated a guy like that — who had a melancholic temperament — the operative word is "once." So if you're given to moods like this morning's, let's call it quits now."

Andrew gazed carefully past her deep brown eyes. There was a spot of acne just beside Penny's right eye — Penny, whose olive complexion never had a single blemish. He backed away from such intrusion into her privacy, and looked directly into her eyes, then down at the floor. "I had a lot on my mind, Penny."

"Oh. Is that all? I know that feeling," she said. "I have a lot on my mind, too, these days." She was smiling again, the full cupid's bow of her lips a bit farther below her nose than most people's, but somehow cuter because of that.

"I keep thinking about what Ed and Bob did last April," she said, "and about the trial, and how it will end. I can't get it out of my mind, and it makes me sick. Actually, it literally made me so sick a couple of times that I had to miss school. That's why I was absent yesterday. Last spring I almost quit school, but when you enrolled this fall, things started looking up. You're about the only one who doesn't know Ed and Bob, and you *are* the only one who doesn't talk about them all the time. Thanks again for the pizza and Halloween Dance," she said. "I had a good time."

Andrew dared to meet the dancing brown eyes with his blue ones. "I wondered why you had been absent after the dance. I didn't know you were sick. I didn't think you cared about the trial because you never mentioned it."

He adroitly changed the subject. "Did you have a good enough time to tell me your last name?

"Why do you need my last name? I thought we were on a first name basis." Her almonds crinkled with mischief.

"We are, but I can't even look up your phone number if I don't know your last name." He put a nonchalant hand on the door frame just above her shining ebony hair, and gazed downward into her beautiful face.

She smiled up at him from a bright spot below his shoulder. "And why would you need my phone number? I don't give it to just anyone."

"I thought I might like to be more than just anyone." He looked into the sparkling, teasing eyes and wanted very much to kiss her.

"OK. I'll give you my ID card until lunch if you promise to eat with me today, but you must also promise to not look at it until I leave."

"I promise." The warning bell saved Andrew from anything further, and she thrust the card at him — upside down.

"See you in the cafeteria," she said with a cute smile, and hurried toward the stairs.

He watched her feminine sway until she was out of sight — watched the black slacks, the crimson sweater, and the swinging black hair.

A confession on his part would ruin their relationship, but his trip to New Zealand would have the same effect, wouldn't it? Maybe it was better that way: that they be forced to break up sooner rather than later.

He didn't want to hurt her for anything because he really did like — he turned over the student ID card — — —

Penny Ando?

# 10

## The Color of Paua

Saturday seemed to arrive early that week, dawning a glorious late-autumn day, with a sky unusually blue for November, and sunshine that belied the chill factor.

Andrew heard Cathryn bounce out of bed, almost more excited than Caleb was. "Alicia," she said, bouncing on her sister's soft mattress. "What should I wear to Caleb's piano competition?"

Alicia groaned, pulled the soft pink duvet over her head, and burrowed into its dark warmth, her strawberry hair the only sign of life.

Cathryn gave up and scurried into their bathroom. She really liked living in the mansion now that everything was settled — everything but the boxes in the carriage house. Cathryn had tried after school yesterday to get permission to look in the carriage house for the P-box, and had received a strange look from Mom. She thought about that strange look now as she watched her mirror hand scrub her mirror face. Did Mom know something about the P-box that she wasn't telling them? Caleb would know. He had a sixth sense when it came to Mom. She'd have to ask Caleb — after his competition. Dad had given dire warnings about what would happen to anyone who bothered Caleb this morning.

Cathryn brushed her hair until it shown. Maybe she would wear it loose today instead of in Pippi braids. She hurried into jeans and sweatshirt for breakfast, and ran downstairs to the big eat-in kitchen. Mom was there, barely awake.

"I can't find Pierrot, Mom. He must be in the carriage house," said Cathryn. "May I look?"

"Meow." Pierrot pounced on her feet.

"Cathryn, you know the carriage house is off limits," said Mom. "Go up and tell your sister and brothers that breakfast will be at eight."

Cathryn raced back up the wide, ornate staircase, thumped on the boys' door and yelled, "Breakfast at eight o'clock! Competition Day!" She skipped down the long hallway to her own room and yanked off Alicia's duvet. "Mom said breakfast is at eight o'clock, and you're to help me choose something to wear." She crossed her fingers as she appended the lie. "I think the red velvet's best saved for holidays, so what do you think of my green plaid jumper with my white blouse?"

"Fine," said a sleep-fogged voice. "Brrr. These old houses aren't very warm." Alicia jumped out of bed into fluffy pink pig slippers and a thick pink robe.

In the boys' bedroom, Caleb prodded his older brother. "Andrew, should I shave?"

Andrew rolled to the floor, struggling for control of his mirth. He gazed solemnly at the chin above him, and said, "You'll be okay, Carrot. I don't see any stubble. Want to borrow one of my ties?"

Caleb brightened. "The green one with the red and white stripes?"

"Perfect. Now shower and dress in something old for breakfast. I'll get the tie and help you get ready after we eat."

Andrew did just that. He applied himself first to vigorous cleansing. He scrubbed Caleb's freshly-showered face — from the back of the left projecting ear, across the freckled, pale cheeks and the thin, freckled nose, all the way to the back of the right jutting ear. Then he scrubbed down the neck to his shoulders. He scrubbed the short-clipped fingernails with a brush, and carefully pushed back each cuticle, much to Caleb's pride. Andrew polished the size seven black dress shoes while Caleb donned his clothing. He made his brother stand for inspection, and brushed every suggestion of lint from the navy suit. He tugged the crisp starched white collar into flawlessness, and circled it with the promised striped tie. He secured the green tie with a textbook half Windsor knot, which he himself had so recently perfected.

"Now, for the pièce de résistance," he said. He picked up his own purple hair gel and applied a generous amount to the unruly shredded carrot heap. He combed the heap into unequal portions, one on either side of a perfect divide, and stood back to admire his handiwork. "You're a new man, Caleb," he said. "Go break a leg!"

Andrew stood Caleb at the top of the stairs and called the family. When they had assembled, he announced in a stately voice: "Ladies and gentleman, I give you the great concert pianist, Mr. Caleb Orin McKean!" Everyone applauded as Caleb descended the stairs.

"You're sure to win, Caleb!" exclaimed Cathryn. "You know what they say: 'cleanliness is next to excellence.'"

"Next to godliness," the family chorused.

Mom fussed over Caleb, looking for some detail to correct, but Dad pulled her away. "He's perfect, Margaret. Let him focus on his music."

* * * * *

At the concert hall, they studied programs, whispering briefly about the boys and girls who would be competing. Then they settled down to await Caleb's turn.

The first competitors were cute little twins, who played a duet version of Fur Elise, their dark faces and curly black hair doing as much of the work as their little brown fingers.

The second competitor began by facing the audience, crossing dark slanted eyes, and staring down his abruptly flat nose. Then he slouched onto the piano bench for a moment, lifted his body and hands above the keyboard, and plunged into an intricate, elaborate tapestry of *Chopsticks*, much to everybody's amusement.

One by one, boys and girls of various ages and abilities went forward and played the music he or she had been practicing for months.

"Our next performer is Caleb McKean. Caleb will be playing *Beethoven's Sonata, Opus 49, Number One, G Minor*."

Mom's hands trembled, but not Caleb's. With sudden and complete stage presence, he strode to the platform, mounted the five carpeted steps, and walked confidently to the piano. He placed his music on the rack, sat down on the shiny black bench, and then stood again.

What was Caleb doing?

The family watched as the intrepid eleven-year-old deliberately turned the adjustment knobs on the left and right sides of the elegant bench. Again, he sat — and again, he stood.

A ripple of laughter ran around the room. Four times, Caleb adjusted the piano seat — he adjusted until it was perfect for him. Then he played. He played as he had never played before.

He began slowly, tendering a G-minor tune that was at once sad and lonely, but hauntingly beautiful. His face reflected the poignant emotion of the forlorn little tune as his fingers accurately, musically conveyed that emotion to his audience, hushing them into their own melancholy thoughts.

Then, he bent low over the keyboard to build the emotion, fingers moving rapidly as he carried his listeners up into a calmer, more extroverted frame, away from the first despondency. As he played, the music grew stronger, with octave trills. Finally, it meandered slowly off to the end of the first movement.

Caleb paused dramatically, breathed deeply, and began the second movement of the sonata — a lovely rondo, marked *allegro*, that brightened to a G major key. The notes multiplied, sparkled, and burst into a vivacious tune. They shimmered. They danced, as did his fingers. He unlocked the listeners' ears with his spell, and poured the rich harmonies into them. He made toes dance beneath seats, and fingers tap in laps.

As Caleb's fifteen-minute performance neared its end, it grew even showier. His left hand, greatly strengthened while the right finger was healing, claimed full attention as it cavorted over a myriad of sixteenth notes, building and building the work to a grand *fortissimo*.

Then, he struck the final stately chord. His fingers lingered on the keyboard, and his head drooped low over it, respect for the great composer holding him captive. The audience, too, was spellbound for a moment — one silent moment.

"Bravo!" A silver-haired man jumped to his feet in praise, and applause swept the auditorium. One by one, they rose to their feet, clapping hands vigorously. "Bravo! Bravo! Bravo!" It almost sounded like thunder claps to the young musician — as though the gods of music were applauding from the sky above the auditorium.

Caleb stood, calmly placed his left hand on the piano, and bowed low. Then, as the applause lessened, he stumbled to his seat, exhausted but magnificently pleased with the experience. His family welcomed him back with whispered praise.

Several pianists followed Caleb, and then came the judges' decision. A girl whose parents recently had emigrated from Russia, received third place for her performance of a Tchaikovsky work. The curly-headed twins were awarded a second, and the audience sat forward in anticipation.

"There is no question in our minds this year," said the awarding judge, "regarding first place. First place goes to Caleb McKean!"

Caleb nearly skipped to the platform, but was all dignity as he received his certificate — a dignity that lasted only until he got back to his seat. Then, he grinned from ear to ear. "I won!"

They all congratulated him, and he had moved on to bask in the praises of total strangers when a man walked briskly to the platform, picked up a microphone and announced, "Ladies and gentlemen, may I have your attention, please? Hurricane Valerie has doubled back, and is headed straight for Wilmington. Thunderstorms have already reached us, and the hurricane's outer wall is expected soon. You are advised to return home directly and prepare for the storm. Thank you for coming, and please drive safely."

"I thought I heard thunder right after I played," said Caleb excitedly. He didn't tell that he had thought it the gods of music applauding.

"Gather your coats and stay together," Dad instructed. "I'll bring the van around to the front of the auditorium." He pulled the collar of his coat around his neck and hurried toward the door.

Although Dad swung the van as close to the stairway as possible, they were quite damp by the time they gained its warmth and protection.

"Wow!" exclaimed Andrew. "I never would have guessed from this morning's weather that today would turn out like this!"

Dad carefully guided the van to I-95, yielded to two big rigs, and merged into the faster traffic on the wide highway. He had gone only a short distance, perhaps a third of a mile, when Caleb said, "Dad, you aren't going home."

Andrew studied the scenery briefly before adding, "You're going to our old home."

Dad muttered unintelligibly, peering through the rapidly darkening scene to find the next exit. A flash of lightning clawed a deep scratch on the leaden sky ahead, then bragged thunderously about the stroke.

Traffic crawled now, and Dad moved to the right lane, trusting the wet red taillights of an eighteen-wheeler for guidance to the next exit.

As he left the interstate route and turned toward what was now home, Mom screamed. "Stop! There's a fallen tree!"

Dad jammed on the brake, and the car slid, coming to a stop with Mom's door touching the huge maple tree. "Everyone all right?"

"Everybody back here is," reported Andrew.

"I'm glad we weren't here when it fell," Mom said, shivering. "We might have been, William, if you hadn't started out for the wrong house."

"Too true." Dad studied the situation the best he could in the dark of the storm, decided he could ease around the tree on the sidewalk, and began his maneuvers. Mom cringed as branches scraped against the paint of her van, but soon they were safely beyond the fallen giant.

"Has the McKean Manor ever been through a hurricane before, Dad?" asked Alicia. She sat far forward in her seat, trying to help Dad's eyes pierce the gloom.

"Big hurricanes went through here in 1954 and 1972, and Hurricane Floyd went through while we were in Europe. The mansion endured those three, and probably a lot more before them, so I don't think we have to worry about being safe, if we can just reach home." Tension coursed from his neck and shoulders to the white knuckles that gripped the steering wheel.

Lightning slashed repeatedly at the dark curtain of the afternoon sky. Sidewalks and houses appeared briefly, only to disappear. The thunder boomed louder, closer, longer. Rain drummed on the top of the van. Wild wind piped unnerving eerie notes. Conversation became impossible.

Dad wove the car between rows of trees, its headlights making mere dents in the darkness. His right tire hit the curb once, and he swerved.

Another luminous flash revealed the McKean home. Dad steered through the big gates, over the flooded cobblestones, and as close to the front steps as possible. The four McKeans in the back seats gave a cheer of appreciation, tumbled into the rain, and flew up the stairway to the wide expanse of dry front porch.

"Everybody into sweat suits, socks and your athletic shoes," Mom called as she hurried to her bedroom, "and hang up your good clothing. Then meet in the kitchen."

Cathryn followed Alicia into their room, uneasiness in her pretty eyes. "Alicia, can you help with my buttons?" Alicia undid them quickly, and hurried out of her own blue dress – the one Dad called *Alice Blue Gown* after some old song. She and Cathryn flew into their sweats and socks and ran for the kitchen's safety, carrying their shoes.

It was surprising how quickly the entire family assembled, all in full sweat suits — all, that is, except Caleb. Caleb had donned the shirt of his green sweat suit, but then had donned, in his haste, the pants of his red one.

"What's in the soup?" Cathryn asked Mom.

"Nutrition," said Mom. "You like it."

"Cathryn likes everything," risked Caleb.

"Well, at least I get my five-a-day of fruit and veggies. That's more than you can say."

"If this storm hits hard, we'll have plenty of veggies — dried veggies," warned Mom. "I was too busy to go shopping yesterday, and we may be thanking Grandfather for the food mixes and drinking water in his emergency store. He even included some treats we seldom buy. It's an ill wind that blows no man good."

"Any batteries?" asked Dad.

"Everything we need is there. Your dad was very wise when it came to preparedness."

""Some call that paranoia, Margaret."

"Good weather paranoia can easily become stormy-weather wisdom, William. I'd far rather be prepared and not need it than face a hurricane without food or water."

Mom quickly sliced soft, golden cheddar cheese and crisp, ruby red apples. Alicia piled lightly browned toast on a large platter.

The storm swirled closer now, blowing huge, angry breaths down each of the manor's eight large chimneys, and sending forgotten soot into the clean rooms. Its voice sent shivers through them all, though they were plenty warm.

Caleb looked at the mantel clock as he slid into his place at the table. "It's already three," he said. "My competition seems so long ago."

Mom smiled. "You'll have time to enjoy your victory once this storm blows out to sea," she told him. "You really did an excellent job, though,

Caleb. You inherited strong musical genes from someone." She placed two slices of crisp apple on his plate beside the toast and cheese.

"Fresh apples are so grotty," he said.

"Grotty isn't quite right, Caleb," said Mom. "The British would use it for a coat that was wretchedly shabby or of poor quality, but...."

"Apples are definitely of poor quality," said Caleb stubbornly, "so they are grotty."

Dad was blown back through the doorway. "Gus pulled all of his nesting material into his little ferret house. He couldn't be warmer."

Dad actually slurped a quick bowl of soup, then took Andrew with him to secure shutters. When all were tightly closed, they returned to the kitchen, and the family began a long watch. At first, the TV streamed storm reports, with soggy, wind-whipped reporters clinging to their jobs. When the channel lost its signal, Dad tuned in the portable radio, and they continued to track the beast as it howled toward Wilmington. They relived Caleb's competition with him, and played board games until the electricity bowed to the storm. Then Dad lit an old kerosene lantern.

"Well, we can't see much with this light, but we can hear," Dad said. "I think this is a good time for Andrew to tell us the big news he got this week." He smiled. "Go ahead, son."

Andrew looked around the table a moment, then blurted, "Grandfather submitted an exchange student application to the Rotary for me, and they're sending me to study in New Zealand for a semester. I'm to leave in mid-January."

The words tumbled into an astonished void. Alicia, Caleb, and Cathryn just stared at him. Andrew was going away. He would be gone for months. They had never considered life without Andrew. Andrew had been there from the day each of them was born. He was their CEO. They had been the McKean foursome so long. How could they be otherwise?

"It's only January through July," Andrew said. Thunder accentuated his statement.

The news was big, so big — bigger than their shadows that the flickering lantern light had choreographed into an intricate dance on the wall.

Alicia's eyes grew teary blue, while Caleb and Cathryn remained wide-eyed.

"Will you write to us?" asked Caleb.

"Of course," promised Andrew.

They discussed Andrew's enormous news in detail then, until the powerful storm finally twisted her gusty skirts around her, and swept out across the Atlantic Ocean.

Then, they went to bed and slept.

On Sunday, they awoke to devastation. The huge Norway pine by the reflecting pool lay fallen. TV news confirmed similar damage to many of the city's buildings, and extensive damage to the courthouse, which would be closed until at least mid-January. "To allow time for repairs to the courthouse, all pending cases will be postponed until late January," reported the news anchor.

Andrew nearly swallowed his entire jelly doughnut whole. Thank you, Hurricane Valerie! Mom was right about it being an ill wind that blows no man good!

The reporter was still announcing closures. "Schools throughout the city of Wilmington will be closed for the entire week."

Andrew shot up off his spine. "Dad," he said, "Don't you think we could have computer access this week since we have no school work?"

Dad put down his coffee mug and stroked the red moustache. Should he relent? He looked at them one by one, still grooming the hairy little pencil. "Well," he said, "I will allow computer use for just two things other than homework. You may look up the meaning of the word *paua*, and you may study New Zealand. But! There will be no games, no e-mail, and no on-line shopping."

"Yes, sir!" said Cathryn, snapping a salute. "I get the computer in our bedroom first."

"No you don't," said Alicia, racing for the stairs. "Last one up is a rotten byte."

"I'm going to practice piano," stated Caleb.

"Aren't you afraid your computer will be jealous?" said Andrew.

"It's in love with yours," Caleb retorted. "It adores your Penny screen saver. Penny, of the mellifluous voice." He batted his strikingly long eyelashes and dashed out of Andrew's reach.

"Thanks, Dad. I've been dying to look up *paua*, but it wasn't homework," said Andrew. "I'll let you know the minute I find it."

He flew up the stairs on wings of curiosity, and was soon opening a huge on-line dictionary. He typed "p-a-u-a" into the blank search box. He crossed his fingers, knocked on the wooden desk, and rubbed the green-blue oval in his pocket as he clicked the cursor on "Look it up." He cracked the knuckles of each hand impatiently.

"The word you have entered is not in the dictionary."

"Okay. There's more than one way to skin a cat." Sitting on the edge of the chair, he accessed a search engine. Carefully, he typed: "p-a-u," and stopped. The oval had seemed to bring luck at school last Friday. Why not today? He pulled it out and caressed the smooth blue-green swirls.

"Do your work, little oval," he whispered. "Help me find the P-word." He struck the final letter.

"Yes!" He scanned the list of eighteen sites. There —*paua.com*. He clicked on it. The monitor blinked to full white, and a blue-swirled egg appeared. The words *paua.com* were inscribed across its long, curved side. Below the egg were the words:

*Southern Shell — NZ Paua Shell*

"What's NZ?" He selected the information button, and gasped. It couldn't be! His heart made express deliveries of adrenaline through every vein as he quickly skimmed the information:

*AN INTRODUCTION TO PAUA*

*A Unique New Zealand Product*

The author called it a shellfish, which is known in New Zealand by the Maori word *Paua* (pä '– wä) — a species of abalone — grows only in the seas around New Zealand — eats seaweed and clings to rocks — is usually found at depths of three to forty feet, right along the shoreline.

"Paua shell," Andrew read, "is the most colourful of all the abalone shells. Others pale in comparison." The photos proved that. The colors varied from pinks and purples to greens and blues.

The author said colors change depending on the angle, and are iridescent like Mother of Pearl shell, but far more brilliant.

Andrew's breath gusted at squall speeds as he focused on the small photo that first had caught his attention — the pendant. Its colors were a perfect match! He snatched up the little oval box and held it near the monitor screen.

"Dad! Mom! Alicia! Caleb! Cathryn!" he squawked. "Come quick!" Schnauzie added his insistence and Andrew ran to fling open his door.

Footsteps pounded from every direction, as Dad called out, "What's wrong?" Dad arrived first, followed quickly by Mom and the others.

The trembling finger of Andrew's left hand pointed to the photo on the screen, while his shaky right hand held the precious oval box beside it.

Dad's eyes followed the finger, he read a few words, and he gasped. "The P-box. It was right under our noses."

Andrew found his voice. "Listen," he said, and he read the brief description, pronouncing *paua* with confidence. "This box is made of New Zealand paua shell. No wonder Grandfather is sending me there to learn its secret." He passed the box around so that each of them could hold it, gaze at it, give it the honor that was its due.

Cathryn pushed back her long red curls and held it to her ear, saying, "I wonder if you can hear the New Zealand ocean in it. Seashells have the sound of the ocean in them, don't they?"

"Only if it's the whole shell," said Alicia. She took the beautiful oval box between slender fingers and held it to her nose. "It has a faint ocean smell," she observed. "I wonder if paua shellfish have a good taste. I think they would be slimy."

Andrew turned back to the monitor screen. "Actually, some people think they taste great," he replied. "It says that paua meat is considered a delicacy in New Zealand as well as overseas."

Mom shuddered and wrinkled her fine nose. "I suppose you could get used to it," she said.

"Not I," laughed Dad. "I'm used to enough things already." He took up the reading of the introduction, paraphrasing as he went:

"The Maori people ate paua — carved the shells. It was part of their tradition. They still gather paua for important ceremonies. It's one of their favorite foods. The use of paua shell has become such a distinctive part of New Zealand artwork that there's a paua shell inlay on the floor in New Zealand's National Museum."

"Did you notice the spelling errors, Dad?" asked Andrew. "Whoever built this web page was careless. *Favourite* instead of favorite; *colourful* instead of colorful." Andrew scrolled back up the page. "He or she even spelled mollusk with a 'c' instead of a 'k' at the end. Maybe I can get a job teaching spelling while I'm in New Zealand."

"Well, now that we've all seen it, what are we waiting for?" asked Caleb, holding up the prize. "Why don't we open this paua box?" It had ceased to be the P-box.

"Can't," Andrew stated flatly. "It's locked."

Cathryn snatched it from Caleb and shook it beside her ear. "I can't hear anything," she said, "and it's supposed to have things in it."

"The key to my piano is in there!" said Caleb, making an excited grab for the box.

Andrew intercepted, and held the paua box above his head. "I've shaken it every night since I found it," he told them, "and I can't hear a thing. If there is a piano key, or anything else, it doesn't make a sound."

Dad reached for the shimmering oval. "Let me see your paua box, please, Andrew," he said.

Dad took it in his large, white hand and shook it gently. Nothing. He pulled his reading glasses from his shirt pocket and donned them, peering intently at the tiny lock. "We would only shatter the box if we tried to pry the lock, so we will have to leave it for now. Perhaps that's part of Grandfather's plan. Perhaps the Bartletts of New Zealand have the key."

# 11

## Kia Ora

Andrew had stayed home from church to pack, but couldn't make himself do it. "I'm really going to miss you, Schnauzie," he whispered in the little dog's soft ear. He scratched the stubby docked tail, and patiently received slimy kisses in return. He would miss them all: family, Penny, Schnauzie. He would even miss Augustus running up and down his legs while he studied.

Speaking of study, he was supposed to read the basic rules for exchange students. He opened the booklet:

*OBLIGATIONS OF STUDENTS LIVING ABROAD*

"Obligations, Schnauzie, not rules. Do you see a difference?" He began to skim the page. "Let's see. First, they expect me to obey the laws of the host country. If I don't, my exchange is terminated. Believe me, I can't afford to disobey the laws, Schnauzie, after the mess I made here."

He rubbed Schnauzie's wiry-soft gray back. "Do they really think I need to be disciplined by the school — and by the Bartletts? I'm old enough to take care of myself. I have a right to make my own decisions." He read on.

"Here's a good one. I have to sign a written statement that I will not, under any circumstances, drive a motor vehicle while I'm under the Rotary program's supervision. Dad would like that rule — obligation, I mean." Anyway, from what he had read on the Internet, New Zealanders drove on the opposite side of the road. Imagine going down the left side!

"Dating will be tolerated." Tolerated? He read on — urge that dates be in group situations only — for obvious reasons, *romantic involvement is strongly discouraged* — a student breaching the rule could be sent home. "You call that dating?" He threw the booklet on the desk. "Well, Penny, you will be happy to know I won't be having any romantic involvements," he said to the girl in the oak photo frame.

Thinking about Penny was painful. Penny Ando. He had wanted to break up right there in the cafeteria — the day he read it on her ID card — but how? He couldn't tell her the truth, so he had pretended everything was normal. He walked her home from school, now that her family was no longer a secret. He had taken her to every dance, every basketball game, and every party, always with the Sword of Damocles above his head.

Fear laughed. "Remember when Bob, Ed, and you sat on the back steps of the church before chorale practice last April?" He remembered. Bob was trying to smoke a cigarette — an experiment that Ed and Andrew rejected, with warnings that only a fool would suck poison into his body.

Ed had asked, "What can we do to get even with Coach for cutting me from the football team?"

"We?" Andrew had countered. "I don't go to your school. I'm a home-school kid, and I don't know Coach, except from seeing him at games."

"You know Coach Ando — short, squat guy with black hair that stands out all over — the Jap." Bob sucked in a lung full of nicotine and coughed. "I think I'm getting the hang of this," he bragged.

"Good for you," sneered Ed. "Slow suicide isn't so hard to master, is it?"

He turned back to Andrew. "Coach Ando has this thing against me because I'm Chinese. My dad said all Japs hate all Chinese — have for centuries. That's why he cut me from the team."

"Coach said so?" Andrew hated prejudice.

"He didn't have to." Ed swore roughly. "I could see it in his eyes. Anyone could. So I was thinking it would serve him right if we...."

Andrew didn't want to remember. He went back to his reading. "Thanks to Mrs. Bartlett, Schnauzie, I have to attend a Christian School. Imagine — me in a Christian school. I don't mind singing in chorale on Sunday, but church school?"

"I may not stay in New Zealand after my exchange program ends, it says, but I wouldn't want to stay away from you," Andrew told his dog, hugging the little warm body against him. Schnauzie still smelled of yesterday's coconut oil shampoo. Memory-making breaths of it filled Andrew's nose. He took the miniature, bearded face between his hands and gazed into the dog's intelligent eyes. "You won't forget me, will you? I promise to come right home at the end of July."

A car door slammed. "Noon!" Andrew plopped Schnauzie on the floor, stuffed the booklet into his backpack, and swiftly unburdened the bed into his luggage. Mrs. Bartlett was certain to own an iron. He slammed the lids of the big black suitcases, and raced for the stairs.

"Packing finished, Andrew?" Dad asked as he began serving plates.

"Yep," said Andrew, accepting his eggplant zucchini casserole from Dad. "This looks better for our hearts than that Italian restaurant meal."

"Andrew, will you be able to eat heart healthy food in New Zealand?" asked Alicia.

Andrew shook his head. "I have to eat what's set before me — my *obligation.*"

"But don't they eat nasty meat pies — stuff like cow's kidneys? You won't eat those, will you?"

"If that's what I'm served."

"Disgusting!" Alicia turned up her nose.

"Then let's not talk about it," ordered Dad. "Andrew, I've forgotten the name of the travel agent who's to see you off on Tuesday."

Tuesday. Tuesday was too soon. "Her name's Ms. Ritchey," he replied quietly.

"Ms. Ritchey. Well, remind me to call Ms. Ritchey tomorrow and be sure all is in order."

"How long does it take to get to New Zealand from here?" asked Alicia.

"Dad?" said Andrew around a sudden swelling in his throat. He put down his fork and tried to reduce the swelling with a drink.

"Well," Dad said, "he leaves home at three o'clock Tuesday afternoon and arrives in New Zealand at eight o'clock Thursday morning."

"Better pray for good in-flight movies!"

"That isn't the end of the trip," said Dad. "After three days of orientation in Auckland, he flies to Nelson on a small plane. The total trip is more than twenty-four hours."

Andrew bulldozed cranberry sauce against fallen broccoli trees. One entire day of his life in planes — and his stomach hated air travel.

"Finish your meal, Andrew," Mom said.

"I've had enough, thank you." He laid down the fork. He was about to leave home, to travel to the opposite side of the globe, the opposite end of the globe. He was no baby, but the reality loomed large on his horizon. By the end of this week, he would be hearing a new kind of English; eating new food; learning new sports. With the contents of only two pieces of luggage and one backpack, he would board the plane for New Zealand. He might as well board a spaceship for Mars.

* * * * *

At 5:30 P.M. on January's second Tuesday, a young man with freshly-conservative copper hair bereft of its spikes, waited with studied calm for the flight from Philadelphia to Los Angeles.

"Send me a wooly New Zealand lamb."

"Did you get your book about rugby?"

The swirling voices in the airport's din gave way to Penny's soft tones. "I bought this pendant for us to wear — half for you and half for me — until you come back." She encircled his neck with a chain from which dangled one half of a silver-plated heart, its ragged edge implying a violent wrenching from its mate. He gave her a silent hug that promised nothing, asked everything. The little heart was likely to remain broken, once Penny found out. Penny surely must sense it, but she told him cheerily, "Now don't read my card until you are over the Pacific — and smile! When you come back, we'll catch up on everything before school starts. We both will be seniors, and I already have a date for the Prom!"

How could she be so upbeat? How could she smile? His muscles refused to do it.

Dad jumped to the rescue. "How's your dad, Penny? I hope he has found a new job."

"Father is fine, thank you, but he hasn't found a new job yet, Mr. McKean."

"Have they convicted those hoodlums yet?"

"No, but Father feels sure they will when the trial reopens. The hardest part seems to be getting them to reveal the name of their accomplice. The fliers came from someone else's printer, but they won't say whose. That's the only good thing about those two — their loyalty."

A speaker crackled: "United Airlines Flight #29 for Los Angeles is now boarding at Gate 5."

"Take care of yourself, Son." Mom smiled, but the greenish hazel eyes became a misty green-brown. "I love you," she whispered in his ear. She kissed him before rummaging for a tissue.

"Smile, you're going to love New Zealand," Dad promised, and Andrew heard: "Smile, you're going to love school." Dad's embrace was intense and brief. "If you need anything, son, send me an E-mail. I know you'll make us proud."

"Enjoy the barbies," said Caleb.

"Have fun." Alicia kissed him on the right cheek, and Cathryn added a quick one on the left.

"I'll write every day," Penny whispered.

"See you all this summer." Andrew's voice squeezed around the swelling in his throat. He gazed toward the impassive jet-way door, and then dared another look at his family and Penny.

Ms. Ritchey came forward, shook his hand, and said, "A New Zealand Rotary representative will be waiting just beyond customs, holding a sign with your name on it. You'll love New Zealand, Andrew, and you'll come back with a lot to tell."

He nodded, and watched his life change.

Dad handing him a black wallet containing tickets, passport, and other papers; shaking his hand again; saying, "You'd better go now."

Mom coming between him and the jet-way: one more hug; one more kiss; wet cheeks; wet eyes; wet nose; dry mouth; knot in throat.

Walking to the jet-way now — looking back — feeling wetness on pale cheeks — wetness that neither stopped nor shrank the boulder lodged in his throat. At the doorway — handing ticket to the attendant — receiving stub — oblivious to her cheery smile. Turning one last time....

Andrew's heart abandoned him and flew back to the sanctuary of his family. They smiled, cried, and waved him forward. He entered the long tunnel, and walked to the plane.

"May I see your boarding pass, please?" A disembodied voice made the request. "Seat 38A, left side, by the window. Are you all right?"

He staggered blindly down the crowded aisle. 38A. He couldn't find numbers, couldn't read them when he did find them. Was that it?

"Are you 38A?" Two men stood to let him reach the window. "I'm Thomas Hearn," said 38B.

"And I'm Edwin Hamilton," said 38C. "Glad to have you aboard. Returning to University?"

"No. Going to New Zealand as an exchange student." Andrew busied himself stowing the gray blanket under the seat with his backpack, tightening the seatbelt, and arranging the pillow. He looked out the tiny window, and tried to see Mom in the huge airport. The dam of tears broke again. He should have told Mom how much he loved her.

A flight attendant demonstrated the safety measures needed in case of an accident, and he listened intently.

The jumbo plane backed away from the gate, and headed for the longest runway. Andrew pressed his face against the tiny window and waved hard, just in case. Tears flooded his cheeks, and he let them flow. They would stop soon, he thought — but they did not. They flowed as the plane raced down the runway; as it rose swiftly into the air, and gained altitude, its aisles tipping sharply. Then the tears almost stopped — until Mr. Hearn asked if he was all right. He could only nod miserably as the canals opened again.

They were still climbing when the flight attendants began to serve dinner. The fruit plate Mom had ordered, "to avoid air sickness" was a bittersweet tether. To Andrew's surprise, Mr. Hearn also had a fruit plate, which he ate while reading his newspaper. Andrew downed all of his crackers and cheese, but could only pick at the fresh fruit. His stomach was a fat water balloon.

After dinner, Mr. Hearn produced a magnetic chessboard. "You can probably beat me, but I'm willing to give it a try if you are."

Mr. Hamilton leaned forward to warn, "Watch him, Andrew. He's a trickster."

"Just because you never can beat me is no reason to cast aspersions," replied Mr. Hearn.

Andrew and Mr. Hearn managed to sandwich three games of chess around the in-flight movie and a couple of snacks. It somehow seemed to abbreviate the long flight to Los Angeles.

"Thanks, Mr. Hearn," said Andrew, as they cleared away the final game.

Mr. Hearn snorted. "Thanks for what?"

"Come on. You let me win those first two games. You won the last one in five moves, which proves you were hustling me."

"I warned you," said Mr. Hamilton.

The pilot's voice announced the landing and asked that seat backs be upright, tables stowed. Andrew cleared his table, looked at the air sickness bag, but decided to leave it there.

Mr. Hearn asked casually, "Want a stick of gum? I always chew it while landing. Helps the inner ear. Before I learned that, nobody wanted to travel with me, if you know what I mean."

Andrew laughed, placed the chewing gum in his mouth, and braced for the inevitable. The world grew as they descended, and his stomach began making threats.

"Don't turn around," Mr. Hearn said, "but another trick I learned is to find a spot where sky meets earth, and keep your eyes on it as we land."

Andrew's misty blue eyes obediently picked a point on the horizon and stared. Suddenly, he realized that full-grown buildings were racing by.

He stiffened as the enormous jet contacted the runway and shuddered across it on hot tires.

Los Angeles. Wilmington was a continent away. In less than two hours, he would be over the Pacific, with the entirety of North America behind him. Well, then, it was time to be a man. He squared his shoulders as the plane taxied to the gate. He stood up as the aircraft stopped.

"Hearn and I are going over to International Departures to continue on to Bali. Shall we walk over together?" suggested Mr. Hamilton.

Andrew grinned. It helped to have a couple of coattails, even if they were business suit tails. He followed them through the airport — three tall men. Just before they parted ways, Thomas Hearn led them into a gift shop, purportedly to see if his products were displayed well, but as they left, he handed a small bag to Andrew. "Pick a point on the horizon," he said, grinning. Inside were a magnetic chess set and three packs of gum.

The two men accompanied him to his gate, teasing about New Zealand girls. They gave him their business cards, and told him to write and let them know all about life as an exchange student. Then they shook hands and were gone.

Andrew was alone.

He sank into a seat near the departure door and pulled his aloneness in after him. He was too tired for tears. He pillowed his head on the Schnauzie-fragrant backpack, and fell asleep.

When he awakened, the area was bustling with activity. "Air New Zealand Flight #9011 is now boarding at Gate 17. All passengers please report to the boarding area immediately."

Flight #9011. This was it. Launch time! He had sole responsibility for himself. Ticket. Where was his ticket? He found it in the wallet Dad had given him, stepped to the door of the jet-way, and handed the stiff card to the attendant.

The man flashed him a wide smile. "*Kia Ora*," he said. "Hello!"

Andrew grinned. "Thank you," he said, and he entered the jet-way with a stride as much like a professional traveler's as he could muster.

The Rotary had provided a window seat again, and he was glad to be first into the row. He fished out the chess game; slipped it into the seat pocket; removed the magazine, and stowed his pack under the seat. He was too tired to read, but the magazine would help avoid eye contact with arriving seatmates who might be unwanted.

"Hello." The gentle voice arrived on vanilla-fragrant air. He looked up to see a girl of about his age struggling with a small blue carry-on, a handbag, a camera, and a long red coat. "I guess we're seatmates," she said.

Andrew leapt to his feet. "I'll help you stow those," he offered — much too eagerly. "Do you want it all in the upper bin, or shall I put your suitcase under the seat?"

Her purple-pink smile broadened. "It all can go above except my handbag. I'm exhausted, so I don't think I'll do much but sleep."

"I know what you mean," Andrew said. Liar. He was not at all sleepy now. He folded her soft coat around her camera, and stowed it in the bin, using her suitcase to push it gently to the back. Then he slid clumsily across to the window seat, tumbling magazine, blanket, and pillow all to the floor in his haste to be out of the way of this tall, dark-haired, dark-eyed feast for the senses.

The girl laughed, and dumped her own blanket and pillow, making his jumble all right. "My name's Morgan Britton. I'm going to New Zealand as an exchange student," she said.

"That can't be coincidence! I'm an exchange student, too. I'm Andrew McKean. If you're in the Rotary program, my guess is that they decided to give us company in our misery."

"I am with the Rotary; I've never been away from home before; and I am in total misery. I'm from Minnesota. How about you?"

"Wilmington, Delaware." They grinned and shook hands, her hand surprisingly strong in his.

"Huh!" The aisle seatmate arrived in an obese bustle, spilling a conglomeration of baggage. "Usual minuscule seat!" He stooped with a loud grunt, stuffing a large suitcase under the seat in front, and losing his cowboy hat in the process. He retrieved the hat, unwound a scarf from his neck, and threw the two items on his seat. Then he repeatedly stretched his grumbling body upward to cram into the storage bin, one by one: a bulky camera bag with large black tripod attached, an overcoat that was surely size XXXL, a red and black golf umbrella, and one large shopping bag. He slammed the bin repeatedly until it closed. He turned to sit down and found his forgotten hat and scarf — but now he could not open the bin.

Complaining in gunpowder language, he hoisted his immensity onto the seat, from which position he forced open the bin and put in hat and scarf. Three hard slams closed the compartment, and the man descended heavily to the narrow aisle, from which he proceeded to jam as much as possible of his triple XL body into the size L seat. Now it was time to fasten his seatbelt. The large man wrestled the standard size belt, swearing loudly about airlines that worked hard to make travel uncomfortable.

Andrew exchanged a grin with Morgan. He had not counted on preflight entertainment. He thought of his CEOP, which Caleb had insisted he take, and pulled it from its pocket. He sketched a quick snowman, captioned it: "MR. OBESITY," and was rewarded with Morgan's soft giggle.

Mr. Obesity pounded his call button with a pudgy finger, and informed the attendant that Air New Zealand should have provided a seat belt extension, since their seatbelts fit only pygmies.

The attendant, all professional courtesy and efficiency, calmed Mr. Obesity, and brought the required extension. He helped attach it to the belt, and waited, an unmistakable twinkle in his eye, until the man had secured it around his ample girth.

Mr. Obesity turned to his young seatmates. "Discrimination." He spat the word. "Airlines never make seats big enough for normal people. You kids have no problem, but you get to normal size and you will." The brief conversation cost him too much breath. He grappled to unfold his blanket — too small — and settled down to sleep.

Andrew looked at Morgan, rolling his eyes in a fat circle. She burst into giggles, and pointed to a single word on the seat in front: "Spacemaker."

As the plane taxied, Andrew and Morgan got acquainted. It was easy to talk to Morgan, and he liked the way her eyes danced energetically beneath perfect brown arches. Her face reflected the same energy from a perfect oval, and her mouth parted generously to reveal perfect teeth.

Morgan's family lived on a farm, she said, outside St. Paul, Minnesota. In New Zealand, she would be in Wellington, attending Hutt Valley High School. She had one brother, but no sisters. She named her cats Michael and Gabriel because they were little angels when she got them. Her description of the cats was so comical that, much to his surprise, Andrew barely noticed takeoff. She was just describing how the cats filled their food dish with toys every night when the plane lifted from the runway. His stomach did a single flip-flop, then settled as Morgan finished her story.

Morgan was laughing over his profile of Schnauzie when the flight attendants served breakfast — breakfast at 2:00 A.M. Weird! Each plate had fresh, juicy red strawberries, too sweet and too ripe for North America's January. Beneath the berries were round slices of a green fruit with fuzzy skin. Morgan said it was kiwi fruit.

"It's the same color as my nail polish," she said, holding up purple fingertips. "Oops! Not that color. The polish is purple in the light, but it turns kiwi green in the dark. I bought it just for this trip because of the New Zealand kiwi fruit."

Everything was delicious, and they cleaned their plates. Then the lights dimmed. Time for the in-flight movie. Andrew had not planned to watch it, but — nestled in the semidarkness under wool blankets — with a pretty girl.... He could handle that. He unfolded his blanket, as did she. He reached up to adjust the air nozzle above his own head, and asked if she would like more air, too.

There was no answer. Morgan was asleep.

Andrew watched the movie for ten minutes, his yawns tearing the corners of his mouth, then he, too, surrendered.

The next ten hours were surreal. In the muted world high above the Pacific Ocean, time stood still. Now and then, Morgan or Andrew would stumble groggily across Mr. Obesity for a drink or to use the lavatory. The silver screen, finally devoid of movies, displayed graphics of their finite existence in infinite skies. Dinner was served sometime in the middle of the flight: roast chicken thigh with honey vegetables and mashed potatoes. It seemed strange to eat again. They finished with a sweet pinacolada mousse topped with berries, after which Andrew challenged Morgan to a game of chess.

"Do you believe we grow into the meanings of our names?" Andrew asked, as he captured her white pawn.

"I hope not!" Morgan laughed, and he watched the way she flicked her long brown hair off her face with one hand, moving her rook with the other. "The meaning I've found for 'Morgan' is 'sea circle' and I would hate to grow into a sea circle. It sounds like a whirlpool, and I do too much whirling as it is. What's your name mean? 'Son of the warrior knight' or something equally grand?"

He captured another lowly pawn, and tossed it into her lap. "It means 'manly courage,'" he said, "and I definitely have not grown into it."

"You're joking, of course," she disagreed. "It takes a lot of courage to make this trip."

"You're here, though." he responded.

"I nearly turned back at each plane change." She tossed a black rook at him.

"Really?" Andrew hadn't considered that option, so maybe he had some kind of courage. He made a swift move. "Check."

"Check Mate — and that calls for courage! It takes manly courage to lose to a woman."

Andrew laughed amiably. "Will you give me another chance to be manly courageous?"

"And miss my beauty sleep?"

"That would be awful! I wouldn't want you to do that," he teased. "Think of the people around you. No. By all means, get your beauty sleep."

She tossed a magazine at him, and snuggled under her blanket, almost in Andrew's seat, since Mr. Obesity had selfishly raised the separating armrest and spilled into half of her seat.

Andrew felt sorry for Morgan, losing half of her seat that way. Someone ought to do something about passengers taking more than their share. Maybe he could help.

He raised his armrest and let her slip a bit farther in his direction. Vanilla filled his brain, but a cool silver half-heart caught on the wool of his sweater as he watched her drift into sleep.

You clod! Laughing with Morgan while Penny tosses to lonely dreams. Letting Morgan sleep against you while Penny can't sleep. Didn't take long to forget, did it? Tears pricked his eyes, and he shoved his body against the window.

He was over the Pacific Ocean — had been for hours — and he hadn't read Penny's card yet. He had promised, and then hadn't even given it a thought. It would be unkind to disturb Morgan, though. He would read it in New Zealand.

He glanced at his watch. Auckland in less than two hours. Andrew closed his burning eyes.

# 12

## *Of Napkins and Nightmares*

"Well, here I am in New Zealand." It was his first E-mail home. "I can't believe I'm actually here. It's hot! The first thing I did after clearing customs this morning was change into summer clothes — in January! I didn't even wait to get to our hostel in Ponsonby, but I'm there now. Ponsonby is one neighborhood in Auckland's big collection of the same. I think I'm somewhere near the harbor."

"They started us off right away, or *straight away*, as they say here, with orientation. Our first session was on One Tree Hill. It is amazing there. You are right in the middle of Auckland, a city of more than a million people, but the hill is sheep pasture, with real sheep roaming the place! There's one tree on the top of the hill — some Maori spot — and the view of the city is great. One Tree Hill is an extinct volcano, but you would never guess it. Everything is so-o-o green here!"

"Hey, Andrew." Morgan was at the door of his room. "Come on. It's time for lunch."

"Time to eat," he wrote quickly. "We are to have late lunch with some Kiwis — that's what the New Zealand people call themselves. It also is the name of an endangered flightless bird that is native to New Zealand. Go figure." He pressed "send" and jumped up to join Morgan.

"If you get any more beauty sleep, you'll be disqualified to represent Minnesota," he teased.

"Redheads can't represent anybody."

"Ouch!" Andrew took off.

Lunch was at Ponsonby Pie Shop, Andrew's worst nightmare come true. He studied the menu board intently, wishing and hoping and dreading.

*Bacon and Pumpkin Pie*
*Lamb and Mince Pie*
*Mince Pie*
*Mince and Cheese Pie*
*Mince, Cheese, and Baked Beans Pie*
*Pork and Apple Pie*
*Steak and Cheese Pie*
*Steak and Kidney Pie*
*Steak and Onion Pie*

Morgan stood beside him. "What are you going to have, Andrew?"

"I'm going to have a barf attack!"

"It's not that bad," she said, giggling. "Try the plain mince pie. I think it's like ground beef — maybe ground lamb. How bad can it be?"

"Bad!" He made a face. "At home, we don't touch red meat, in or out of pies. We don't even eat chicken all that often. I'll have a dessert pie."

"Can't. We have to adapt, and this is what Kiwis eat. Come on. Order a mince pie."

Andrew ordered, and they joined two Kiwi students at an outdoor table. Andrew unwrapped the pie and inspected it. It was small. He could encircle it if he touched his two index fingers and two thumbs around it. He sniffed surreptitiously. The crisp veneer of crust failed to mask the smell of — was it lard? He watched the Kiwi students, surprised to see that they held their pies as though they were hamburgers. Pies without forks?

"Come on. Have a go," invited the nearer of the two Kiwis. Her name tag read *Raewyn.*

Andrew gave Morgan a pinched smile of mute appeal, gathered his courage, and took a hot bite. Streamlets of juice and grease oozed between his fingers and dripped to the table. His taste buds shuddered, while his lips, tongue, and throat slowly thickened with a coat of fat. "Cholesterol overload!" screamed his heart. He calmed the taste buds with a drink of Coca Cola, and promised his lips a napkin. Too bad about the heart.

"Well?" Kiwi Peter asked.

Truth and tact collided in Andrew's brain, and he sidestepped. "I need a napkin."

Peter and Raewyn nearly choked with laughter. She regained her composure quickly, but Peter simply buried his head in his pie and snorted. He stamped his foot, and pounded the small wooden table.

Andrew looked to Morgan for help, but she was as stymied as he.

After an eternity of torment, the Kiwi gained control of himself and apologized. "Sorry, mate," said Peter, blotting his eyes on his sleeve. "Couldn't help myself. The word means something different here — something like a baby's diaper. Nappy." He snickered again.

"Peter," scolded Raewyn. "At least you could get him a serviette." She went herself.

Andrew scrubbed his lips with the paper serviette, happy when the discussion turned to other subjects. Peter and Raewyn asked if they were going to the barbie tomorrow.

"Back home," said Morgan, "Barbie is a fashion doll, but you obviously don't mean that, so what's a barbie?"

The Kiwis laughed merrily. "Here's a hint," they said. "We're having a big one for tea on the beach tomorrow evening. It should be listed on your orientation schedule." They pronounced the final word *shed-yool.*

Andrew risked, "Tea on the beach?"

"We often call meals tea," said Peter.

Morgan pulled out her schedule. "It's on the *shed-yool,*" she said. "Is it a kind of fish?"

"It's a barbecue," said Raewyn.

So, that is what Caleb meant when he told Andrew to enjoy the barbies! He thought his little brother was talking about New Zealand girls.

He made a secret note of it in the CEOP, along with a personal directive: "Meat pies are atrocious! Do your own cooking."

* * * * *

The second day of orientation included a sight-seeing tour of Auckland, and Andrew sat beside Morgan on the bus. The big city seemed to consist of many small neighborhoods connected to one another: small restaurants, small stores, and small vehicles. They visited a supermarket, also small, and Andrew realized that shopping was not going to be easy. Things had different names: bell peppers were capsicum; cookies were biscuits; and gelatin was jelly. The mall they toured was two floors, six small shops on each, connected by a narrow escalator. Lilliputian!

By the time they arrived at a wide sand beach for dinner, everyone was chattering, and eager to do justice to the barbie. The meat of choice was steak, but chicken and fish were available, and Andrew chose fish. When he asked for a grape soda, the Rotary host beamed and said, "One grape bubbly!" Bubbly. He made a mental note of it.

Saturday's orientation was more formal, filled with information about exchange student responsibilities, hints to make life easier, warnings about dating, encouragements, etc. Then, it was time to travel. Andrew and his new friends were eager to meet their host families, though Andrew suspected that his own eagerness was more to open the paua box. Either way, he must meet them tomorrow. Last Sunday, he had skipped church to pack. It seemed an eternity ago, a universe away, a life that no longer existed.

Saturday evening, over a dinner of fish and chips that soaked its newspaper wrapping with oil, he told Morgan, "I guess this is good-bye."

"Until we see each other at camp on Valentine's Day," she said.

"I may not live to attend that," Andrew said. "You stay on the North Island, but I have to fly across Cook Strait — and I hate flying. Even worse, my hosts are Christian fanatics, who probably won't let me to do anything but study and go to church. I just don't think I can handle this."

"Whether you think you can, or you think you can't, you're right," said Morgan.

"What?"

"Henry Ford. If you think you can handle it, you're right — you probably can. If you think you can't handle it — you probably can't."

"I don't think that statement always holds true. Look, if I think I can fly across Cook Strait tomorrow without mechanical assistance, it won't change the fact that I can't — and I won't be right." Girls were so ready to accept simplistic things. It was a wonder any of them became scientists. He registered a wish that the Bartletts would have no daughters — and only one son. He said very little to Morgan after that, excusing himself early.

Andrew slept fitfully Saturday night. Three times, he used the loo — necessary Kiwi word. A small electric fan mocked him with hot ocean air as he struggled into troubled sleep, and a dark dream. In the dream, he became a boa constrictor's dinner; a boa constrictor named Bartlett.

"Welcome." Her hot, vile breath smothered him. She slowly and firmly crushed his throat, her beady eyes staring into his. "I'm glad you're going to be part of our family." She spiraled downward to mash and heat his torso, thrusting upward on the greasy fish and chips dinner. Her tongue flicked in anticipation.

Andrew tumbled to the floor, stopped his mouth with a trembling fist, and made the first trip to the loo. A stranger gazed back from the mirror above the basin. He threw cold water on the face, and returned to his room. 12:15 A.M.

Opening the loosely woven drapes, he stared at Auckland — Kiwis pronounced it almost like *Oakland*. Tomorrow night, he would be looking at Nelson. He sighed, left the limp brown drapes parted for air, and went back to bed. "Don't think about the boa constrictor," he warned his brain, which organ promptly disobeyed. He rolled to his stomach and dozed.

"Andrew, Andrew." Echoes whispered around his bed.

"Who are you?" he muttered aloud.

"The Bartlett girls," tittered a giggling voice. They pelted his body with rotten eggs, the strong odor prodding at his nostrils. "We are ten," screeched a soprano in a white science lab coat.

Andrew rolled to his back, rubbing at the dream mist. "Do you have brothers?" he moaned

"No, but if you think you can be our brother, you're right. You can!"

Andrew waved his arms to beat them off. Chemical-soaked hands wrapped around him. His sheets were wet with their vile experiment — wet and tangled. He fought upward, pulling his body and mind to consciousness. It was nearly 2:00 A.M. He made a second flying trip to the loo.

That clammy body. That hot, sour breath. The pale face, stained now with shadowy magenta circles beneath the eyes. Were those his? He washed his hands, and splashed his face. Less than eight hours. Eight hours until the real Bartlett family. Nothing was as bad as dreams — was it? He wandered, dripping, back to his room and sat on the edge of the bed in front of the useless fan.

The cool water dried quickly, and Andrew lay backward, descending into new torture.

"The Honorable Judge Bartlett. All rise, please." A burly man appeared, cumulus white wig floating above his craggy features. A long black robe dusted the steps as he mounted the dais, and sat heavily behind the huge bar.

"Andrew Trevor McKean, ancestor of the Honorable Thomas McKean," intoned the judge. "You are charged with aiding and abetting one Edward Tao and one Robert Stedman in the defamation of Coach John Ando. How do you plead?"

"Guilty." The hot pillow absorbed the voice.

"Do you understand what defamation is?"

"Yes." The voice broke in the stifling room.

Judge Bartlett banged the gavel. "You will serve sentence in my home, McKean," he declared.

"Yes, sir," mumbled Andrew.

"My ten girls shall prepare meals for you every day — porridge every morning, fish and chips every noon, kidney pie every evening. Also," ordered Judge Bartlett, "At every meal, you shall have a large helping of capsicum."

"No, not capsicum! Not capsicum!"

"I say, McKean. Was that you shouting? Are you all right?"

Andrew struggled upright. "Sorry," he called wanly. "Had a nightmare, I guess." Faint first light appeared between the weary brown drapes, and a cool breeze finally found its way through the fan. It was 4:45 A.M. He traipsed to the loo for the third time. The tile floor felt cooler, but an ashen mirrored face stared sadly from beneath a mass of bright copper hair. He turned away, and stumbled to his room.

"To sleep; perchance to dream; ay, there's the rub...." The whisper hung forlornly in the cool air as Andrew walked to the window. In the dawn, a small Victorian neighborhood spilled down the hill at his feet — the demons of the night lingered between him and it. Better stay up. Breakfast is at six, my flight at eight-forty-five. Dad and Mom are in church. No, it's Saturday morning there. Poor Schnauzie. Probably lying in front of the fireplace sighing big doggy heartache sighs.

Swallowing fought with regurgitation, and lost. Andrew disgorged his roiling stomach in the loo. Then, exhausted, he collapsed on the bed to think about home. He fell rapidly into a dreamless sleep instead.

Incessant pounding on his door awakened him sometime later. "Andrew. Your ride leaves for the airport in fifteen minutes."

Andrew jumped up. "I'll be in the lobby in ten." To himself, he added, "No breakfast down, no breakfast up. I feel like death warmed over."

A quick shower was better than no shower. He made it very quick, rubbed on a first-impression-thick layer of deodorant, and dressed in navy khakis with a pale blue knit shirt. He laced up his shoes, and tossed his belongings in his pack.

At 7:41 A.M., he arrived in the lobby. At 7:45 A.M., he boarded the van, sat back, and watched Auckland thin from metropolis to suburbs to farmland — with sheep. He was on his own. He had full responsibility for himself now. What a great feeling!

Lifting from Auckland Airport at 8:45 A.M., he picked a spot on the horizon — a spot where the blue-green waters of the bay licked gently at the emerald-green pastures surrounding the airport. He watched the spot descend, and lost it as the plane banked toward the south.

Next stop — Nelson.

He settled back, happy to have no seatmate. Nausea was a private matter, and he wanted his personal space, what there was of it. This plane was much smaller than the previous ones had been, with only two seats on each side of the aisle. This plane had a lower flight path, too. He looked out the window to his right. All he could see was ocean. They were flying south along the North Island's west coast, and the turquoise ocean waves below seemed much too close.

A flight attendant came by to tell him, "Mount Taranaki is on the left. It's one of our most beautiful mountains — an active volcano. You may get up and sit over there while we pass if you want. We have a lot of empty seats today."

Andrew loosed the safety of his seatbelt and slid across the aisle. The volcano was beautiful! Its sides flowed gracefully downward from the cone's top to a wide base, a base whose west side slipped into the ocean. He stayed at that window until they had passed the mountain, then slid back to his own seat, and refastened the gray seatbelt.

"Would you like some bubbly?" The caring attendant was at his seat again. "We're going to have a wee bit of turbulence over the Cook Strait, and you might like some ginger beer."

"Is it like ginger ale?"

"Yes, I think so." She poured it from the small, dark bottle into a clear plastic glass. She gave him a packet of nuts with it, and a serviette.

"Thank you." Andrew waited until she left, and tasted the drink. "Soapy," said his taste buds, "and not at all like ginger ale." It was his first food or drink since last night, though, so he sipped it, and put the salty nuts in his pocket.

That must be the south end of the North Island — must be Wellington — where Morgan would be living. If only the Bartletts had lived in Wellington. What was that on the right? It looked like a stadium, but it was completely round. What kind of sport did you play in a round stadium? There was Wellington Harbor — then Cook Strait. It looked so wide. The water looked so ominous.

Not caring to think about the deep blue ocean roiling so close below the frail silver plane, he took a magazine from the seat pocket, and skimmed it. There was an article about Nelson:

> *Nelson area, found in the northwestern part of the north end of the South Island, is dramatic, with mountains that stretch southward to the northern edge of the Southern Alps. It also offers many curving, expansive beaches. This is a busy area, filled with enthralling events, and a diverse, fascinating culture: people who are attracted by its rich resources and easy climate. You are sure to*

*make friends among Nelson's population of artists, craftspeople, educators, anglers, farmers, orchard owners, Maori marae groups, alternative communities, and just plain adventurers.*

Make friends, hm? His bon voyage cards! How could he have forgotten? He retrieved them from his backpack. The soccer team had given him a booklet, each page signed by a teammate, each containing a joke about flying:

*The propeller, located in the front of your plane, is a big fan used to keep the pilot cool. When it stops, you can actually see the pilot start sweating.*

*When the jetliner, delayed for an hour, finally took off, a passenger asked what the reason was for the delay. "Oh," the flight attendant said, "The pilot was bothered by a noise in the engine, and it took us a while to find a new pilot."*

*Helicopters can't fly; they're just so ugly the earth repels them.*

Those were his favorite three. He put the booklet aside and read cards from others in his class — most funny — a few sad and lonely.

Penny's was the saddest, her flowing script reminiscent of words on a Japanese scroll. Rereading it made it sound even sadder.

He returned it to its fragrant envelope and took out the last packet — intriguingly thick, and about the size of a half sheet of letter paper. He tried to ignore the dull ache in his head as the plane lurched, helping him rip off the wrapper.

Inside was a blank book, a journal. On its front page, his English teacher had written:

*Capture your mem'ries,*
*Hold them dear.*
*They'll never grow old,*
*Locked in here.*

A diary? Diaries were for girls. That was the trouble with women teachers. Every thought was flowers and lace — sugar and spice. A male teacher would never give a guy a journal.

The plane dropped into an air pocket, pulling his stomach down with it. He snatched one of the plastic-lined bags from the seat pocket and heaved into it. Was that ginger beer a help or a hindrance? He took a sip. Then he folded the air sickness bag shut and set it on the empty seat, hoping the flight attendant would collect it soon.

Another vicious pocket of clear turbulence bounced the airplane. Gag reflexes working overtime, Andrew slowly put the journal and the cards in his pack, and checked the supply of little white bags. There had been two in each seat pocket. Little wonder — and good thing he had two seats!

He fumbled for the airline safety card again, and reviewed it — just in case.

> *Your SAAB 340 airliner is equipped for your comfort and safety. Please note your nearest emergency exit and how to evacuate.*

Equipped for safety, but we expect it to be not so safe, so be sure you know how to get out.

The plane convulsed through another cloud, and Andrew sacrificed again to the god of the bags.

Wanly, he pulled out his pad, and began to write words for someone to find and send to his family — when they someday retrieved his dead body from the tumultuous Cook Strait below.

> *It is too clear below. It would be better if I could not see the waves. They seem tall as skyscrapers. I see five boats racing across the strait, and a large ferry just below. Are they positioning to rescue us? I love Mom, Dad, Alicia, Cathryn, and Caleb — all of you. I'm only sixteen — too young to die, but that may not matter to God. It feels as though this plane is in an earthquake.*

After a wrenching pause, he finished:

> *I have used three of my four bags. How will I ever be ready to meet the Bartletts?*

# 13

## The Bartletts

"There's Andrew!" The boy was Caleb's age or a little younger — and could have been his twin, so identical was the hue of his red hair.

"James, let him get his breath. He just landed." A girl about Andrew's age ran after James, a lighthearted smile dancing beneath her comical hat. It was a tall, mad hatter sort of hat, a patchwork of orange, red, green, and brown. Her flowered skirt lapped in waves about slim ankles — above outrageously heavy, black, laced shoes. Penny would never dream of wearing such shoes, let alone such a skirt.

"Watch out for Katherine," said a slightly younger girl, with more conservative clothing.

Andrew tried to make his tongue say hello, but it tangled and slipped out "H'lo." He smiled timidly and tried again, "Hello. You must be the Bartletts."

"Some of them," laughed Katherine. She crunched the silly hat down over her long, curly brown hair.

"Katherine, don't frighten Andrew to death." Mrs. Bartlett, he guessed. "Welcome to Nelson, Andrew. Did you have a good flight down from Auckland?"

"It was pretty bumpy," he replied.

"Oh, did you *chunder*? I always *chunder*," said redheaded James. He broke loose from his mother and came closer to inspect the American.

"I didn't lose my breakfast, if that's what you mean," said Andrew. It was the truth. He had not eaten breakfast, so he did not lose it. He had not even eaten the packet of salty nuts.

"Dad and Richard are in the car park," said the second sister. "My name's Anna." She extended her hand in well-bred fashion, shook his, and then pushed her short, straight brown hair away from her face. "I'm fifteen. Katherine, the clown in the funny hat, is sixteen. James is nine, and Mum is...." She laughed teasingly at her mother and stopped.

"I'm glad to meet you all," said Andrew. "I guess you know that I'm sixteen, but a year ahead in your school." Why did he add that? It sounded arrogant. "It's only because Mom is such a good teacher," he added quickly. Maybe that would make it better. The word *Mom* caught in his throat, though, and tears threatened.

"He says *mom* instead of *mum,*" observed James. "Mom. Mom." He practiced the accent.

"You have got a good teacher here, too," said Mrs. Bartlett, pulling James to her side again and covering his mouth. "Oh, there's Mr. Bartlett — Dennis. He'll be going to baggage claim."

To Andrew's amazement, the terminal was limited to one rather small room, the one into which he had first come — and baggage claim was outdoors.

Uneasily, he followed Mrs. Bartlett and James. Must the two girls walk behind him? What were they doing — studying him? New Zealand girls probably were like some of the girls at home, whispering behind a guy's back. He hated that. He was glad when they met Dennis and Richard.

"You have a nice family, Mr. Bartlett," he said, courteously shaking hands.

"Oh, you have met only part of the Bratletts," said Mr. Bartlett.

"Dennis, don't give him the wrong impression!" laughed Mrs. Bartlett. "Our children are not brats."

"I'll let Andrew be the judge of that, after he has been here a month. If you can take it for a whole month, Andrew. You will have your hands full. We have five of them altogether — three boys and two girls."

Only two girls? These two? Not the ten that were in his nightmare? Andrew breathed a sigh of relief. The girls were not bad — very different from each other, but not bad.

He found his luggage and let Richard help him load it into the family bus. "How old are you, Richard?"

"Thirteen, but a year ahead in school," said Richard.

Andrew was glad Richard had duplicated his own rude remark, and chanced punching him lightly on the shoulder. "Good for you," he said.

"Good on ya!" corrected Richard with a grin.

As they climbed into the minibus, Andrew stood back to let the girls go first. "Wow! A gentleman!" said Katherine. She pretended a curtsy as she stepped in front of him to get in. "It will be nice to have a brother who treats us like royals!" Katherine and Anna had saved the seat between them, Richard was tormenting them about that, and James was trying, against Mum's will, a chant about Princess Anne and Prince Andrew.

"Janette, did you want to have tea on the beach?" Mr. Bartlett asked, as he started the long red minibus.

"Yes, you know what."

He nodded, and pulled away from the air terminal. "Katherine and Anna, I'll let you be the tour guides until we get downtown," he called over his shoulder. "Then James and Richard can take over while you do an errand for your mother."

The girls grinned past Andrew's nose at each other, and launched their narrative: Dad was taking the long way into Nelson, and they were passing Tahunanui beach, which had a petting zoo, roller skating, and a water slide that was brilliant.

Andrew interrupted to ask, "*Brilliant*, meaning smart, gifted, clever or talented?"

The girls giggled. "Meaning fabulous or wonderful or — well, you get the idea," explained Anna.

He did and he did not. How was he going to communicate if the meaning of every other word was up for grabs? *Chunder. Mum. Good on ya. Brilliant.* What was next?

Katherine and Anna chattered at him from both sides. Nelson had it all, they told him: ocean, sandy beaches, plains, hills, mountains, clear trout streams, lakes, vineyards, orchards, and all kinds of sports — even skiing. You never ran out of things to do here. When you got tired of playing in the sun, there were places where you could learn to make pottery, or create wearable art.

Anna produced a handful of post cards and managed to show one now and then in spite of Katherine's ongoing recital. This was one of two Nelson Lakes. They would take him fishing up there. The golden beach encircling a quiet bay was in Abel Tasman National Park, as were the sea kayakers. Did he like sea kayaking?

"I never tried it," said Andrew.

"Oh, we must take you sea kayaking," said Anna. "It is so peaceful and quiet."

Katherine's running travelogue sparked another question. "Did you know you were coming to the area where they filmed the *Lord of the Rings*?" she asked. "It was filmed all over New Zealand — in fourteen or fifteen places, and one of them was Nelson."

"Remember Dimril Dale and Eregion Hills and the Rough Country South of Rivendel?" asked James. "Those were near Mount Owen and Mount Olympus. They were the mountains in the background."

As they left the beach area, Mr. Bartlett approached a large circle in the street and came to a stop. Katherine smiled at Andrew's quizzical look. "You haven't got roundabouts in America, have you? A roundabout is a traffic circle without lights, and you have got to be careful of traffic entering the circle from your right. I'm getting my driver's license," she bubbled.

Andrew resisted the urge to tease about the danger that would pose to New Zealand citizens. She might not understand his style of joking.

"Queen's Gardens," they announced next.

Mr. Bartlett stopped and Mrs. Bartlett turned to give Katherine and Anna each a canvas tote bag. "We will meet you back here," she said. "Be sure you buy just what I told you."

"Of course, Mum," said Katherine. She squashed her tall floppy hat onto her head and crawled quickly over Andrew, giving Anna a good-natured push from the van, and calling back, "Cheers."

The girls dashed away across the park, and Richard took up the travelogue, with help from James. Andrew only half-listened as he looked out at the narrow streets of the tiny, colonial town center. The most impressive of the very old buildings was the English-style cathedral, but otherwise Nelson was very small. How was he going to live in such a tiny town? What would he do when he was not in school? The girls seemed to think there was plenty to do, but he definitely did not like crafts, and he already knew their main sports were cricket and rugby instead of baseball. He knew nothing of either cricket or rugby. He thought of Wilmington, of home. Bad move. He blinked rapidly several times and tried to focus on Richard's words.

"We don't live in Nelson," Richard was saying. "We live out that road — in Richmond." Andrew's eyes followed the narrow road into the countryside. Maybe Richmond would be larger than Nelson. Maybe there was a shopping mall in Richmond. What was Richard saying? They lived beyond Richmond? On a hill above the town? It was possible, in the strange English of New Zealand, that town meant large city. Possible.

Mr. Bartlett stopped in front of Queen's Gardens, and his tour of Nelson was complete. Katherine and Anna's canvas bags bulged, and they were laughing together. Probably discussing the dumb American exchange student. Probably had filled their bags with steak and kidney pies for their beach picnic, and were giggling about making him eat one. His stomach knotted at the memory of the pie in Ponsonby, and his taste buds threatened mutiny.

"All right, then," said Mr. Bartlett as the girls climbed in, Katherine crawling over Andrew's lap again, "We're off to the beach for tea."

That evening, Andrew began writing in the new journal his English teacher had given him:

> *I arrived at Nelson airport, New Zealand around 10:10 A.M. today. My host parents, Dennis and Janette Bartlett, seem friendly and generous. They took me from the airport into Nelson, where their two girls*

*bought bags of Kentucky Fried Chicken for a picnic (tea) on the beach. Just imagine — Kentucky Fried Chicken in New Zealand! We drove about 12 miles (learn metric: 20 kilometers) to Rabbit Island, an idyllic spot. The chicken tasted just like it does at home, but get this: Katherine told me that the counterperson assured her we do not have Kentucky Fried Chicken in the U.S.A. What?! Where does she think Kentucky is? I never eat fried chicken at home because of all the grease, but compared to that awful mince pie, this was like eating a broiled salmon fillet.*

*After lunch, we went beachcombing. I saw a lot of small shells that looked like paua on the inside. I didn't want to ask, but they must have been. A little blue penguin had washed up on the golden sand. Its feathers were bluish gray, and it was only nine inches long. I never knew there were blue penguins, or such small penguins, or that penguins don't all live in Antarctica.*

*The Bartletts' house is really in Richmond, I discovered, and is large compared to other houses I saw on the way. It sits high on an emerald hill back of Richmond, with Mount Richmond Forest Park behind it — and white heather in front of it! My nerves were shot by the time we got there, and I really was looking forward to being alone in my own room.*

*Surprise, surprise! I don't get my own room. I room with Matthew, the 18-year-old son. It is probably the best room in the house, if I have to share. The window overlooks the Nelson Airport, the aqua waters of the Tasman Bay, ubiquitous green fields filled with sheep, and all of Richmond (which is not a very big all). Matthew is simpatico, as near as I can tell. I have no older siblings, so it will be interesting to room with him this semester. I hope he does not snore!*

*Anna and Katherine asked their mum to bake a "special" pizza for me tonight, like the ones served at a restaurant in Nelson. It certainly was special! It had ketchup base instead of tomato sauce, and was covered with sweet pickles, creamed corn, onions, kidney beans, black olives, pineapple, and a generous sprinkling of grated Swiss cheese. It was, to say the least, different! And while...*

*a rose by any other name would smell as sweet,*
*a pizza by this name ain't fit to eat!*

*It was thoughtful of them, though, and their family all seemed to love it. Wonder what they would think of the pizzas Penny and I eat every Friday evening in Wilmington.*

> *Thus far, the Bartletts seem to be a good host family — warm and understanding. I expected them to be more straitlaced and aloof, especially Dennis, but he is very friendly. He does insist that I join them for family devotions at breakfast — guess it won't hurt me to read the Bible more. I was surprised that they skipped church to meet my plane today.*

Andrew stopped writing, and began to close the journal, but there was still space on the two-page spread, so he decided to share a private thought:

> *I don't think the Bartletts know what a hard time I'm having adjusting. I couldn't even flush their toilet — after I found it, that is! I went in the bathroom to use the toilet, but it isn't in the bathroom. It's in a separate room. The bathroom has only a sink and a tub. The toilet itself has no handle. It has two buttons instead, chosen for the desired swirl. My friends back home would have found it funny. Friends. Penny. Home. Has it been only four days? That would make it January 19 back in Wilmington. I wonder if the trial has resumed.*

He stopped then, and slipped the journal into a secret compartment of his pack. Maybe he did need a locked journal.

The entire Bartlett family had gone out to some Sunday evening church service, excusing him this once because they thought he was still suffering jet lag. He was not, having been in New Zealand since Thursday morning, but why change their minds? The house was peacefully calm and quiet, demanding nothing of him.

Curious, he explored from room to room, feeling the pulse of the Bartletts. Downstairs, he dared to peek into his host parents' bedroom, and was surprised to see only a bed, crowded by twin nightstands. The room was small to be a master bedroom. Then who used the master bedroom upstairs? Probably Anna and Katherine. Girls get the largest bedrooms every time, remember?

He paused before a closed door, which bore a small ceramic plate. The plate's circumference was wreathed in ceramic heather, and its center proclaimed in raised ceramic letters: "Toilet." He grinned. Labeling one's own toilet door!

The kitchen, dining, and living rooms all supported an open plan. He centered himself in it, turning slowly to take in the possibilities. Ferns and other plants veiled the cookware hanging over the island bar. Beyond lay the now-immaculate scene of the crime: the creation of that pizza. The long wooden dining room table was surrounded by comfortable padded chairs. He shook his head. Why linger over New Zealand cuisine?

At one end, a big upright piano intruded itself into the dining area, minimizing access to the outside door. Extending from the piano, out around the living room's wall of picture windows, an array of ample chairs and couches bore silent testimony to the Bartletts' hospitality.

Accepting the invitation of a long orange couch, he flopped lengthwise and closed his eyes. Remember Penny. Picture Penny as she looked at the airport. He could imagine her essence, could imagine looking back at her, but his mind refused to fine-tune the picture. He reached inside his blue knit shirt and rubbed her little silver half-heart between his fingers, his eyes still shut. It was no good. Penny remained a phantom.

A huge reddish-orange tomcat jumped up, purring loudly, and began kneading his stomach with its toes. Then it licked an arm, licked the silver half-heart, and licked the ear of this stranger. Andrew compared its sleek enormity to Pierrot's fluffy compactness. What had they said the cat's name was? Oh, yes – Skippy: named for a brand of New Zealand cornflake cereal.

Absently, he rubbed Skippy's back, and massaged the cat's ears. "Hey, there, Skippy. Your battle scars are showing." Skippy rolled over for a belly massage. There was a velvety feel to the stomach hair, like Schnauzie's stomach. Abruptly, Andrew slid Skippy onto the floor and stood up. "I have to find something to do, or I never will get through the next six months."

A carpeted stairway led downward from the far side of the living room, and he followed it to the bottom, where he stopped short.

"Paradise!" A large doorless room spread across the entire ground floor. A red felt pool table beckoned from the room's center; a green and white ping-pong table stretched luxuriously in a large corner; and gloriously striped beanbag seats plopped invitingly wherever they found space. The walls were dressed in colorful murals and clever hand-lettered signs, exhibiting every interest a teen could have: sports, popular music, dating, clothing, food — he could hardly believe his eyes!

The cat had followed, and jumped up on the ping-pong table. "You're probably too good for me, Skippy." Andrew grabbed up a ping-pong paddle and hit the ball. The big cat chased it and batted it back to him.

"You've done this before, big guy." The bounces of the ball echoed with his voice in the silent room, and he stopped the game.

"What else do you play here, Skippy?" He continued his investigation. Pool balls, racked in black plastic on the red felt, waited eagerly for a game. The long wooden cues shared wall space with a dart board, beside which a black chalkboard proclaimed Matthew the winner of a recent game. His opponents' names sounded foreign to the American: Lynton, Ian, Chaffey, and Wilfred.

Andrew's blue eyes scanned the remainder of the four long, colorful walls, and he laughed aloud at some of the mural's offerings. A large square section under the stairway, bordered by strips of photo negatives, held a hundred or more snapshots. He grinned at the antics of the teens in the photos, and continued around the room, an enthusiastic smile growing on his face until the eyes came to rest on an enormous yellow and green poster that proffered, in two languages, a long list of "Character Trait Objectives."

| | |
|---|---|
| *Attentive* | *Puakaha* |
| *Available* | *Wätea* |
| *Committed* | *Kaingäkautia* |
| *Confident* | *Mäia* |
| *Cooperative* | *Paheko* |
| *Courageous* | *Toa* |

He stopped. "Should have known it would include courage!" Everything reminded him of his inadequacy. He looked at the second language. It must be Maori. "How do they define courage, Skippy?"

Skippy meowed, changing the subject back to exploration, and led his new friend to the room's farthest corner. It held a wide array of sports equipment — but no baseball bat.

"We aren't snooping, Skippy — just getting acquainted."

The cat gave another low "Meow," and led the teen back up to the main floor. It continued upstairs to the boys' room, and jumped on Andrew's bed.

Andrew sat down and absentmindedly rubbed purrs out of Skippy's back. Maybe Dennis and Janette had been right. Maybe his jet lag had not ended. He felt exhausted.

He dressed for bed, and lay down on top of the blankets, thinking of the poster downstairs. Was God pursuing him? Was that why he seemed to see the word courage everywhere? God was not that personal, though. Was he?

If it was God, Dennis would know. Dennis probably did think God was personal. He must think something like that, if he made his family read the Bible at breakfast every morning. Trouble was....

His eyes drooped shut of their own volition, and he fell swiftly into a troubled sleep.

# 14

## Long Drops, Pikelets and Shouts

When Andrew opened his eyes on Monday morning, Matthew was grinning down at him.

"Gidday. How ya goin'?" he said. "I'd bounce out if I were you. Mum's made pikelets for our breakfast, and Dad has got heaps of things planned for you. So has Katherine, but she's a bit crackers — you may want to refuse her ideas. Brother James is crook this morning, so he won't be bothering you."

Andrew stared. That was the most foreign paragraph of English he ever had encountered. "Thanks, Matthew," he replied, hoping such an answer was appropriate. He hurried to dress, but was the last one to reach the table.

"We've got heaps of pikelets, Andrew, so I hope you're hungry," said Mrs. Bartlett. She held out a plate of delicious-looking, small pancakes. "We're more likely to eat these on a cold winter afternoon, but I thought you might like them for your first breakfast." She passed a brimming bowl of hot oatmeal next, urging, "Eat enough porridge to hold the pikelets in place."

Andrew took cautious portions of everything, except the fresh juicy strawberries, of which he took an almost embarrassingly large serving. The porridge was much thinner than what Mom made, and hot for a summer breakfast, but it was not at all bad. The pikelets were something else. They were delicious. He watched the Bartletts to see how they ate theirs, and was soon spreading jam and whipped cream on his own.

He had barely eaten two bites of the warm, sweet pikelet when Katherine nudged his elbow, and began bubbling over with plans. "You have got to go to Richmond Mall with us this evening. Everybody will be there! Before that, though, we climb Botanical Hill, go swimming at Tahunanui Beach, and wind up with a snack at the *dearie*."

Now what kind of place was a *dearie*, and what kind of snack did one eat at a *dearie*? He knew better than to ask, but he could wonder. He could wonder, too, who Katherine thought she was.

"If we hurry, we can fit in kayaking this afternoon," Richard added.

Dennis interrupted, "Andrew and I have errands to accomplish today."

Whoa! Back up the Kiwi-mobile! Andrew's Irish eyes flashed as he looked from Katherine to Richard to Dennis. Hey everybody! What about what I want to do? This is my life. Go plan your own and stay out of mine. I have charge of my own life here — things he wanted to say.

Dennis turned to him. "You and I must go to the bank and set up an account: get you some New Zealand dollars. After that, and only if you wish to do, we can tour the area; and you may go to the mall, but that will be your decision." He looked meaningfully at Katherine.

That was better! Now, the first order of the day was a necessary trip to the bank with Dennis, his host dad. Excitement burst in his head as he realized that he and Dennis would be alone in the car. He could ask about the paua box. It would be such a natural opportunity. Mr. Bartlett might be able to tell him where Grandfather got the box; who gave the box to Grandfather; why it was given to Grandfather; and how it was made. Being an exchange student meant getting along with people, though — especially one's host family. So, partly to be a good ambassador, partly because it did sound like fun, he agreed to the suggested tour. And when Anna caught him taking another pikelet, he grinned, and dumped two on her plate.

Janette said she would stay with James, causing Andrew to forget the day's itinerary long enough to ask hesitantly, "What's wrong with James? Matthew said he's *crook*, but back home that word refers to a thief or a robber."

Richard, Anna, Katherine, and Matthew all found that hilarious, and chortled, but in a friendly way. Janette explained that it was New Zealand slang, "New Zildish," and meant James was sick.

Andrew made a mental note to add every new word to his journal. Maybe the final few pages of the journal should be a "New Zildish" glossary.

As the last luscious pikelet disappeared, Mr. Bartlett reached for his Bible. It was time for the dreaded family devotions. Andrew cracked his knuckles and slid downward in his chair. Maybe there was a good reason for comfortable chairs at the Bartletts' table after all.

Mr. Bartlett opened the Bible and found a place he wanted to read. He was awfully quick at it. Dad would never know where to find anything in the Bible. Did Dad have a Bible? Mom did — a little one she had carried in their wedding. She never got it out, though. The only time anyone read the Bible in his presence was when he sat in church on Sundays. He never listened. He always changed channels when the minister got up. He did the same now, and waited for the devotional time to end. It ended with everyone singing a hymn that, thankfully, he knew. The chorale director would have killed him for the way he muttered it.

When they left the table, he escaped to the car with Dennis. Not that he anticipated being confined with the fanatical Bible man, but ....

A wave of shyness engulfed him as they started down the hill toward Richmond, and he cracked his knuckles repeatedly. He cleared his throat twice, and finally said, "Mr. Bartlett, do you know anyone who could open this box for me?" He took the gleaming oval from his pocket and held it toward his host.

"The paua box! It's been years since I saw that." Dennis' attention shifted back to the road as he turned right across the traffic, much to Andrew's confusion. "Where did you get that?"

"Grandfather left it to me in his will, but it's locked, and we don't have a key. We thought there might be a place here in New Zealand that could open it."

Dennis smiled. "I believe there is," he said.

They entered a roundabout, from which Andrew almost expected to be shot forth like a marble in a maze.

"Masterton, a town near Wellington, has a paua factory that makes these boxes, or used to do. Actually, it is not in Masterton itself, but in a small town called Carterton — they should be able to open it for you."

Wellington. A trip to Wellington would be great, except that it meant another flight. "Could we go to the paua factory before school starts?"

"Well, if you lived with a man of leisure, he might go," said his host, "but I run a tomato farm, and this is my busy season. I'll give you a tour of the hothouses tomorrow so you can see what I mean. You will be working in them soon."

Working in the hothouses? When did exchange student translate into exchange slave?

Dennis pulled into a gas station, where a uniformed girl offered to "pump petrol" and "clean the windscreen while it's topping up."

Andrew busily noted the new terms, then got back to the subject of the paua box. "Do you know how my grandfather got this box?"

"It was given to him by an elderly Maori chief." Dennis paid the station attendant and they were on their way again.

"But my grandfather was never in New Zealand, Mr. Bartlett."

Dennis turned and parked across from the bank. "Actually, your grandfather did visit New Zealand. He was on a ship that was blown off course, forcing it to dock at Wellington for a time."

"Grandfather never went anywhere on a ship as far as I know. Are you sure about that?"

Dennis was out of the vehicle, and Andrew jumped out to join him. "We'll talk about it later."

Period. "Full stop," as Katherine said later.

There was no further time for discussion of the box or of Grandfather that day. When they returned from the bank, Richard, Anna, and Katherine joined the tour. At Andrew's request, they drove to Nelson first, to climb Botanical Hill. He was amazed to see how many sheep there were along the way, even in private front yards. Richard said there were twenty sheep per person in New Zealand, and it was easy to believe. Nobody around here ever said "Got sheep?"

Botanical Hill was an easy twenty minute walk to the summit, where a large white obelisk curved upward, tapering not to a pyramid, but to a vertical arm. From the arm, a rod pointed to the geographical *Centre of New Zealand*, on which they stood. The 360-degree view sparkled in the morning sunlight. The view across Tasman Bay was spectacular. Andrew snapped pictures of the scenery with and without his hosts.

Then Katherine snatched his camera. "You have got to have a photo of you standing on New Zealand's geographical center," she insisted. One was not enough, though. There had to be one of Andrew and Anna; Andrew and Katherine; Andrew and Richard; Andrew and everyone — for which they enlisted Mr. Bartlett's help.

The summer sun had climbed with every snapshot, assuring they would be hot by the time they had descended to the car. "Dad, may we stop at a dearie and get ice blocks?" asked Katherine.

"Good idea," said Dennis.

A few minutes later, Andrew observed that a *dearie* is really a dairy, which isn't really a dairy, but a corner store that sells a bit of everything; and that "ice blocks" were, of all things, Popsicles!

"Would you like to swim at Tahunanui Beach now?" asked Katherine as they started back toward Richmond. Her sparkling brown eyes urged him to agree.

"I'll let you decide," said Andrew.

"Good! We're off to Tahunanui," she said.

"Let's go to Rabbit Island, and combine beachcombing with our swimming," said Anna.

Everyone agreed eagerly, and they headed toward Rabbit Island, where they had picnicked yesterday. Katherine begged for permission to drive, but Mr. Bartlett refused.

Andrew breathed audible relief. Riding down the opposite side of the highway with Katherine at the wheel? No way!

The girls sang as they rode — mostly children's songs. Richard joined in, adding corny actions, and making their guest imagine the jeers of the guys back home. *Bunny Foo-foo* was followed by *Mices are the Nicest,* which gave way to a silly laughing song. By the time they reached Rabbit Island, Richard wanted a toilet, and Andrew later described in his journal:

> *Today I learned about "long drops." When Richard and I found the toilets in the park, this poor "townie" discovered that they all were — well — long drops, if you get my meaning — very long. It's been a long time since I saw such a long drop! In case you need another hint, long drops don't flush!*

After a refreshing swim in the crystal clear, turquoise waves, the group prepared to set off on a beachcombing hike. All four Bartletts wore sun hats, and were alarmed that Andrew had none. "You need a hat, Andrew. There's a hole in the ozone layer," worried Anna, pushing her shiny brown hair under her own broad-brimmed hat.

"Yes, I've heard there's a hole in the ozone layer," agreed Andrew, bending to pick up a shell.

"That hole is mostly right here over New Zealand," Richard said.

"Really? It's shrinking, though. NASA takes pictures of it all the time," said Andrew, "and they say this year's hole is smaller than last year's."

"Shrinking, but I read that at the present rate of shrinkage, it will be 2060 at the earliest before it disappears." Richard was amazingly well-read for a thirteen-year-old.

Mr. Bartlett cut to the heart of the matter. "You do burn much more quickly here than you would in America. Did you bring sun block?"

"I left it at the house," Andrew said, "but don't worry about me. I'll be all right."

Famous last words! The sun soon was laughing derisively at the cocky American, and kept it up all afternoon, right through the hole in the ozone layer. By the end of the hike, his body made a burning confession that the hole in the ozone layer was real, and large.

Their beachcombing hike had rewarded them well, though. Richard had found two dead sharks on the beach, which he eagerly buried in the sand. Katherine, Anna, and Andrew gathered an amazing number of unbroken shells. Dennis even found a glass fishing ball.

"We don't have many people on our beaches, so you find heaps of pretty shells here," Anna said.

"Heaps of lobsters, too," laughed Richard, with a quick look at their American guest. "Oh, look. There's one now!"

When they reached the bus, hot and thirsty, Mr. Bartlett announced, "I'll shout lunch and ice cream for you at Seifried's Vineyard Restaurant."

Shout lunch and ice cream? Andrew waited for an explanation, but everyone climbed into the red bus and Dennis started the engine. A few minutes later, they pulled into a parking lot.

The restaurant reposed elegantly in the midst of acres of grape vineyards. As far as the eye could see, huge clusters of purpling grapes hung on thick, twisted vines. The lush greenery whispered softly in the afternoon breeze.

As they entered the building, Andrew looked around quickly. This place was upscale! From its high cathedral ceilings hung colorful painted banners, while every wall was decorated with original works of art. Surely, Dennis did not plan to shout in here. He wouldn't do that. Would he? Maybe it would be better to act as though one was not in the Bartlett party — just in case.

But Mr. Bartlett did not shout. He simply asked quietly for a shady table in the vineyard garden. That was good. If he shouted out there, it would not be so gauche. As the waiter seated them, Mr. Bartlett politely ordered cool drinks for everyone. He still did not shout anything. The four Kiwis studied their menus, each suggesting what he or she thought Andrew should try, but otherwise appearing normal, and not shouting.

Finally, curiosity got the better of Andrew and he blurted out, "I thought you were going to shout 'LUNCH AND ICE CREAM,' Mr. Bartlett."

Even Dennis lost his composure at that, convulsing with glee.

Anna smiled archly, and rescued the poor American. "If you *shout* something, it's your treat — you buy for everyone. Dad meant he would treat us all to a late lunch and ice cream."

That decreased his ignorance, but not his embarrassment. "Thanks." He buried his coppery head in his menu, waiting for his freckles to cool.

When the waiter returned, Mr. Bartlett began the ordering. "Let me have the Redwood Valley Steak, please." Katherine ordered Grapepickers Treat — a delicious-looking quiche with a side salad. Anna chose the Pruners Salad — with smoked salmon, hazelnuts, cheese, and figs; while Richard opted for Rabbit Island Shells — big pasta shells filled with ground lamb.

Then it was Andrew's turn. "Will you have a steak with me, Andrew?" asked Dennis.

"No, I'll try Fieldhands Favourite," decided Andrew. It was the only vegetarian thing on the menu. It had the distinction, also, of costing less than most of the items ordered, and actually sounded good. He read the description again:

> *Baby capsicums filled with swiss brown mushrooms and herbs, served on a smoked flat mushroom ragout drizzled with walnut oil.*

He did like capsicum, especially if you called them green bell peppers.

The waiter suggested wine for Dennis, and graciously acknowledged his decision to abstain. Andrew fidgeted in his seat. Dad would have had the recommended glass of Cabernet Sauvignon. This was, after all, a vineyard restaurant.

Richard spoke as soon as the waiter left. "I guess we haven't got time to go kayaking today."

"I think not," replied Dennis. "There will be time later. Andrew is to be here an entire year."

An entire year? "My exchange is only for six months, Mr. Bartlett. I go home in July."

"I was sure the Rotary had asked us to host you for the full year," said Dennis. He frowned. "Well, I shall have to straighten that out when we get home, but even six months gives you plenty of time later for sea kayaking."

"Maybe tomorrow?" Richard was tenacious.

"Matthew is taking us fishing tomorrow," said Anna. "He wants to show Andrew the lakes."

The conversation continued to hum as they ate, making Andrew feel welcome, but overwhelming him with possible schemes.

"We could go to Richmond's 'Sunny Side Up' this Saturday. It's an all-day with music, ultimate disc, aerosol art, and heaps of fun."

"Have you ever seen a deer farm, Andrew? We have a large one just outside Richmond."

"This Pruners Salad is lovely. I like the poached figs. Is this brie cheese?"

"I'd rather have shells. These are choice."

"Everything on the menu here is choice!"

"How about horse trekking, Andrew?"

"I don't know if horse trekking is *choice* or not, but this food is." Andrew desperately hoped he had used the word properly. He must have, because nobody even snickered.

"Isn't the A & P Show this week? I wonder if Mrs. Borlase will show the biggest onion again."

"Let's take Andrew to the Fjordlands." Richard's idea met with excited support from his sisters, who began packing verbally.

"What are the Fjordlands?" asked Andrew.

"Possibly the most beautiful part of New Zealand," responded Dennis. "They are southwest from here — an area where narrow, deep fingers of the Tasman Sea flow among snow-covered mountains, towering waterfalls, and steep cliffs."

"It sounds beautiful," said Andrew.

"It is beautiful when you are with someone who knows the forest and has a map, but it's a good place to get lost. The Fjordlands contain acres of untouched wilderness; forests so dense that people say some of it still remains unexplored."

"Unexplored?" Andrew cut into another tender baby capsicum. "I thought every inch of New Zealand would have been explored by now."

"Our population is not big enough to use all of our land," explained Mr. Bartlett, "so that incredible, pristine wilderness is seldom seen."

"That's why we should see it with Andrew," urged Katherine. "We have time, don't we?"

"I wish we did," replied Dennis. "I would love to find some of those places that have never felt the tramp of a man's boot, but that would mean a two-week holiday, at least."

"There's a five day guided walk we could do on the Milford Track," said Richard. "It goes through forests and canyons out to the Milford Sound in the fjords. Everybody has to do the Milford Track once in his life, Dad."

"You have to book huts months in advance, though," said Anna. "I read that they only allow forty independent walkers a day."

The ensuing discussion of New Zealand's uninhabited wilderness carried them to the end of the delicious meal. They all had cleaned their plates, but that meant they all were too full to accept Dennis' offer to shout ice cream.

Andrew reminded him of it, just for a laugh: "Nobody's out here, so you can shout now."

Mr. Bartlett laughed, but Richard stood up, and shouted loudly, "Lunch and ice cream!"

Andrew yanked him back into his chair, involving brotherly struggle and laughter. It was the first time he had felt normal since leaving the United States. He scrubbed Richard's head in the bargain, and escaped for a few laps around the garden before falling back into his seat.

"I almost caught you," gasped Richard. He, too, sank back into his chair to catch his breath.

As they prepared to leave, Katherine returned to the original question: "What shall we do between now and time to go to the mall?"

They decided to end the tour with a visit to a glass shop, and then to Richmond's craft megaplex, specifically to find a sun hat for Andrew before tomorrow's fishing trip.

It took Andrew several pages to record that first Richmond Monday. He ended by writing:

> *It's getting a little easier to adjust now. I was so busy today! The area around Richmond is beautiful and bursting with life. I'm exhausted from everything we did: hiking, swimming, beachcombing (sunburn). I saw two Presbyterian churches today, but I*

*know I will have to attend the Reformed church with my host dad and mum. Funny word – "mum."*

*I have lost several pounds since arriving because I eat so little. The food is very different here. I'll have to acquire a taste for it, but I do like "pikelets," which I had for breakfast, and "ice blocks," which I had for morning tea break. I had a good lunch, too, at a restaurant in the middle of a vineyard. I wouldn't mind eating there everyday, if they would prepare things as good as those stuffed capsicum (green bell peppers).*

*After lunch, we went to a little craft place that makes glass. Anna bought me a glass blue penguin. It's about three inches tall, and the outside is clear, tinted a very faint blue. The inner core has a dark blue-gray back and a white stomach. It looks so like the penguin we found dead on the beach. Anna seems to be very sensitive. I like her — as a sister. As though one craft place wasn't enough, they took me to a megaplex of craft shops, purportedly to buy a sun hat. I think the girls just wanted to look at all the crafts, but I did get a hat. Of course, nobody in Thomas McKean High would be caught dead in it, but it's what's favored here by the Cancer Society, and sold everywhere.*

*We went to Richmond Mall after dinner, and "heaps" of kids were there, but the mall was microscopic. We sat in the courtyard and talked until closing time. Everyone was nice enough, but I miss my friends, and am already counting the weeks till I go home. Want to hear something pathetic? I'm homesick.*

*E-mail was still down tonight, so no letters from family or Penny. She promised to write to me everyday, but nothing yet.*

*Most interesting thing was learning about New Zealand's unexplored wilderness. I'm tempted to ditch the Bartletts and see some of it. School doesn't start for two weeks.*

*I wish I could go to Masterton and get the paua box opened. Then I could go home.*

Andrew closed the journal and slipped it under the bed. Automatically, he took the little bluish-green paua box from his pocket and put it on the nightstand. He pulled on his pajamas, and allowed sleep to take him home to Wilmington.

# 15

## *Reading, 'Riting, and Rugby*

The weeks that had seemed so long on Andrew's first day at the Bartletts' rapidly filled with activity and fun, thanks in no small part to Katherine and Anna.

Tuesday morning, those two turned the tour of the hydroponics greenhouses into a game of hide and seek among towering tomato plants.

Tuesday afternoon, having gone with Matt and Andrew to fish in a crystal mountain stream near Lake Rotoiti, the girls sat on the bank and made wreaths of purple and white flowers for their hair, wrists and ankles. In response to Andrew's laughter and teasing, they made a rich green fern wreath for his coppery head. Then they dubbed him Lord of the Rings, and placed the wreath, amidst ceremonial gestures and speeches.

When Richard's godfather, André, arrived just before evening tea on Tuesday, it was Anna and Katherine who badgered the poor man until he regaled them with stories of his boyhood in the Netherlands. His deep youthful voice went with his dark beard, but not with his bald head, which he referred to as *eggshell blonde.*

The girls coerced André to spend the night, and he agreed, phoning his wife to let her know he would be home in the morning.

Tuesday evening, when Andrew's feet and legs itched unbearably, it was the two sisters who pronounced him "King of the Itchy Bites," and set about preparing a royal throne. A tepid footbath substituted for a footstool. They told him sand flies were New Zealand's worst *nasties*, since there were no snakes in the country. The insects, a cross between fleas and mosquitoes, would have ignored him if he had kept moving.

It all was quite silly, but Andrew enjoyed their relaxed approach to life. The Bartlett girls were less pretentious than those he knew back home, and easier to be around.

He was tired when he went to bed, too tired to check E-mail, and so tired that he wrote only briefly in the journal.

> *Two wondrous things today — sand flies and tree ferns. Sand flies are prodigious, ferocious, voracious, and atrocious! My poor feet and ankles will never be the same. They sucked the last drop of blood from both. The*

*tree ferns were an opposite wonder. Never have I seen ferns that grew as tall as trees — that are, in fact, trees. If I lived here, I would surround my house with fern trees.*

He snapped out the light and fell asleep.

* * * * *

Wednesday morning broke early and abruptly with a rude, insistent pounding on the front door.

"What's that?" cried Matthew, jumping out of the bed next to Andrew's. "It's only five o'clock!" He stumbled into the hallway, with Andrew close behind.

"Stay up there," Dennis ordered sharply. He approached the door with caution, and shouted, "Who is it?"

"Police! Open up!"

Police! Fear pulled Andrew back into dawn's shadows, and shouted to his brain. "Caught! Trapped! Ed and Bob blabbed! Penny heard! Parents know! Deportation! Paua Box still locked! Have to hide! Can't go home!"

Fear jerked him back into the bedroom as he heard Mr. Bartlett fumble with the locked door.

"One moment, and the police enter. One moment, and they ask for Andrew McKean."

No! He could get away. Those unexplored areas of New Zealand. The Fjordlands. He could hide there. He was strong, athletic. He knew something about surviving in the woods. How hard could it be?

Swiftly, he tore off his pajamas and donned khaki cargo shorts, stuffing the pockets with a few necessities: first aid kit, flashlight, matches, compass, sun protection, fishing line, hooks, and the CEOP. He made sure the paua box was deep in another side pocket, and secured it with a pair of extra socks. He put on a sweatshirt — hot, but essential. Hiking boots went on over clean socks and he jumped up. Time was of the essence. He must leave immediately!

"What are you doing?" Matthew separated the individual words with astonishment.

"Uh — thought I might as well get dressed."

Matthew grinned as he stepped toward the younger boy. "Come downstairs." Matthew was strong, and Andrew dared not resist the big hand that clutched his arm. Terrified, panic stricken, he let Matthew lead him down to the main living quarters.

The whole family had gathered — had been ordered to gather. Even Richard's godfather, André, was there. Two big police officers stood in front of the door, their arms crossed. They carried no guns, but clubs and handcuffs gleamed at their waists. Andrew moved with head down, his glance shifting from side to side, desperately willing his brain to create a miracle.

The larger of the two police officers stepped forward. "Which of you is An...."

Here it came.

The police officer consulted a paper, "...André Hendrikse?"

André. They wanted André. Not Andrew! Relief shook him like an aspen leaf.

"I'm André Hendrikse." As the older man spoke, the larger police officer stepped forward and arrested him. He handcuffed Mr. Hendrikse with cold, hard steel cuffs, and took him to the police car. A chill went through Andrew, in spite of the hot black sweatshirt.

The other officer ordered, then, that they all go down to the station, and soon Andrew found himself in the back seat of a dreadful black and white squad car. He captured the event later as a letter to Penny, but wrote it in the journal:

*Dear Penny,*

*Richard's godfather was arrested this morning on charges of misdemeanors committed over a period of 60 years! He was handcuffed and taken to the police station, fingerprinted, and put into jail clothes.*

*Then, with all of us present, he was tried, convicted on all counts, and jailed!*

*Actually, it was a surprise party for his 60th birthday, planned by his wife and friends, and it was hilarious! After the sentencing, there was a great breakfast in one of the old jail cells. It's the first time I've ever been in a police car or a jail cell (and I pray it will be the last!).*

He decided, then and there, to make all of his journal entries letters to Penny. It felt better than writing to a book, and maybe she would read them someday.

The remainder of Wednesday seemed dull compared to the jail party. The Internet server was up, and he got E-mail from Dad, Mom, and Alicia, but none from Penny.

A Rotary meeting concluded his day, and led into a whirlwind period of activity before school commenced.

* * * * *

Andrew was becoming fast friends with Anna and Katherine, and spent hours with them and their friends. They swam at Tahunanui Beach. They went sea-kayaking in Abel Tasman National Park. They visited Richmond's mall, craft stores, and Queen Street shops. They went into Nelson by bus to visit a museum and park — and went sight-seeing any time they could get a ride.

There were family chores, too, much to his chagrin. Mr. Bartlett insisted that everyone who was part of the family, including Andrew, work in the greenhouses for at least an hour a day.

When would anyone respect his rights? Eat here. Sleep there. Attend family devotions. Go to church there. Attend this school. Work here. What was next? Telling him how to dress?

Exactly! With only a week to go before the start of school, Janette announced at breakfast that she was taking Andrew shopping for school uniforms.

He could go alone, couldn't he?

No, Janette wanted to be sure they fit him properly. Also, the uniform had to be purchased at *Postie Plus* in Nelson, and she had other shopping to do there, so they would leave straight away after family devotions.

It was ghastly. The store clerk handed him the official uniform code published by the school:

~ *shirt - pale sky-blue polo*
~ *longs - long blue grey polyester*
~ *shorts - blue grey walk shorts to be worn with pale sky-blue walk socks*
~ *jumper - sky blue V-necked*
~ *tie - navy blue with scarlet diagonal stripe*
~ *shoes - black lace-up leather*
~ *sun hat - monogrammed school hat only*

Janette was sympathetic, but firm. School uniforms were required of everyone, and had to be worn on the way to school, in school, and on the way home. No exceptions.

The mirror in the fitting room exacerbated his opinion of the costume. What was wrong with jeans and tee-shirts? This wasn't Great Britain. This was New Zealand — land of relaxed people — people with a laid-back attitude. He yanked the clothing off and took it to the clerk.

"These fit," he said curtly.

"Will we be wanting a blazer?" she asked.

"I think he will wait until later." Janette did not allow him to answer, but she did allow him to pay for the trash.

"I'll take a tee-shirt, too," he said, asserting what was left of his free will. He chose a white one that proclaimed, "Next Stop Antarctica." He was beginning to wish it were true. At least, he would be allowed to wear what he wanted there.

The shopping trip consumed the entire morning, and ruined the entire day.

His letter-to-Penny entry complained:

*Sweaters are jumpers, and pants are longs, i.e., as opposed to shorts. Now. Want a good laugh? Picture me in blue-gray walking shorts with sky-blue knee socks and black lace-up leather shoes. Add a sky-blue polo shirt with a red-striped tie, and top it off with a wide-brimmed blue-grey hat. That ought to keep you giggling for a month!"*

He checked E-mail that night, as usual. There was no letter from Penny, as usual. The little silver heart felt colder each time, it seemed, and he guessed that she had learned the truth.

* * * * *

On the last Sunday evening before school was to begin, Morgan called. The only phone was in a corner of the kitchen, and none too private.

"I just had to see how you are surviving," she said. Her joy effervesced over the distance.

"I'm great now!" — in a stage whisper. "I'd forgotten how beautiful American English is! Are you surviving?"

"I love it here," bubbled Morgan. "I live in a tiny house on the hill above the harbor. The people are very nice, and I've been invited to lots of things already. Three girls phoned me today and said they'd be looking out for me at school tomorrow. Do you go tomorrow, too?"

Andrew faced into the corner. "Yes, but not willingly. Get this. The name of the school is Hebron Christian College, but it's not a college. It's just high school."

"Oh, I ran into the same thing," Morgan offered. "My host mum said that most secondary schools here are referred to as college. What we call college is a university, I guess."

"Oh." He paused. "Are you nervous?"

"About school? Sure! I'm excited, though, and I can't wait to make some friends. I'm bored with having nobody but adults in my life. Tell me about your host family. How many sisters did you get? Are they cute? Do you have any brothers?"

They talked for thirty minutes — until James wandered into the kitchen for a drink. "I have to go, Pen ... Morgan."

"You have to go pen? What do you mean?"

"Twongue-twangled," Andrew said quickly. "Bye."

* * * * *

Monday evening, he could hardly wait to write in his journal. He chose a fine, black-ink pen, and wrote:

*Dear Penny,*

*Today was my first day of school at Hebron Christian College, but I don't start classes until tomorrow, so today I just followed my counselor around to his classes. His name's Craig. It is, no doubt, too early to make a judgment of the school, but I made one anyway. I hated it!*

Andrew exchanged the black ink pen for a fluorescent marker, and marinated the last three words in green. Then he continued:

*The girls were giggly, the guys were socially inept, and if either bothered to talk to me, it was just to make me answer a question so they could hear my American accent. Not exactly what I thought Christian school would be. I almost checked in the mirror to see if I had contracted leprosy!*

*The only decent person I met (besides Katherine, who's in most of my classes) was a South African exchange student. I hope Tuesday will be a better day.*

Tuesday was better. There were English, math, chemistry, Maori, French, and Performance Music. But best of all, there was rugby!

Andrew was eating lunch with the South African exchange student, Phillip, who already had been in New Zealand for six months. As they talked, the topic of sports arose. "Do you like sports?" asked Phillip.

"Every one I've tried," said Andrew.

"Brilliant! Why don't you try out for the rugby team with me — or cricket?"

"Are you kidding? I know nothing about rugby — and all I know about cricket is that it's like American baseball — but entirely different."

"And played in a round stadium. I'll teach you both," said Phillip. "Come on. We can start rugby during interval. We have two hours."

"Okay." Andrew followed to a grassy area behind the school. Round stadium was cricket!

As Phillip introduced him to the oval rugby ball, larger than a football, more boys congregated, each eager to share his knowledge of rugby.

"A rugby game requires fifteen players."

"The object is to score as many points as possible by carrying, passing, kicking — and grounding the ball in the scoring zone at the far end of the field — the in-goal area."

"When you ground the ball, you get a try — worth five points. Then you go for a conversion by placekicking or dropkicking. If the ball goes over the bar and between the goal posts, you have two more points."

Andrew followed their instruction eagerly. "It sounds a lot like American football. Do you have long forward passes like in football?"

"No. You pass backward, kick forward."

"And you aren't allowed to tackle someone who isn't holding the ball."

They went on to tell him that play only stops when a team scores a try, the ball goes out of play, or an infringement occurs. "Three words you have got to remember are *scrum*, *try*, and *line-out*. When the ball goes out, it's thrown back in at a *line-out*. The opposing forwards line up and jump for the ball."

"Or throw one man in the air to grab it!"

"Fouls get a penalty or free kick — or a *scrum*. Scrum's an abbreviation for 'scrummage' or 'scrimmage.' The scrum is the most brutal part of the game. In a scrum, the opposing forwards bind together in a unit to push against the other forwards, trying to win the ball with their feet. They hang onto shirts, shorts, or whatever they can grab. One mate got his shorts pulled off once."

"*Try* will be the hardest to remember," said Andrew. "I call it a success, not a try."

Good-natured laughter ensued, and they practiced a few scrums to help Andrew get the idea. By the end of the second hour, sweaty and disheveled, Andrew had become one of them. He was definitely going to try out for rugby. "What's the best rugby team in New Zealand?" he asked.

"All Blacks," answered Phillip.

"All Blacks?" Andrew raised an eyebrow.

"Not all black men." Phillip grinned. "I was told the name came from a typographical error in a news article. Observing that the team played as though every man was a 'back,' the article said mistakenly that the men were 'all blacks' instead of 'all backs.' The name stuck."

They went back to classes, physically, but Andrew's mind stayed on the rugby field.

That evening, he talked to the Bartlett men about rugby, and about his decision to try out for the school team. "Their first game is in Masterton," he said.

"Oh, that reminds me," said Dennis. "Something came up and I have got to go to Masterton Friday and Saturday. You have school holiday on Friday. Would you like to try the ferry with me?"

Would he! Not that he expected sea travel to be any better than air travel, but he would do anything to get the paua box open. Anything!

He hurried to his room and went online, found no waiting E-mail, but wrote to Alicia, "I'm going to Masterton Friday, and see if I can get the paua box open. Don't tell the rest. Just wish me luck!"

# 16

## *Beastly Holiday*

The trip to Masterton was ghastly. There was no other word for it. The dreadfulness began the moment they left Richmond, early Friday morning.

They drove east along the top of the South Island to Picton, where the ferry dock was located. Riding the left side of the narrow, mountainous road, Andrew fought to avoid the inevitable motion sickness. It seldom bothered him back home, where roads were wide, curves were smooth, heavy guardrails lined dangerous drop-offs — and cars drove on the right side of the road.

This road was a major national highway, but it had only one lane in each direction, sharp curves, and imaginary guardrails.

He tried to segregate his mind from his stomach — to enjoy the scenery, which actually was breathtaking.

At first, the Tasman Bay sparkled in the rising sun, gently reaching for the coastal route, reaching to embrace it — but swampy estuaries kept pushing the road away. Repeatedly, the road tried to return to the turquoise water, but being often rebuffed, gradually yielded and turned to ramble through the hills — green, rolling hills dotted with white sheep and frolicking young lambs. Contentedly, it led them through pastoral scenes for a time. Then, tiring of the smaller hills, it climbed upward into towering mountains of dark, silent pine forests. The frightening drop-offs multiplied, plunged into deeper ravines, and dared one to sneak a quick look. Finally, the road conquered the summit and descended rapidly to the Marlborough Sounds. Fingers of blue-green ocean stretched into lower hills, caressing more bright green pastures and dark green pine farms.

The redheaded teen wanted to enjoy it all. He wanted to drink in every vivid color, every soothing aroma; to form clear memories for his journal — but motion sickness defeated him.

He swallowed. He swallowed again. But as they entered picturesque Picton, his freckled cheeks bloated suddenly, and he motioned for Dennis to stop. Humiliated, he leapt from the minibus and threw up.

That was the beginning of learning the full meaning of the word ghastly. At the quay, Dennis suggested that Andrew stay outside and get some fresh air. Dennis went inside to buy tickets.

Andrew got out of the vehicle and walked slowly around the quay. "Suck in huge gulps of ocean air, and you'll be better," he instructed himself. He walked farther, and dismally watched the large ferry rise and fall on the gentle harbor tide. "Yeah, I'll be better. Fat chance!"

Long before his qualmish stomach was ready, the call came to board the ferry. They climbed back into the minibus, and Dennis drove into the ship's dark bowels. They parked, locked the vehicle as a crew member chained it down, and climbed to the top deck.

"Let's sit at the front, then, where you can see," said Dennis. He headed down the length of the ship, pausing at a snack bar to buy a ginger beer for Andrew. Dennis was a thoughtful host, he had to admit, but if this trip was anything like the flight from Wellington, he might as well have saved his money.

They found comfortable, padded armchairs, with a small table between, and settled their bags. Dennis said something about visiting the on-board shop, and hurried away.

Andrew sipped slowly at the soapy ginger beer, watching families scurry to claim the best seats. When he heard a mother asking a young girl to get a napkin out of her bag for the baby, he leaned forward in curiosity. Then he wrote to Penny:

> *A napkin really is a diaper. Can you believe it? I'm glad I learned that! Imagine sitting in a restaurant with friends and asking the waiter to bring a napkin with your meal!*

Dennis returned. "Here are a few things you might like," he said, an empathetic note in his voice. He handed Andrew a packet of tablets to ward off motion sickness, and two wristbands that used pressure points on the wrists to accomplish the same goal.

Andrew smiled apologetically. "I'm sorry," he said. "I've never been a good traveler on curvy roads or in the air." He quickly swallowed a dose of the tablets, and slid the gray knit bands onto his wrists, positioning them as pictured on the box.

Somewhere above, a big horn sounded. The ferry slipped its bonds, slowly crawled down the long finger of the sound, and crept out onto the widespread hand of the Cook Strait. Andrew was fascinated. "How long is the trip to Masterton?" he asked.

"Three and a half hours to Wellington, then a couple of hours up the mountain to Masterton."

"Is the Masterton road...." Andrew began.

"Curvy," said Dennis. "That's why I got the

pills and wristbands. They'll prevent sickness." He pulled out his Bible and began to read.

Read? He had better pray. Pray that the pills and the knit bands worked!

Andrew turned away, and concentrated hopefully on the wide expanse of the choppy Cook Strait. It was good to not feel nauseous, but he really could not say he felt well. A dull ache was developing at the nape of his neck. He turned his head slowly, and discovered that a vague dizziness accompanied the ache. He turned slowly back, and opened his journal to write a Penny note:

> *On my way to Masterton. I have to pinch myself to believe this is not a cruel dream. The scenery on the way over to the ferry was colorful — blue, gold, and the ever-present emerald green (he saturated the last word with the green marker). The road, though, was torturous, and I chundered again, just barely making it out of the van in time. My host dad bought motion sickness medication and "seabands" for me. I guess he doesn't want a repeat. He says we won't reach Masterton until well after noon, but the paua factory will be open, and if my luck improves, the box will be unlocked by the end of the day!*

His head really ached now, so he closed the book and rested against the seatback. His hand found its way into his pocket, and he rubbed the glossy paua box, eagerly anticipating, wondering, imagining. He looked across the table, wanting to ask more about Grandfather's visit to New Zealand — but Dennis was deeply engrossed in reading his Bible.

Andrew sighed and leaned his head back again. Dennis was a good host, charitable and thoughtful and all that, but when it came to church stuff, he was fanatical — rude, too, reading his Bible instead of paying attention to his traveling companion.

The upper muscles of the teen's right leg pumped up and down like pistons, causing his feet to tap nervously on the carpeted floor. His fingertips drummed on the small table. He cracked his knuckles. He just had to ask. He had to know. He could not, would not wait.

"Mr. Bartlett, will you be done soon?" He was ashamed instantly. What kind of moron tried to stop a man from reading the Bible? "I'm sorry."

"No, no. That's all right." Mr. Bartlett read a few more words, placed a paper-thin gold bookmark in the Bible, and closed it. "Are you feeling sick?"

"Oh — no, I'm not sick. My head hurts a bit, but I'm not sick. I just wanted to talk — but only when you've finished your reading. It can wait. There's no hurry. Please continue."

"Want a wee chat, do we?" said Dennis. He slipped the Bible into his briefcase. "What's on your mind?"

"Grandfather's visit to New Zealand."

"Aha. We never did finish our discussion about his visit to Enzed."

"Enzed?"

"Not heard that one yet?" Dennis laughed. "Enzed is our abbreviation for New Zealand — NZ." His fingers traced the two letters in the air. "I guess you would pronounce it Enzee."

Andrew grinned. "You pronounce 'z' as *zed*?"

"We speak the King's English, you know. Have you learned to spell words the New Zealand way yet — colour, honour, saviour, harbour, and especially aluminium?"

"I'm learning by making mistakes." Andrew sighed, and willed Dennis to get to the important question.

"Good way to learn — mistakes. Beastly, but good."

Andrew coughed. "Mr. Bartlett, you said that Grandfather's ship was blown off course and docked at Wellington. Can you tell me more? I didn't even know Grandfather had been to sea, let alone to New Zealand."

"I'm not surprised by that, Andrew. Your grandfather was a very private man — had heaps of secrets, it seemed. He was on holiday by some government arrangement when he blew in here. It was not much of a holiday at that point, though. He looked as though he had been dragged through a hedge backwards, he did. I was a young bobby in Wellington, is how I got acquainted."

"Bobby?" Andrew frowned in puzzlement.

"Policeman. The British nicknamed them bobbies after Sir Robert Peel, who organized the London police force. They called him Bobby for short, and bobbies were like Bobby, I guess. Rather the same as Christians being like Christ."

Andrew shifted his shoulders.

"Anyhow, I had just joined the force, and I volunteered to help your grandfather's group. One chap, who must have owned a German vehicle, tried to put his luggage under the bonnet of my motorcar instead of in the boot. Then, when I took them on a tour of Wellington, another fellow said my muffler needed mending. I thought he meant the cloth around my neck, but he meant the motorcar's silencer."

"But — your grandfather." Dennis' eyes brimmed with joy as he returned to the subject. "Your grandfather was a wonderful man. He took time, once he knew they would be docking in New

Zealand, to study our way of speaking. He stepped off the boat ready to be a mate, knowing where to look for the loo, and prepared to order crisps. He was no clever mate, but neither was he backward about coming forward."

Say what!? Grandfather had been a better linguist than Andrew was if he could have understood all of that!

For the next two hours, Andrew listened, aching with a growing desire to have known the grandfather Dennis described.

Grandfather had come to New Zealand about seventeen years ago. His work remained as secret as his holiday. There were many strange things about the man and his sidetrip to New Zealand, but the most peculiar thing was Grandfather's keen desire to meet a Maori chief. It was unusual to see such interest in a pakeha.

"The Maori were surprised," said Dennis.

Mr. Bartlett took Grandfather to visit the Papawai Marae near Masterton, since there was a chief there at the time. The Maori people all invited Grandfather to visit in their homes, and he accepted. He learned Maori words, and memorized Maori Bible verses. He learned the haka and other rituals. His new friends were so impressed that they gave him the paua box as a token of abiding friendship. As far as Dennis knew, it was empty when Grandfather received it.

"So, Andrew," Dennis concluded, "Whatever is in the box now was placed there by your grandfather." He peered through the ferry's now-salty front window. "There's Wellington Harbor off to the left."

Andrew sat up eagerly, and looked across the deep blue water. The harbor's wide mouth was probably another fifteen minutes away, but he could see Wellington flowing down the surrounding hills to line the busy crescent. The city looked much larger than it had from the air.

"Let's go to the outer deck for the ride into port," suggested Mr. Bartlett. "Oh — you had best take more pills, too, before we start driving again."

Andrew swallowed two pills with the last of his stale ginger beer. As they gathered their belongings and picked their way among seasick passengers, he was thankful anew for pills and wristbands. Even if his head did feel like a nail at the business end of a hammer, he had not chundered, if indeed chunder had a past tense.

The two men stood silent at the rail of the uppermost deck as the ferry exchanged greetings with a departing twin. Then, the big vessel turned with dignified slowness, and entered the harbor. It crawled laboriously among the pleasure craft, tugs, and freighters, and came to rest at the quay with a solid bump. They had completed the rough crossing without incident.

"Well, then," said Dennis. "We'd best be in our bus when the gates open." He led the way through a rapidly swelling crowd that poured down the stairs to the vehicle deck. They reached the minibus quickly, got in, and waited for the crew to loosen their ties. As the big gate opened, Dennis started the engine and they drove out — out onto the road to Masterton.

Soon now! Soon! Andrew's excitement swelled as he anticipated the opening of the paua box. He took it from his pocket and carefully rubbed a fingerprint from the shimmering blue-green iridescence of the cover.

The divided highway, a pleasant surprise, hugged the bank of a wide riverbed as it passed through lovely Wellington suburbs, and out into lush green summer meadows. The curves were gentle, the traffic light, and he relaxed. He felt almost at home.

Almost. The thought was barely formed when the road slimmed to a single lane in each direction, and started up the mountain through an endless series of linked elbows.

Andrew wished mightily that Dennis could drive on the right side. He would not mind at all being very close to those solid rock walls. Instead, the view from his side window raced downward, the yellow-blooming gorse bushes failing to hide the chillingly steep, unguarded ravines.

The dull ache pulled itself up from the nape of his neck and over his head, settling behind his eyes. It threatened dire consequences if he glanced anywhere other than straight ahead.

Dennis was describing the Rimutaka Mountains, but the teen stopped hearing. He stopped thinking about Grandfather. He forgot the paua box. He lost track of time. He knew nothing but the center line that curved left, right, left, right, left....

The sickening repetition of the tight curves imprisoned him. There was no escape — no end.

Suddenly, he felt a trapdoor open in the floor of his stomach. It gave no warning. "Bleah!"

"A bit crook?" Dennis kept his eyes on the road. "I can't pull off now — but there's a car park at the summit. Try not to think about it."

Count to ten without thinking of being sick. Right. One, two, three — as they pulled into the summit parking lot, he leapt from the slowing vehicle and threw up the remainder of his ginger beer and medicine.

Dennis was beside him quickly, putting a gentle arm around his shoulders. "Feeling better?"

Andrew shook his head greenly, slowly. He dared not speak yet. The cool mountain air felt good on empty cheeks, but not that good.

He raised his head, and silently stared back over the vast green and yellow scenery toward the Cook Strait. If only he could walk the rest of the way to Masterton.

Dennis read his mind. "We have another hour to go, mate, but you'll be better now. I know five teens who get sick every trip on this road, and they all feel better straight away when we leave this spot. Come on. Let's find the loo and wash up."

Twenty minutes later, Andrew took one last clean breath and settled reluctantly into the front seat. The curves did grow fewer and gentler straight away, and the highway descended into the three tiny towns of Featherston, Greytown, and Carterton.

Just north of Carterton, Dennis turned onto a dead end street and into a car park. "Well, you're here, Andrew."

"Carterton? I thought you said Masterton." Then he saw the sign:

*~ Paua Shell Factory ~*

That's right. A small town near Masterton. The factory was minuscule. Never mind that. What mattered was whether they could open the paua box for him.

He jumped from the bus, and hurried around to the driver's side. "I can't believe I'm actually here!" Andrew tugged at his light green shirt, trying to hide the remaining stains. He whisked a hand up over his copper red hair, and smoothed it into place. Matching his stride to Dennis' long stride, he entered the little factory showroom. It glowed with the iridescence of paua.

"Kia Ora." A darker-skinned girl with black hair stepped forward to greet them. "May I help you?"

"Yes, I think so," said Dennis. He explained about the little paua box.

"I'm not sure, but I'll ask," she said. She returned to say that the master artisan was busy. "If you will come into the factory, you can watch the workers while you wait for him."

The factory seemed more like a small home craft shop than a factory. A woman guided them through the manufacturing process while they waited, explaining that the paua lives in New Zealand coastal waters only, and is a common sight on the beaches. Andrew knew that from his Rabbit Island experience.

"The average," she said, "is an oval about five inches long. The shell is well known for its scintillating blue-green and turquoise colors. Our native Maori people used paua often for jewelry, and for the decoration of our tiki. Later it was favored for inlay boxes."

Boxes! That was the word he was waiting to hear. Andrew listened intently.

"The outer part of the paua shell usually is covered in hardened lime, and sometimes there are barnacles attached, but the inside of the shell shows its true color." She led them to the first workstation.

"First, we clean the exterior lime off the shell by immersing it into a weak hydrochloric acid solution for approximately thirty minutes, depending on the thickness of the lime. Too long in the acid can make the shell too thin to work. Next, we thoroughly scrub each shell in water." They moved to the next workstation, and the guide raised her voice above the drill noise.

"We remove any remaining residue with a paint-stripping wheel attached to an electric hand drill. Stubborn encrustations have to be ground off on a bench grinder." She handed Andrew a piece of shell.

"At this point, the shell shows the color of the finished item. This one is iridescent blue, but they range from this through to pearly pink. Next, we buff the shell on a cloth buffing wheel. If the shell is to be used for inlay or jewelry, we cut and shape it with a Carborundum wheel."

"And if it's for a box?" Andrew had to ask.

"Final polishing is with the buffing wheel. Then we coat the piece with a clear lacquer."

"Why do the workers wear masks?" asked Andrew.

"The particles of dust from grinding the shells are barbed like tiny fishhooks, and very toxic to the lungs. We use a vacuum extractor for the whole factory, so you need not worry, but the masks are extra individual protection for the workers who are so close to it every day."

"Now," she concluded. "Here is the man who can help you." She introduced a tall, very austere looking Maori man.

The man smiled briefly as he extended his hand in greeting. He left the hand extended after shaking Andrew's and Mr. Bartlett's, and said crisply, "The box, please."

Andrew fumbled it from his pocket. His handkerchief came out with it, and dropped to the floor. He ignored the white cloth and, trembling with excitement, placed the precious paua box in the sinewy hand of the artisan. His hand burst with emptiness as the little box left it.

"This!" The craftsman gave a startled gasp of recognition, but quickly stifled it. "Come with me," he said.

"You go, Andrew. It is your box," said Mr. Bartlett.

Yes. It was his box. It was his box, and it was about to be opened. Maybe. He accompanied the Maori man to a small office.

"Please tell me all about the box, in detail," ordered the quiet man.

Andrew leaned forward, his eye guarding the precious treasure that lay in the stranger's hand. Rapidly, he explained everything, from the letters Grandfather had left, which bequeathed the box and its contents to the four McKeans; through the riddle of the meaning of *paua*; to his selection as exchange student, Grandfather's note on the map, and the subsequent trip to New Zealand.

"We desperately wanted to open it, but we were sure it would break if we tried to force the lock, and since it is my gift from Grandfather, I don't want it broken," Andrew ended. He hoped the man would take the hint.

The craftsman's brawny hands turned the paua box with amazing gentleness. They held it to the light, rotating it as his eyes examined each seam. The hands paused briefly once, began again, and returned to the spot that first had caught the attention of the keen eyes. One hand reached for a pair of magnifying glasses that lay on the desk, grasped them, and pushed them onto the man's nose. "That is it. I am sure. That is it."

Andrew wanted to shout, "What is it?"

Why did he not hurry?

What did he find?

Andrew shrugged his left shoulder, then his right shoulder.

He sighed deeply.

He cracked his knuckles.

He clenched his hands in his lap, and his stomach clenched in harmony.

He strained to see what the man saw.

He strained to cling to his patience.

"HURRY!" screamed his heart.

# 17

## *Masterton's Secrets*

As Andrew agonized, the man turned a bright lamp to shine on his hands and on the box. He opened a desk drawer, and carefully selected a tiny screwdriver, no more than an inch in length.

With amazing accuracy, he touched the tiny instrument to a spot at the back of the box's lid, just opposite the site of the tiny lock. Exercising infinite care, he pressed lightly on the spot. The lid sprang up.

Andrew gasped.

The paua box was open!

He held out shaking hands to receive the treasure. "I thought you might have a key," he whispered.

"Fake lock. Secret latch." That was all the man said. He placed the paua box in Andrew's hands, stood, and opened the door. Before Andrew could think, he had gone. He went only a few steps, however, then returned and asked, "Would you like to know about the box?"

"Yes! Yes, I would." The teen struggled for maturity, but his voice cracked.

The Maori man's blue eyes softened, and his voice held a note of mystery as he began.

"My father told me the story ten years ago, and swore me to absolute secrecy. It seems that your grandfather was under a witness protection plan due to his part in bringing a federal criminal to justice. He had to be gotten out of the United States until the time came for him to take the witness stand, so your government put him on a cruise, without his wife. It was hoped that his whereabouts would remain a secret until word returned to America that his ship was lost at sea."

"You mean they purposefully steered into that storm to make it realistic?"

"His ship never encountered a storm, but that report formed part of the protection plan. It made it appear that all aboard were lost at sea. Meanwhile, your grandfather visited us for a week, and my father gave him this box, which he had made years before."

"Your father made the paua box?" Andrew gazed solemnly at the story teller. "Why did he give it to Grandfather?"

"It was the greatest gift he could give to show his friendship to this noble person." The man paused to brush a tear from his dark cheek. "My father spoke often of your grandfather. He held him up to me as a role model. He said that your grandfather could have kept his silence, could have refused to witness. It would have been easier on both him and your grandmother. But he was a man of character. He was a man of courage."

Staring into space, he continued, "Your grandfather held the conviction that a man must always speak truth, and he was willing to accept the consequences of acting on that conviction. A lesser man might have refused to witness, but your grandfather believed one's true character shows in the difficult challenges of life."

The artisan turned and gazed straight into Andrew's soul. "Your grandfather, Andrew, had the courage of his convictions."

"The courage of his convictions," Andrew echoed.

With a few simple words, the master craftsman went on to explain the construction of the paua box, and Andrew tried to listen respectfully, but his mind was busy with the implications of the man's story, so busy that he was startled when the story teller stood again.

"Thank you so much, Mr. ...."

"My name is not important compared to McKean," said the man. "Be worthy of the name, Andrew." He turned once as he went out the door. "Stay and explore the contents of your box alone," he said. He closed the door behind him.

Andrew slowly raised the freckled hand that had rested protectively on the paua box. How did one dare to look into such a box? There should be some ceremony — something to mark such an auspicious occasion.

Slowly, the sunburnt, freckled hand covered the iridescent blue-green box again. The serious blue eyes closed. The husky voice of a near adult whispered, "Grandfather, wherever you are, thank you for being a man of character. Thank you for this paua box and for whatever is in it. I want to be a man like you — a man who has the courage of his convictions." He almost added amen, and blinked his eyes open in slight confusion.

Now it was time. He carried the little paua box to the desk and placed it carefully on the thick, soft desk pad. He removed his hand and gazed spellbound into the box.

A folded piece of paper lay in the top. This, he placed to one side. Beneath it, bedded in soft cotton, lay a gleaming brass key — the perfect size for Caleb's beautiful grand piano. He reached in clumsy fingers, and tenderly removed the key to the soft black desk pad.

Another cotton ball parted to reveal a more delicate key. A small strip of attached paper read, "Alicia, this is for your kaleidoscope, which was handmade by dearest Grandmother. Look for the dream inside."

Andrew smiled mistily. Alicia would love this gift. It was so perfect for her. He wished Caleb and Alicia were here right now so he could hand them their keys.

He looked into the box again. The bottom held another folded paper — crackly blue paper like that on which Grandfather had written their letters. "Dearest Cathryn, your name is derived from the Greek katharos 'pure,' the name of your dear grandmother. I am giving you her wedding china and her cookbooks, especially her *Joy of Cooking*. Be sure you look at the front page, signed personally by the author, Irma Rombauer." Grandfather knew what mattered most to Cathryn, that's for sure. Food!

Well, those were the gifts for his siblings. Now for his own note. There was no name on it, but it had to be his. "Last, but not least — I hope!"

He unfolded the note eagerly, anticipating his wonderful gift. His eyes rapidly scanned the note, blinked with incredulity, and tried again. It was not English! It was not any of the romance languages — not Latin, not French, and probably not Spanish or Italian — not one word bore the slightest resemblance to anything he had ever seen or studied.

*Kia maia, kia toa, kaua e wehi, kaua e pawera ia ratou: no te mea ko Ihowa, ko tou Attua, ko ia te haere tahi ana ia koe; e kore ia e whakarere ia koe,e kore hoki e mawehe atu ia koe.*

It had to be Maori. Was the Maori man still outside the door? He yanked it open and looked around. He was across the room. "Excuse me, sir."

"Did you want me?"

"I need your help, please."

The man returned readily, and Andrew detected a conspiratorial smile, or thought he did.

"It is from the Maori translation of the Bible," began the Maori man.

*Deuteronomy 31:6:*

*Be strong and courageous, do not be afraid or tremble at them, for the Lord your God is the one who goes with you. He will not fail you or forsake you.*

Andrew's face fell, and his anger rose. That was a gift? That was what Grandfather had left? That was meant to be an inheritance — a Bible verse? The teenaged McKean liked to think of himself as a Christian, and had told Grandfather he was, but this was no inheritance — no gift.

The Maori man let Andrew wrestle for a moment. Then he said, "There's something else, Andrew — something not written here."

Andrew glared through red anger. "What? I get a personalized copy of the Maori Bible, too?"

The man's keen disappointment slapped the boy, bringing forth a curt apology. "Sorry."

"Andrew, your grandfather left something with my family. He asked us to give it to nobody but the one who came carrying the paua box. We thought he had forgotten, but now you are here. Will you come home with me?"

Puzzled blue eyes lifted to the Maori face. "I guess it would be all right, but I have to ask my host." He looked around the factory room. Mr. Bartlett was not there. He picked up the little box, and carefully replaced its contents. The Maori artisan showed him how to disable the lock's catch, and Andrew closed it, pushing the box habitually back into his pocket.

"Your host is in the shop," said the man, leading the way from the manufacturing room.

Andrew hurried to where Dennis was looking at paua jewelry. "Mr. Bartlett, the man that helped me open the box wants me to go home with him to see what else Grandfather left for me. Is it okay with you?" His anger was changing rapidly to curiosity.

The Maori added, "Today is an important day for me also, Mr. Bartlett. Will you come to our home later for a *hakari* in Andrew's honor?"

Dennis agreed, and suggested that Andrew change from his vomit-stained clothes. Dennis would take care of his business in Masterton, and meet Andrew at the hakari this evening.

The shopkeeper showed the American youth to a small, clean toilet room. There, Andrew quickly changed into a clean pair of blue jeans and his favorite blue-green polo — to match the paua box. Then they were off.

"My name is Mr. Raumati," said the Maori, as he steered his blue Honda onto the highway. "I live with my wife by the Papawai Marae near Masterton. Our children, six of them, all are grown and married, but they live nearby with our grand-children." His tongue grew suddenly loose, and he began to share his beloved Maori history with Andrew.

As the long canoes of his people neared this land, crossing the Pacific from *Hawai'iki*, a long white cloud hovered above these islands. Therefore, they named this land *Aotearoa*, "land of the long white cloud." They found it to be a good land, lacking people or mammals, but offering lush growth and beautiful birds, fishing in stream or ocean, and farming in rolling hills and coastlands. It was a land of great variety, with icy glaciers flowing to the ocean through dense rain forests; with volcanoes steaming in snowy deserts; with thermal pools reeking near fresh, clean ocean beaches.

Mr. Raumati described *The Treaty of Waitangi*, celebrated today, and the reason that Andrew had a school holiday. "It was signed at *Waitangi* in the Bay of Islands on 6 February 1840," he said. "Captain William Hobson, several English residents, and approximately forty-five Maori chiefs signed it. In the Treaty, our Maori chiefs gave to Queen Victoria the government of our land. The queen agreed to protect the Maori people and let us live in our own villages as before, with the same rights as the white people who had become settlers in New Zealand. It was a good start, but there were problems."

Hating history as he did, Andrew tried to change the subject. "Tell me about your family, Mr. Raumati."

"My *iwi*," said Mr. Raumati. "My people. I trace them back through the *whakapapa*, the generations, to the canoe in which they arrived. In my *iwi* were separate *hapuu*, family groups. When Maori people ask, '*Ko wai koe*?' (Who are you?), they are not just asking your name. They want to place you in your historical, tribal, and geographical context. They can do that only if you can tell your tribe, your canoe, and your ancestors."

Andrew grinned. "I'm glad my school made me sign up for a course in Maori," he said. "Maybe the next time we meet, I will be able to tell you who I am. Maybe I will understand a few of your words, too. Right now, I don't understand much of anything — like when you invited Mr. Bartlett to a *hakari* tonight. What is that?"

"A *hakari* is a Maori feast. Tonight, we will cook in the ground with hot rocks. You will help me cook."

Andrew cook? Good luck! You should ask Mom what happened whenever Andrew tried to cook. He longed to beg off, but instead he asked, "What does *pah-kee-ha* mean?"

"You are a pakeha, a white person," laughed Mr. Raumati. "A sun burnt one, but still a pakeha. Here we are." He turned left into a long driveway, and parked near a small, neat house. "Andrew, meet the family."

People poured out of the woodwork: big people, little people, men, women, and children. A phone call had announced the hakari, and all had gathered quickly. Everyone shared in the preparations, enveloping Andrew with warm smiles and friendly words as they worked. He and Mr. Raumati helped for a half hour.

Then Mr. Raumati said, "Come, Andrew. Let's go for a tramp in the bush."

They left the family happily involved in the commotion of lining the earthen pit oven with rocks, and hiked into the quiet of the native bush, the virgin forest.

Andrew caught his breath at the entrance. Never had he experienced such intense beauty! Bellbirds, so fearless that they brushed his sleeves in passing, warbled the clear, resonate sounds that earned them their name. Landing briefly on a low branch, they sang as though for him alone. Flitting upward, they darted through leafy branches, palm fronds, fern fronds, and pine needles. Only the pines seemed at all familiar to the American teen.

A pensive, thirty minutes of silent walking ended at a fallen eucalyptus log. Mr. Raumati sat, and patted a space beside him. He fumbled in his pocket, and drew out two objects: a yellowed paper, and a red velveteen bag.

"For you," he said brusquely.

Andrew took only the paper, and slowly unfolded it along deep-creased lines, sensing its import, breathing in the solemnity of the moment. The forest, worlds away from wintry Delaware, draped the occasion in beauty. Trees blossoming in Christmas red rubbed branches with tall, verdant fern trees and taller dark pines; the colorful bellbirds rang in celebration; a transparent fishing stream bounced and tumbled toward the sea

— and a dark native man, possibly the son of a chief, sat beside him on a log, passing on gifts from a deceased grandfather.

Andrew smoothed the paper across the slim legs of his blue jeans, his eyes never moving from the features of the man before him. Repeatedly, he ironed it beneath his strong, athletic fingers, sweaty droplets dampening the surface.

This was his inheritance. This was the real reason Grandfather had sent him to New Zealand. It had been left there for him, in the safekeeping of the stern Maori artisan. Grandfather had left it for him.

"Look at the paper, Andrew. It is yours."

Andrew's eyes slowly moved downward to the paper and read.

"All around you," said Mr. Raumati. "This land is yours. This is your forest, your bush. We walked through your paddocks as we came. Your grandfather bought it from my father — for his yet unborn descendent. My house is marked there at the border. We are to be neighbors."

Andrew blinked repeatedly, trying to understand the foreign deed. Fifty hectares. Hectare. A metric measurement. How much was it? "What is a hectare, Mr. Raumati?"

"One hectare is about two and a half acres."

"That means...," Andrew calculated quickly, "that means I now own — I own almost 125 acres of land!"

"Your grandfather bought the land from my father when he visited us, Andrew. He also bought this precious gift from our craftsmen, and left it for you." Mr. Raumati extended again the little red velveteen bag.

Andrew opened the bag, and withdrew a small green carving suspended on a satiny black cord. The rich, dusky green of the carving seemed to vibrate with its own inner memories, and with the memories of its gifted carver.

"What is it?" he breathed.

"Greenstone — New Zealand jade. This is the koru shape," explained his Maori friend. "It is a scrolled shape, like the curled-over tip of the New Zealand fern shoot, which unfurls and becomes a fern frond."

Mr. Raumati swept his brown hand toward the fern fronds overhead. "The koru reaches to the light, striving for perfection, encouraging new beginnings. It represents the unfolding of new life, of everything that is reborn. May I?"

He took the greenstone pendant and hung it around Andrew's neck, firmly securing the cord with a knot. "You are highly fortunate, Andrew McKean, to receive the paua box, the land, and the koru. Your grandfather must have expected you to be like himself — a man with the courage of his convictions."

He extended his hand, then. "I am honored to have you as my friend and neighbor. I hope you will return soon and often. God bless you."

Andrew never remembered walking back — across his land — nor did he remember the hakari. He must have talked as they walked — must have eaten. His stomach felt full. He did remember wondering how an honored guest behaved; hazily recalled fixing a smile on his face. Mostly, though, the latter part of the day swirled, its dancing patterns misty beyond the bounds of reality, gradually slowing as he parted from his new Maori friends — his new neighbors.

Exhausted, he climbed into the quiet of the minibus. Dennis had finished his business more quickly than expected, so they would take the night ferry home rather than wait until morning.

Andrew let Dennis monopolize the conversation on the way down the dark mountain road to the ferry, and for some reason, he did not get sick enough to vomit this time. He did not throw up on the ferry either, as it plowed through night seas to Picton. Dennis was reading his Bible again, but that was fine now. Andrew wanted to be alone with his thoughts. He closed his aching eyes.

# 18

## *Empathetic Valentine*

On Monday morning, February 9, a man awoke in Andrew's bed. A man awoke in Andrew's body — a man who reached to the light, wanting to make a new beginning, to unfold in rebirth and new life. Had the jade koru cast a spell?

"I may be a New Zealand citizen, now that I own land here," he mused. "If so, I can stay in New Zealand. I can desert the Rotarian exchange program — go AWOL. If I'm not a citizen yet, I can become one. I suppose I have to wait until I turn eighteen, but I can wait."

His eyes remained behind closed doors, painting the enticing picture at the dictation of his imagination.

"Mr. Raumati will sponsor me, and I will attend school up in Masterton on my student visa. I'll build a cabin on my land, in the glen of leafy tree ferns. I'll build it with my own pine trees."

He rolled onto his back, his eyes refusing to come out. "I'll use my pine for any furniture I need, too. I'll grow my own vegetables, and I'll catch fish in the stream. I'll be self-sufficient and live the way the Maori did when they came to New Zealand."

Fear stretched and yawned. "Hi, stupid. Time for me to go to work, is it? All right. Think about this, jerk. When you apply for citizenship, the authorities will do a background check in America, and if Ed and Bob told, your name will pop up in guilty scarlet."

"Maybe they do background checks on adults only. If Dad and Mom come over and become citizens, all of us kids will automatically be citizens, won't we?"

"You wish!"

Andrew's eyes opened their doors slightly and peeked at the clock. Yikes! He shot out of bed.

* * * * *

At 9:00 A.M., in Maori class, he offered to do a report about the jade koru. He had decided, somewhat guiltily, to wear it in place of Penny's silver half heart. He volunteered, also, to take part in a group study of New Zealand's native bush. His teacher expressed surprise, and approval. Math class saw his interest in metrics strengthen: hectares and kilometers were important, after all.

After school, he hurried home to complete his chores, ate dinner with the family, and then dashed to his room.

His mind raced as he waited for his E-mail account to open. "I'll tell about the keys and Cathryn's note first. No, wait. First, I'll explain how Grandfather got the paua box. I wonder if I should include something about the trip and the factory tour. Maybe. I'll tell about my jade koru after explaining the other things, but I'll keep the news about my land for last."

Words poured from his fingertips. He wrote, he cut, he pasted, he deleted and wrote some more. The finished E-mail included it all — all except the Maori Bible verse, which he was trying hard to forget.

"Can all of you come over to New Zealand at Easter?" The suggestion bounced out with his mind barely noticing. "I have a two-week school break in April, and we could be tourists together. Love, Andrew." He positioned the cursor, and sent the E-mail on its way.

Immediately, a pop-up message announced, "You've got mail." It must be Penny! After four weeks, she finally had written. He clicked on the pop-up.

"Hi! Remember — Rotary Weekend at El Rancho starts this Friday! See ya there! Morgan."

Morgan. Not Penny. Friday. This Friday would be February 13. Wasn't that McKean High School's Winter Ball? Penny would go, but alone. Would his valentine arrive in time? He had one for Morgan, too, but only a silly one.

He closed the computer and crawled into bed. A weekend like that left a guy exhausted.

* * * * *

Friday arrived on Olympic feet, and Andrew welcomed it eagerly. He had not realized how much he wanted to see Morgan. He stuffed his backpack, and was off to school early.

"I need to cram for my vocabulary exam," he said in answer to Katherine's cry for him to wait for her.

It was the truth. Slouching on a bench outside the school, he skimmed the first page and the second. Good. Good. He started down the third page, and stopped. Was that word unique to New Zealand? Not that he knew every word in the American English language, but this one was totally unfamiliar, totally hostile, in fact.

*CALUMNY (noun) (KAL um nee)*

*a false and malicious statement designed to injure another person's reputation.*

Did the English teacher know about Coach Ando? Did he suspect Andrew? Nonsense! Don't get paranoid. They probably have this same list every year. Forget Coach and just remember the definition — as though he could forget!

He finished his review, and rushed into class, his only class for the day. When it ended, he would be off to El Rancho Camp. A message on the board instructed:

> *You may leave when you have completed your work.*

Terrific! Andrew opened the exam booklet, sailed through the questions, and embraced the offered liberty.

Outside, the bus to Nelson Airport was just pulling to the curb. He dashed toward it, waving wildly, and panted up the steps. Safe! He lurched to a back seat.

He could get an earlier flight than planned. Maybe he could ride the Wellington to Waikanae train with Morgan. Or, if he caught the very first Auckland flight and the first Los Angeles flight, he could attend the Winter Ball tonight with Penny — half a world away. Weird!

The scenery along the Richmond coastal route was familiar already: the sawmill, the drying estuary, the craft center, the fields of sheep next to the meat packing plant, the berry farms, the orchards, the small houses, and finally, the Nelson Airport.

Andrew disembarked and hurried to the ticket counter. "I wonder if I would be able to change to an earlier flight," he said, showing his ticket to the man at the counter.

"Good as gold! Can you be on that plane in two minutes?" He gestured to a tiny white plane, its twin props whirling.

"Deeefinitely!" Andrew tried to pronounce it as though he were a Kiwi.

With a quick stamp, the attendant changed the ticket, rushed him out across the tarmac, and into the aircraft. A quick word of explanation gained Andrew a seat, and the ticket man waved as he dashed away.

Good as gold! Andrew grinned and shook his head. He pulled out the wristbands and, as the frail craft taxied to the runway, positioned them over the pressure points on each wrist. Maybe this time he would not get sick. Well, he could wish.

Morgan was not on the Wellington train. Andrew shared a seat with an older woman who helped him pronounce station names, especially *Paraparaumu*.

"That's Maori: Para-para-u-mu. With Maori words, you mind the vowel sounds and end every syllable in a vowel. Here. Let me give you a guide." The woman pulled out a scrap of paper and wrote:

| | |
|---|---|
| a = a | father |
| e = ea | measure |
| i = ee | seem |
| o = o | low |
| u = oo | room |

Andrew thanked her, and put it in his pocket. Now that he was a landowner, he must learn such things. Maybe they taught this in lower level Maori classes, but sixth form discussed only the culture of the Maori people.

A few minutes up the track, the conductor announced Waikanae, and Andrew stepped out onto a deserted platform.

As the train departed, a white van pulled up. The driver jumped out and strode toward the platform. "Bound for El Rancho, are we?"

Andrew nodded wordlessly, and climbed into the front seat. This had better be a short ride. The train trip had about finished the stomach demolition work started by the flight across Cook Strait.

To his relief, a few minutes along garden-decked streets brought them to the turn, and a short drive between pasturelands terminated at the campground.

"Here you are, then," said the driver. "You can sign in here at the office. I dare say you'll have your pick of bunks, being so early."

Andrew did have his pick — of bunks and of cabins. He settled quickly, and went to explore. He found Morgan about a half hour later, and that night wrote in his never-to-be-sent Penny letters:

*Dear Penny,*

*So far, this Rotary weekend is incredible! We are staying at a Christian camp called El Rancho, and there's so much to do here — tramping, a beach walk, a flying fox, mini golf, tennis, trampolines, horseback riding, swimming, sailing, a water slide, a petting zoo — well, I happen to like animals.*

*Get this. There's even a guy on staff from Pennsylvania. I haven't met him yet, but I can't wait!*

*Everybody did skits this evening. Kyoko, a Japanese girl who looks a lot like you, Penny, played the piano — almost as well as Caleb does. Of course, she's five years older than Caleb is. A boy from Argentina did one of their native dances, as did a boy from Australia.*

*I liked the Maori haka that the Kiwi men did. It's a very aggressive and warlike dance-chant sort of thing. Kiwi sports teams often do it at the beginning of a game to intimidate their opponents, and I'll bet it works. It's actually a bit frightening to watch, even when you know it's in fun!*

The pen paused. If he was writing to Penny, how could he tell about Morgan? Penny might never read these letters, but maybe she would. He capped the pen and wrote the remainder of the entry in his thoughts:

> *Morgan and I went for a late evening walk. I held her hand, and she let me. We didn't kiss or anything, probably because our lips were so busy chattering about American things.*

Saturday, Valentine's Day, began with a glorious summer sunrise. Andrew decided to add roses to his valentine for Morgan, and hitched a ride into Waikanae to buy them. She would really be surprised. He imagined her delight. What girl didn't like red roses?

He was back within a half hour, thanked his driver, and hurried to meet Morgan, the roses in a large shopping bag behind his back.

Morgan was sitting in front of his cabin. She gave him a faint smile, and he quickened his pace as he crossed the dirt road, but irritation chilled her usually cheerful face.

"Did you and Rachel enjoy your morning drive?" she asked icily.

"Rachel? She drove me into Waikanae... ," He produced the ruby rose buds from behind his back, and finished, "...to get you these."

He laid the flowers on her lap, with his funny valentine nestled among the long stems.

"Happy Valentine's Day!"

Morgan flushed pink to the roots of her soft brown hair. "But I thought...."

Her cheeks burned redder. "Never mind what I thought. Thank you, Andrew. Let's go find a vase for them."

She jumped to her feet, gathering the sweetly fragrant blossoms to her face, and shyly took his hand in hers. They found a vase in the dining room, and went to her cabin to arrange the roses.

"If you want to go to the beach," he invited, "I can change and be back in five minutes."

"Make it ten, and I accept." Her sanguinity had returned.

Fifteen minutes later, in bathing suits and sun hats, they wandered the beach hand in hand, reliving their first few weeks in New Zealand.

"Did I tell you about my paua box yet?" asked Andrew.

"I'm afraid to answer. It's probably a joke, but, OK. What is a paua box?"

"It isn't a joke. It's quite serious. My Grandfather left it to me when he died last September, but it was locked, and there was no key. It's a long story, but I got it open last weekend when Dennis took me to Masterton."

"So what was in it?" She spread a beach towel on the sand, and dropped gracefully onto it.

He plopped down beside her. "There were gifts for my sisters and my brother." He paused.

"Nothing for you? I thought you said your grandfather left this box to you."

"The only thing for me in the box was a verse from the Maori Bible, if you can imagine."

He sat straighter, and the canvas behind his freckles flushed as he continued. "But the Maori man who opened the box was the son of the chief who gave it to Grandfather. The chief told this man to give to the holder of the box, and only to the holder of the box this greenstone koru."

Andrew touched the green scroll that hung in bold relief against his freckled chest. "Oh, and a deed for 125 acres of land."

"You inherited 125 acres of land in New Zealand?!" Morgan's brown eyes popped. "Where?"

"Just outside Masterton. I wish you could see it. It is the most beautiful place there could be on earth — and it's all mine! I keep thinking I must have dreamed it. I can hardly believe it's real. It has rolling green hills, a beautiful fishing stream, and an incredible forest of pines, ferns, flowers, birds, and a lot of things I've never seen before. I'm planning to shift to a Masterton school, throw up a little cabin, and live on my own land instead of staying in Nelson. I'll probably go there as soon as this weekend is done. I'd have gone sooner, but I wanted to see you first. I brought my passport with me, just in case." He grinned, eager for Morgan to join in his happiness.

Morgan frowned. She was happy for him, she said, but he had to have a Rotary-approved sponsor; he had to live with the sponsor, not in a shack on his land; he must have the agreement of the school; the Bartletts deserved time for input; and his parents might oppose it. She agreed that it was a wonderful inheritance, and she would love to see it with him, but had he considered all of those things?

"You mentioned a Maori Bible verse, too," she said. "Did the Maori man translate it for you?"

"Yeah, it was nothing," Andrew answered.

"Oh, but don't you think the Bible is some of the best literature ever written? I do. It's so beautiful. Can you recall what it said?" Morgan's soft smile urged him.

Andrew expelled a sigh. "Look, Morgan, I wanted you to be happy for me. I wanted you to visit my property with me. I didn't come down to the beach to discuss some Bible verse. Don't get me wrong. I believe the Bible and all. I like to think I'm a Christian, but I think the land God created is more important than a single verse from the Bible."

Morgan simply gazed at him, waiting.

"Oh, all right. It said something about me being strong and courageous and not being afraid of them, whoever them are. Then it said God goes with me, but I don't intend to go anywhere except to Masterton." He rattled off the words, hardly realizing that he had nearly memorized the verse.

"Be strong and courageous. Do you suppose it was one of those 'courage' things like you said your parents hang on your wall every birthday, or do you think your grandfather knew you would be afraid of something?"

Morgan was getting too close to the truth. She was dangerously close to what Andrew himself had wondered every day since he opened the box: did Grandfather know about his crime?

He shifted uncomfortably, and jumped to his feet. "How about going back to camp for a game of tennis?" he challenged hoarsely.

Morgan sat still, absently sifting the fine sand through her fingers. Andrew was afraid. Was this why he wondered about growing into the meaning of his name — manly courage?

"It would help to talk about it, wouldn't it?" She patted the flattened circle of sand where he had been sitting. "I can be a good listener."

Andrew slumped to the spot, and stared at the ground. His strong index finger traced swirls in the warm golden sand. His left shoulder shrugged, and his larynx gurgled briefly. His blue eyes moved upward just enough to reflect the cool aquamarine waters. His right shoulder aped the left, and his larynx sputtered more strongly until it finally produced words.

"It's a long, long story," he warned.

She nodded and pulled her white sun hat lower over the long brown hair.

"It happened last April. You see, I never went to school until this year because my mom home-schooled us. So I didn't have friends, but I did know some guys in the church choir — not friends, just guys I talked to at practice every week. Their names were Ed and Bob. Well, one evening last April, we were talking and Ed said he had to get even with the Japanese coach for cutting him from the football team. He claimed that the coach cut him only because his family was of Chinese descent."

"That sounds like hate language."

"That's what I thought, but he said his dad taught him that Chinese people are anathema to

Japanese people. It's something that goes way back in history. At first, Bob and I disagreed, and told him he would have been cut even if the coach were Chinese. He just wasn't that great. The more he begged us, though, the more it seemed like a good practical joke was in order, regardless of why he had been cut."

The tall teen picked up a fragment of shell and tossed it into the ebbing tide.

"I was never in their school, and I knew nothing about the coach, but I like practical jokes. So we started thinking:

~ mix minestrone soup with vinegar, and pretend to vomit it in Coach's face
~ hoist Coach's car onto the gym roof
~ move all of Coach's office furniture to the top of the science building
~ download fake error messages to Coach's computer, so he formats his hard drive

"We thought of a couple dozen things, but nothing was bad enough to please Ed. He kept saying that the coach had practiced purposeful discrimination against him and the punishment must fit the crime." Andrew shifted uncomfortably in the hot sand.

"Go on," urged Morgan.

"Well, Bob finally described a news story he had seen on TV, in which a girl accused her coach of sexual abuse. The coach lost his job. His wife divorced him. The court tried him, convicted him, and sent him to prison as a child molester."

"You didn't!" Morgan's eyes blazed.

"I would give anything to have you be right, but we did. I was scared, but I was too cowardly to stand up for what I believed. I knew the guys would ridicule me if I didn't go along with it. I did say something about not copying everything you see in the media, and that the girl was not playing a prank, but they just laughed. They concocted a big story about how the coach seduced selected girls by first giving them special attention in gym classes, then guaranteeing them places on whatever teams they wanted — in return for sex. The chosen teens must continue trading sex to stay on the teams. It was a vicious lie, but they made it very believable."

"I thought you were above creating such a lie. Boy, did I have you wrong!" Morgan pulled her hat over her flashing eyes and threw herself back on her big yellow towel.

"I wasn't the one who created the lie. That is, I refused to help construct the story. I simply agreed to help spread it." What a jellyfish defense!

"Continue," she mumbled from the hat.

"We printed colored flyers about the alleged molestations — printed them on my printer. I never touched them. I just provided the printer. Ed and Bob handled the flyers, and distributed them after dark, attaching them to windshield wipers, doorknobs, lamp poles, trees — anywhere they could place them." His voice had risen half an octave, taking on a hoarse, constricted tone.

"The next morning, our whole city pulsed with anger. Everybody was ready to lynch the coach. The man had worked nine years to earn a great reputation, but they — we, I guess — had destroyed it in one night."

"What happened to you?" asked the hat.

"Nothing. That is, nothing yet, except that I walk around with an eerie feeling that someone is pursuing me. Strange things happen, like finding the word *calumny* on a vocabulary test. Know what it means?"

She nodded, and the floppy white hat bobbed. "A false, malicious statement planned to ruin a reputation. It was on my test, too."

"I keep having things like that thrown in my face, as though some god is trying to beat a confession out of me."

Morgan pushed back the hat and squinted up at him. "Did the other two confess?"

"They confessed to their part, and the last I knew they were waiting to stand trial."

"Sounds as though you're off the hook."

"No, I'm not. Everyone knows there was a third person, because neither Ed nor Bob has a color printer. Detectives canvassed the school, looking for the printer's owner, but I was not in school, so they never questioned me. So far, Ed and Bob have refused to finger me, but it's only a matter of time until they crack."

He laid a sweaty palm on her arm, willing her to understand. "That's why I have to live on my own land, Morgan, and stay in New Zealand. I've been possessed by a devil named Fear ever since it happened, but if I stay on my land, I can exorcise the devil."

Morgan sat silent, her young face framed below by her trim turquoise bathing suit, above by the floppy white hat. Her brown eyes stared toward mysterious Kapiti Island, basking just beyond a strip of sun-dappled water.

"Do your parents know?" she asked.

"No. You're the only one I've told."

"Didn't you tell your girlfriend at home?"

Andrew threw himself facedown in the warm sand and groaned. "I started dating the coach's daughter — before I knew who she was."

"Onerous." It encompassed the whole of Morgan's shock.

"Onerous?" he shot upright and glared at her. "Onerous? Onerous is my favorite dessert these days! Onerous is carved on my friendship bracelet! I carry onerous around like a blankey! This is not onerous. This is the kiss of death!"

The words knifed through the air and plunged into the deadening sand. The two teens fell silent, neither moving nor speaking for a long time. A late afternoon breeze sprang to life, teasing the gentle blue waves, perching white caps atop each one — but the humor of it was lost on the silent friends. The rising tide scrubbed higher and higher on the beach, removing the footprints they had tracked in — but they didn't notice. Other couples from camp wandered past — but Andrew and Morgan never saw them. He lay back in the sand, retreating behind closed eyelids. She sat and gazed at Kapiti Island, now silhouetted in late afternoon sunlight.

Andrew was a felon. Morgan tasted the guilt herself. She recoiled from his pain of having bowed to cowardice, suffered the frustration of not standing for truth and right. She ached with his longing to turn back the clock, to set things straight. She empathized with him, but she could not sympathize. She could experience vicarious guilt, but she could never participate fully.

At last, Andrew sat up — facing her, and facing the mountains, behind which was his land.

He could not meet her gaze. He focused on the mountains, above her floppy white hat.

"Look at me, Andrew," she said. "Please look at me." Her voice was quietly intense.

His focus shortened, and obeyed.

"You must confess. You can't keep running from this. You want to be a man of courage. You told me that in the plane. This is your chance. You have very strong principles, but you made a mistake. You have to take the consequences of that mistake before you go on with life. Exercise your manly courage, Andrew. Tell your parents. Call your dad and ask for his help."

Her eyes held his for an eternity.

"It's tea time," he said, leaping abruptly to his feet. "We'd better get back to camp."

The rest of the weekend was spent in the safety of groups. Morgan's eyes pled with him many times, but her lips remained locked. On Sunday afternoon, they shared a quiet train ride into Wellington, and said their good-byes.

"I'll be thinking of you," said Morgan.

"Thanks," Andrew murmured.

She hailed a cab, and he caught the next bus to the airport.

# 19

## *A Beard in the Hand*

Andrew did not go to his own land Sunday night. He caught a flight back to Nelson, as he was expected to do. The taxi dropped him at the Bartletts' while they were at evening church services, and he took his train sick, air sick, car sick body straight to bed, resigned to staying.

In the wee, sleepless hours of a warm Monday morning, however, he reconsidered.

Fortuitously, Matthew was in Christchurch for a week, so Andrew bothered nobody when he jumped up and wrote an impulsive brief note by flashlight. He scrawled a hasty signature on the note, slid the page into an envelope addressed to Mr. and Mrs. Bartlett, and propped it on the desk.

All right. If this was going to work, he would have to hurry. His backpack, still packed from the El Rancho weekend, was a start. He dressed in layers, all dark blue, and his black school shoes.

Everything else went into the two pieces of luggage he had brought from America. Passport, cash, traveler's checks, and his return flight tickets remained in a jacket pocket.

He tiptoed to the window, selected a thick clump of bushes, and aimed his luggage into them. The impact seemed deafening, but nobody stirred.

Skimming the stairways undetected, and bypassing locked doors, he fled toward the always-open window at the end of the game room.

The die was cast. He was out. He was on his way back to Masterton. The moist air of a late New Zealand summer filled his lungs, and he gulped it hungrily, realizing that he had been holding his breath. An army of second thoughts marched toward him in the darkness, but he avoided them, and double-timed down the drive to the phone in the hothouse.

Yes, the cab company would send a driver to the intersection at the bottom of the hill. Hopefully, his luggage wheels would make it that far. It was too risky to use the noisy wheels near the house, though — and he had only six minutes to reach the intersection.

He assigned one cumbersome piece to each hand, and wrestled them down the long drive to the road. Then he rested each on its wheels, and sprinted down the hill. The tiny wheels bounced and ground along behind him, scattering plastic chips with every revolution, but he paid no attention. This luggage would be extinct in a few hours.

The Nelson Airport, silent in the early dawn, would not open for thirty minutes. "You're an early one," laughed the cab driver.

Andrew agreed, dismissed him, and settled on the edge of a bench. He had no idea when the first flight would leave, but he must be on it.

When the doors opened, he charged to the counter, piled his luggage atop the scales, and presented his ticket with hasty maturity.

"One return flight from Nelson to the U.S.A. I hope you enjoyed your stay," said the counter attendant. He looked more closely. "Say, you're the American student. You can't be leaving so soon. You've been here less than a month!"

Andrew's face flushed. "It's an emergency."

"Oh, I'm sorry," said the man. "I hope it's nothing serious." He handed back the tickets and a boarding pass. "This is the newspaper run, so I could only check your bags to Wellington. Be sure you claim them there and check them through to Philadelphia. Your flight leaves in ten minutes. I hope you have a good trip."

That was a narrow escape — hadn't thought about strangers asking why he was leaving. Have to relax. Look calm. Be casual. He took out the document wallet Dad had given him, and made sure his passport and checks were safe. Then he sat down and closed his eyes against the world. It was good he had made the newspaper run, whatever that was. He had to be out of here before Mr. Bartlett found his note. He hoped the plane seat beside him would be vacant.

Outside the quiet terminal, an engine started. Andrew lunged to his feet and bound to the door. A tiny prop plane was warming up. Was that the newspaper run? If so, he was in trouble!

He made his feet carry him back to the seat with clarion nonchalance. He needed wristbands. He intensely needed wristbands, if he was going to ride in that.

He dug them from his pack, positioned the first pressure knob over a large freckle on his left wrist, and was reaching for the second when he heard: "Mr. A. T. McKean, your flight is ready at Gate One."

He was the only passenger! He grabbed the heavy backpack, remembered his maturity, lifted his fair Irish chin, and walked briskly to the plane.

* * * * *

Back in Richmond, Mrs. Bartlett got no answer when she called their American guest to breakfast that morning. She dispatched Richard to check on him, and finished putting the meal on the table.

"Andrew's not up there, Mum, but I found this on his desk."

Janette took the envelope and handed it to Dennis. Breakfast waited as the family watched him open it. He frowned, then read aloud:

> *Thank you for your hospitality. You are very good people, and I have enjoyed my visit. I must go, but am not at liberty to explain why or where. I'll contact my parents, so please don't worry. They will be in touch with you later. Please tell your family I said good-bye. Andrew McKean.*

Curious conversation buzzed as Dennis placed rapid phone calls: first to the McKean home in Wilmington, then to the Departures Gate at the Wellington Airport.

* * * * *

Andrew, at the Wellington Airport, snatched his bags from the carousel and dragged them to the door. A city-bound bus sat at the curb. With a businesslike gesture to the driver, he tugged the hapless luggage onto the bus, paid the fare into town, and sank into a front seat.

Now. Think of an explanation to give Dad and Mom. How can I make them understand?

The passing scenery intercepted his silent brooding, and demanded attention. On his right was the harbor, teeming with ships, fishing boats, and ferries. On his left, stately architecture, much of it Victorian, mingled with modern government buildings, one shaped like a huge beehive — which fascinated him, but awakened Fear.

"New Zealand's government probably will cooperate if the United States looks for you here."

The bus pulled to the left curb before a huge brick building. Andrew tumbled his luggage from the bus, and hauled it into the station. Hunger shouted at him, but his rapid pace carried him from the ticket window past the food stands, and to the platform where the train for Masterton waited. He selected a single seat just inside the end door, and stowed his bags quickly beside and behind it. Good. Privacy. Blessed privacy.

He glanced around. The car was still empty. His backpack gave up a gray tweed cap, which would have been more at home on an old man's head than on his, and he pulled it well down over his forehead. The coppery hair showing at the back would be no problem, given New Zealand's high percentage of red heads. Next out of the pack was a book from the airport shops — how to sustain life in the New Zealand bush with no money. He spread the book open on his blue-clad knee, and feigned deep concentration. There. Incognito.

A moment later, boarding passengers ignored the old man bent over his book. The doors closed, and the train lurched out of the station.

The train trip seemed interminable, but the conductor finally announced Carterton, and Andrew's heart leaped. His land was near. He shoved the book into his pack, and stood. He must be ready to get away quickly.

"Masterton," called the conductor.

The old man in the tweed cap gathered his luggage with amazing strength, and stepped nimbly to the exit door. The conductor noted a strange look in the surprisingly young eyes and wondered, but when the door opened, the tall man was gone, lurching swiftly toward the single cab that waited.

The conductor shrugged as he waved the train out of the station. "He's probably up the boohai shooting pukekos with a long-handled shovel," he muttered to himself.

Fifteen minutes later, the cab stopped along a deserted stretch of the narrow road. The driver jumped out to help with the young man's luggage, and gave a three hundred sixty degree stare. There was not a house in sight. "You got a bach in the bush?" he guessed.

Andrew looked up. "Yes," he lied. "Can't see it from here. It's in the back-blocks." He paid his fare, and assured the driver he could handle his luggage without help. A minute later, he was alone — sequestered on his own land.

* * * * *

William McKean could hardly believe his ears. "He did what?" He glanced at the clock in his den. It was two o'clock Sunday afternoon. "Do you have any idea what time he might have gone?"

"After midnight. He took everything. We will have the bobbies looking straight away, but I did think you should know. He wrote that he will contact you." Mr. Bartlett sighed.

"What time is it there, Mr. Bartlett?"

"Six o'clock Monday morning."

"He may have as much as a six-hour jump. Thank you for letting us know right away."

Mr. McKean threw the receiver at the cradle and stormed out to the broad stairway. "Margaret," he called sharply. "Margaret, come to the den." He stalked back to his computer, a muscle twitching at one jaw. His hands raced across the computer keyboard. Andrew's E-mail. Maybe there would be a clue there.

Mrs. McKean dashed into the room, strands of auburn hair flying free from an otherwise tidy coiffure. "What, William? Is it one of the children?"

"It's Andrew. He's run away."

"What?" Margaret sank into a chair, the breath coming raw in her throat. "When?"

"During the night, with only a brief note. I'm checking his old E-mail for a clue."

William tugged the moustache. "Andrew has been upset about something for months — wanting to be alone — more than can be explained by age and hormones. He probably wanted to be alone in New Zealand, too. I think he has gone to the land he inherited." He made an unusually abrupt decision. "Pack and be ready to leave on a late afternoon flight, Margaret. I'm just glad we had planned to surprise Andrew on his birthday. At least we have our passports and visas in hand."

"The children are tobogganing, William...."

"I'll get the children."

Margaret sprinted toward the stairs as though she were sixteen, exhorting herself to remember that it was late summer in New Zealand.

William placed a frenzied call to his accounting partner and dumped the remaining tax season in his lap. That done, he phoned an airline, and purchased five tickets to New Zealand. Then he dashed off to pick up his children.

"What's up?" asked Alicia.

"A sudden chance to move forward our New Zealand vacation," Dad replied. "We're leaving today instead of waiting until Andrew's birthday."

A few hours later, the McKeans were flying high over the wintry landscape of the U.S.A. and, at 10:30 P.M., they lifted into the endless skies above the Pacific Ocean.

* * * * *

Somewhere outside the small town of Masterton, on New Zealand's North Island, Andrew's shoulders ached as he struggled deeper into the native bush, puffing and wheezing his way uphill. It was not so much the backpack that made the shoulders ache. He was accustomed to carrying that to school everyday. They ached because they must contend with the backpack while bending low enough for his hands to tug along two heavy suitcases — over rough terrain. There was no path here. Nor was there a paddock, as the Kiwis called it. This part of his acreage never had seen a bulldozer within its boundary. This was raw forest, thick with the growth of centuries.

The path from Mr. Raumati's home would have been easier, but it was too soon to meet the Raumatis again. He had to be alone on his land first. He had to embrace it; talk to it; listen to its voice; explore it; find the spot where he would camp; the spot where he would later build a cabin; and someday build a solid house. It was too soon to let Mr. Raumati know he was here. In a week, maybe, or two weeks. Not yet.

Andrew paused, sweeping a damp lock of hair off of his sweaty brow. His chest heaved. How far had he come from the highway? How far was it to his stream? He needed a drink. He dumped the pack to the ground and unzipped the water flask. He drank heavily before remembering that it was his only water until he did find the stream.

Nearby, four glorious, flutelike chimes rang out. A bellbird — a bird found nowhere but in New Zealand. He waited for the bird to appear. In a moment, the four notes sounded again, notes that were the most melodious wild music he ever had heard. Even the big pipe organ at church never had managed such perfectly-tuned chimes.

The bird flitted down to land on the heavy black luggage, making a whirring sound as it flew. Andrew caught his breath. Its beauty matched its shimmering notes. A yellow-green head and back were camouflaged with black tail and black wings. It had a bright yellow under-body, and its eyes were ruby red. Its curved black beak glistened with a single bead of nectar.

Very slowly, Andrew moved one hand. The bird cocked its head, then started up, hovering upright by a low tree branch. It chimed once more, then flew deeper into the bush.

Andrew sank to the ground and inhaled deeply. Who cared about school and Rotary and trials when there were bell birds in the forest? One could set priorities straight in a place like this — and it was his. This was his forest.

He recognized beech trees, willow trees, tree ferns, and pine trees. He would learn later about the other flora — trees and bushes with rosy-pink berries, dark purple berries, orange-yellow fruit being eaten by pigeons, and small white flowers.

Besides the bellbirds, he knew the tui, the New Zealand pigeon, and the shining cuckoo. He supposed there would be kiwis — he would listen for their nocturnal musings after dark tonight. Native bush. His home. It would teach him about its other birds: morepork, kea, weka, and pukekos, which could provide food — he had heard that the weka was a large bird, good for food.

Andrew grinned wryly as he thought, "A bird in the hand is worth two in the bush, and I hope there are a lot in my piece of the bush. I'll worry later about how to get them into my hand."

He got to his feet. This spot was too close to the highway. The center of his acreage was the place to be, wherever that was. At the very least, it must be a spot near the small river. He gazed around once more before engaging the bush. The jade koru promised new life, if one could believe superstition. This certainly would be a new life.

The koru did not preclude questions from the old life, however. Had Mr. Bartlett called the police? Had they called his parents? Would they find him? Ridiculous question. Of course, they would find him. It was only a matter of time. They would know he had to be on his own land — in his own space. Mr. Raumati would lead them to him.

On that day, at that time, he might have to go back with them, but only temporarily....

* * * * *

Across the farthest boundary of Andrew's property, Mr. Raumati picked up his car keys, ready to leave for a day at the paua factory. His wife was sleeping in today, so he would leave as quietly as possible. The phone rang, and he grabbed it. His initial low greeting was followed by extended silence. He mumbled assent to the caller's request, depressed the receiver hook, and placed a call to the paua factory.

"I'll be late coming in today," he said calmly. "I must help a friend." The tall Maori man replaced the receiver and stood thinking for a moment. Then, he made a second quick call. Yes, a cabbie had taken a young man from the train station this morning. Yes, red hair. Mr. Raumati hung up and hurried to his car.

A few miles down the highway, he steered the blue Honda onto the shoulder and parked. He jumped out, and scrutinized the tall green grass. He smiled. The young American had much to learn. Heavy bags blaze an unmistakable trail.

Mr. Raumati ran lightly over the trail, far less encumbered than his young friend, and far more accustomed to the land. It took only twenty minutes for him to sight Andrew, and he remained silent when he did. His pace slackened, and he continued the mental preparation initiated after the first phone call. His keen eyes flicked constantly between the youth he followed and the trail left by the young man. Bending once to avoid a branch, the tall Maori saw a long black object in the grass — Andrew's passport, traveler's checks, and cash. Mr. Raumati secured it in a shirt pocket, and continued his trek until he saw that Andrew had stopped.

Andrew sat on the ground, throbbing knees supporting his weary head, luggage in disarray at his feet. Tramping uncleared forest was much more difficult than running bases. The slight twists as occasional small rocks rolled beneath his feet had taken their toll. The lack of food also had begun to tell on him. He was weary, hungry, and hurting in his shoulders and his trick knees.

Mr. Raumati approached softly, not speaking until he was directly behind the exhausted youth. "You have come home, Andrew."

That was all he said. He stepped forward and sat with his back to that of the teen, giving Andrew the option of sustaining the conversation.

Andrew let it perish. He did not turn. He did not so much as raise his head. Why? He wanted only a few weeks. That's all. Even a few days. Why not a few days alone? Why not a week to enjoy the land before it was snatched away? Was that too much to ask? He knew the voice. It was the voice of his Maori neighbor. Hope uttered a dying sigh within, but the sigh never found Andrew's lips.

Mr. Raumati maintained mute patience. Time was a priceless gift, but he would share what he had. He shared twenty minutes before saying, "You are afraid of something."

Andrew did not speak.

"I think your fear is the reason for the Bible verse in the paua box. Had he lived, Grandfather McKean would have helped you, Andrew, but now you must help yourself. You must be strong and courageous."

Extreme exhaustion, hunger, the stress of the escape — all descended with a crushing weight. A spasm squeezed the young adult face, and anguished sobs gushed forth. "I want to be alone, Mr. Raumati. I can't go back. I can't. I can't!"

The stern Maori's work-toughened hand was gentle on the shaking shoulders. "I believe it was an English author," he said quietly, intently, "Ralph Waldo Emerson, who wrote:

> *When a resolute young fellow steps up to the great bully, the world, and takes him boldly by the beard, he is often surprised to find it comes off in his hand, and that it was only tied on to scare away the timid adventurers.*

"You are ready to find a beard in the hand, lad. You do have within you the courage of your convictions. You can be a man of character, but you must put character into action."

Andrew still did not turn as Mr. Raumati said, "Character in action will face the bully, lad. It will have courage — and when courage acts, it takes the world boldly by the beard."

"But I can't do it, I tell you."

"You can, if you remember that God goes with you, that He will help you."

Mr. Raumati stood and extended one hand. "Come home with me. Breakfast will take only a few minutes, and you can clean up while you wait. Then, we will let your parents know where you are. I suspect your father is already on his way — if your father is like your grandfather."

Desolately submissive, Andrew stood and shouldered the black pack. Mr. Raumati was wrong. Dad would not come. He was right about Grandfather — Grandfather would have come — but Dad would not come — not all the way from Wilmington to New Zealand.

Andrew trudged obediently behind as his Maori neighbor carried the two black suitcases, and soon reached the car at the side of the road.

No. Dad would not come.

# 20

## *Cold Foreboding*

Dad did come.

The entire family came, arriving at the Raumati home around noon on Tuesday.

A torrent of emotions flooded the heart of the tall youth as he watched the rented van drive toward Mr. Raumati's small white house: ardent joy at being reunited; hot humiliation at meeting in such circumstances; and a cold foreboding of the future that loomed darkly ahead.

Andrew bridled the joy as he walked out to meet them, cracking his knuckles individually. He gave a timid smile when Mom embraced him.

His siblings bubbled excitement. What had he thought of that long flight from America? Had he gotten sick? Was he bored? Did he get to see much of Auckland? Was everything always this green? How many sheep were there here?

Andrew looked down at the three with newly serious blue eyes. "Hi, Carrot Cake." He flattened his little brother's carrot top with a pat. "We can talk about those things later."

Caleb looked at his sisters. "Who is he, and what have they done with our brother?"

They would have understood, had Dad told them of Andrew's escape, but Dad had not. He had given them a surprise vacation, and they thought Andrew should be as ecstatic as they were.

The Raumatis offered lunch and overnight accommodations, but Dad declined. He did agree to visit again before leaving New Zealand, and Mr. Raumati instantly promised a big *hangi*.

Dad went upstairs to help Andrew repack, dismissing his stuttered alibis, and telling him that they would discuss it later — alone. "Only Mom knows why we are here, son. The family has come for a vacation, and I want all of us to be able to enjoy it, but there are some things we need to take care of first. You need to go back and face the Bartletts, and you need to explain to the Rotary why you are not in school. There will be plenty of time after that for you and me to talk — alone."

Dad put the backpack in the van, and asked Mr. Raumati to store the other bags. Farewells were given, and the McKeans departed, driving the curving mountain route to Wellington.

Dad was mute, preoccupied with reverse driving skills, but Mom steered everyone into a discussion of seeing as much of New Zealand as possible, now that they were here. Did Dad think they could cover both islands in two weeks? Had Andrew studied the nation enough to guide them to the most scenic spots? How far was it from his host home to Mount Cook where Sir Edmund Hillary had trained to climb Mount Everest?

Dad stopped in Upper Hutt, soon after the last hairpin curve — partially to buy a guidebook and maps, partially to let blood circulate through his whitened, wheel-gripping fingers. Andrew pointed out a dairy, and greenly suggested ginger beer for all, but the ginger came too late for him.

That Tuesday night, he stayed up to help Dad and Mom plan an itinerary — anticipating harsh words — expecting punishment. Neither Dad nor Mom mentioned his escape, though. The next two weeks were precious, they said, and they wanted to have a marvelous family vacation.

"If we stick to national highways, we should be able to circle both the North and South Islands," said Dad. "The mileages are like doing Colorado in two weeks. The difference is, that can include every extreme, from glaciers and rain forests to mountains and beaches."

"There's so much to see! The time is going to fly!" exclaimed Mom.

Well, the time might fly for Mom, but for Andrew, whose conscience nagged him to do the right thing — while he was afraid to do the right thing — two weeks would be an eternity.

Early Wednesday morning, Dad sounded reveille, and marched the family forth to conquer. He treated Andrew as though everything was normal. He asked Andrew's help in reading maps, and thanked Andrew for warnings to stay on the left side of the road — especially after turning a corner. He relied on Andrew to take the family to the proper check-in counter at Wellington airport, while he returned the rental car and arranged for one to be waiting on the other side of Cook Strait.

In Nelson, Dad put Andrew in the white rental van's front seat — to be his navigator and tour guide. He hoped, too, that it would help the pale green subside from below Andrew's red hair.

"First stop will be the home where Andrew has been staying," Dad announced, "and I want you children all to remember your manners. The Bartletts are good Christians, and I do not want them to see you behaving improperly. Be careful what you do — and what you say."

Yeah, they had better be careful. Andrew had better be careful — what could he possibly say after what he had done? How could he explain, after all Dennis had done for him? Dennis had provided a home for him and a whole lot more.

Dennis took him to Masterton; cleaned up the van after Andrew hurled; bought him ginger beer; bought the wristbands for seasickness; took him to the paua factory, which clearly was out of the way for Dennis; took time to attend Andrew's hakari; and then went through the whole process in reverse to return to Richmond. On the return ferry trip, Dennis had even taken an interest in Andrew's problems — not that he knew about Coach. He had just said that he wanted to explain how God would forgive sin, no matter how bad.

So how was Andrew to face such a man now? How was he to apologize?

Thankfully, only Mrs. Bartlett was at home when they arrived. The children were in school, and Dennis had gone to Nelson for hardware.

Andrew breathed a measure of strength into his introductions, and avoided explanations of his actions.

Janette, in turn, avoided all questions, but insisted, "You must have a cuppa before you go."

She took Mom and the girls to her kitchen. "Give your dad and brother a tour, Andrew," she called over her shoulder.

Andrew's uneasiness lengthened his stride as he escorted Dad and Caleb around the house. "This is Matthew's bedroom, where I roomed." It was now barren of his own belongings.

He hustled them through the living area, and out to the hothouses. He filled the air with copious details, showing them what his daily chores had been, and why Mr. Bartlett's work was brilliant. Returning to the house, he relinquished his duty and let Janette lead.

"We have got hot tea, and lemon scones fresh from the oven," she said. "I hope you like scones. Do you drink tea with milk?"

The children were polite, taking only one scone, and agreeing to tea and milk in proportions of about one part tea to seven parts milk.

Cathryn's eyes sparkled as she tasted her first scone. "These are delicious, Mrs. Bartlett," she said. "Would you give us the recipe?"

Janette was captivated. "I certainly will do."

By eleven o'clock, they stood and thanked the host mum for her hospitality. "We must be on our way," Dad said. "We have many kilometers scheduled for today." He gave Andrew a meaningful look and guided the others to the van.

Andrew turned a pinched face to Janette. "I'm sorry for the hasty departure. I will explain someday, but for now, will you please forgive me? I did enjoy my stay in your home. Please convey my apology to Dennis and the rest — and would you please call the Rotary representative and tell him I have to leave the program?"

Janette hugged him briefly, and whispered, "Yes, Andrew. Write, and visit when you can. We will miss you. Go with God."

Andrew squeezed her clumsily, and turned away. Why this bleak, wintry feeling inside him? He crawled into the navigator's seat, and waved. Janette had treated him as one of her sons. He never had known a woman, other than Mom, who cared so much what he thought and how he felt. He actually was going to miss Janette.

He knew, too, that he would miss Dennis, Katherine and Anna. He had seen much less of the Bartlett boys, but their memory would linger. He would write, and maybe someday they would visit him in Wilmington — or in jail. He brushed his eyes with one hand. He waved again.

"Right, then," Dad said, trying to mimic something he had heard on TV that morning. "No wowsers allowed, mates! We're off on holiday! Andrew, where can a mate get some petrol in his motorcar?" He drove away with a toot of the horn.

"Say what?" Andrew stared, and laughed for the first time since his parents' arrival.

He pulled his tall, thin frame straight in the seat, lifted his chin, and said in his best New Zealand accent, "You can top up in Richmond. Then I'll shout lunch at the vineyard restaurant if you want to motor out to Rabbit Island before heading west."

The old Andrew fought for life. "We can spend a little time at Rabbit Island, can't we?"

Dad was amenable. He stopped for gas, and then followed his navigator's directions out of town. He was beginning to feel comfortable with the driving customs, but he hit the windshield wiper every time he wanted the turn signal.

The roundabouts were no picnic either, and still brought beads of perspiration to his forehead. So when Andrew directed, just beyond Richmond, that he turn *left* into the roundabout so he could take the road to the *right*, Dad panicked. He entered the circle, and tried to revolve clockwise, with other cars entering the ring from other roads. He bumped the curb several times in the process, and the family was giggling when he emerged.

From that moment, the vacation became a delight — for brief spells — interspersed with the lonely times — times with his nagging conscience. Andrew's journal captured good times and bad:

Dear Penny,

*We started with a scrumptious lunch at Seifried's Vineyard Restaurant. Then we went beachcombing — all of us, including Dad, in sun hats — not a pretty sight!*

*Dad wanted to reach the west coast before sunset, so we were soon on our way to Greytown, aptly named, since the sky was gray there. My mood matched it. I can't shake this cold fear. I just know I'm going to prison. I can forget for a half hour or so if we're doing something interesting, but it always comes back and snatches my fun. I'm waiting for Dad's other shoe to drop.*

*We got takeaway fish and chips at Greytown and ate in our motel room. Everyone froze during the night there — thanks to New Zealand's lack of central heating. We got up early, and drove down to Shantytown, an amusement park in the middle of nowhere. We panned for gold there, and I actually got a tiny nugget. I wish it were a good omen.*

*An hour later, we were at Pancake Rocks, where the ocean-carved rocks look like tall stacks of golden brown pancakes beside the deep aqua of the Tasman Sea. Dolphins played just offshore, and we could hear them talking. I wanted to swim away with them.*

*We drove south another two hours through what the guidebook calls "a wild, sparsely populated region of magnificent coastline, primeval forests, unruly rivers, mountains and glaciers." We love the glaciers — big rivers of ice flowing between mountains, with waterfalls rushing down to meet them, all just 19 kilometers from the ocean, and the glaciers flow into big rain forests.*

*A Maori legend calls Franz Josef Glacier "The Tears of the Avalanche Girl." It says she loved climbing, persuaded her lover to climb with her, and was brokenhearted when he fell from the peaks to his death. Her tears froze to form the glacier. Will your tears freeze when you learn what I did?*

The glaciers were the high point for all, and Dad decided to see them thoroughly, even if they had to skip some other part of New Zealand. He found a quaint motel within sight of the Franz Josef Glacier, and rented the family unit.

Then, in a nearby village, they watched as the sun set, throwing its fiery colors on the icy brilliance of the glacier. A small restaurant invited them in, and Andrew snickered as he watched his family try New Zealand pizza.

On Friday morning, it was Cathryn who blew reveille, but it wasn't necessary. Everyone was eager to see the river of ice. They made short work of cornflakes, coffee, and milk, and followed the road to the glacier. Amazingly, the primeval rainforest lasted all the way to the glacier's bed.

Dad pulled into a space beside another man, and parked, saying "What is he doing?"

They all watched as they slowly left the van.

The man carefully removed both of his windshield wipers and stowed them in the trunk.

He then draped a towel over each of his four tires, tucking it well up over the top of the tire. He smiled when he saw them watching. "Protection from the kea — parrots," he said. "They'll eat your rubber if you park here long enough. We're tramping in to the face of the glacier."

"Let's hike it, too, Dad," urged Andrew. A good hike might take away this inner chill — might help him forget for a while.

"How long does it take to get to the face and back?" Dad asked the Kiwi.

"Shouldn't take more than a couple of hours." He looked at Mom's high heels. "Might want sturdier shoes, though, mum."

Mom laughed. "I think we girls will leave the hiking to the men," she said. Caleb begged off, too, so it was only Dad and Andrew who hiked.

The going was easy at first — a brisk walk along the rocky, dry portion of the wide Waiho riverbed. They soon had to climb to higher ground, though, and the pair found themselves moving forward over a path barely wide enough for a single foot. Dad almost turned back when he saw that they would have to traverse the face of a high, thin waterfall, but he was as eager for the goal as his son was, so they dug their toes into the mud, and stepped warily through the mist.

The reward was incredible. The aquamarine of the great ice river seemed to draw them into itself, as it hung suspended high above. A sign on the rope barrier warned that ice could break off in chunks as large as a truck or bus, and that visitors should stay well back.

Dad wanted proof, though, that they had been there. He asked a fellow hiker to take a photo of him with Andrew, and they stepped as close to the hulking face as possible, pushing the rope inward toward the ice. It formed a majestic background, but before the man could get clear focus, a thunderous crack sounded above their heads.

"Run!" someone screamed.

Andrew grabbed Dad's arm and raced from the spot, rocks tripping them, cold fear driving them, curiosity turning them just in time to see an explosion of ice plunge from the titanic glacier to the rocky river bed. The cold chunks tumbled along the rocky bed, a few reaching the icy stream that stormed frigidly from beneath the glacier. The sound resonated throughout the valley.

"Whew! That makes you remember how short life can be," Dad said breathlessly. He ran both hands through his red hair the way Caleb so often did. "That was too close for comfort!"

The cameraman returned their camera. "I clicked as the ice broke, but I don't know what I got," he said. "I can try again if you want."

Andrew declined, thanked him, and took the camera. Then he looked at Dad, his blue eyes still startled wide. Dad was right. They might have been killed. He might have died just now — died as a cold coward. He made a sudden decision.

"Dad, do you mind if we sit on those big boulders for a few minutes before we hike back?"

"Sure. We need to sit down after that."

The huge gray rocks sat squarely in front of the blue ice wall, but at a safe distance from it this time. The two settled on them, and faced the awesome glacial power. They listened to the roar of the stream formed by melting ice. Waiting for tranquility to return, they gazed at the scenery — the long misty waterfall whose face they had crossed, its twin on the opposite mountain, and the mind-boggling ice river that was frozen, yet flowed constantly toward the nearby Tasman Sea.

Finally, Andrew spoke — carefully chosen words — words of truth. He bravely confessed his part in the crime against Coach Ando. He made it clear that he had known the deed was wrong, that he had been without doubt it would hurt the coach. Voice wavering, cracking, and straining, he told about learning that Penny was Coach Ando's daughter. Voice growing hoarse, determined to be courageous — at last — he made full confession. Then, he turned slightly toward his father and choked out, "Dad, Mr. Raumati said Grandfather had the courage of his convictions and was a man of character. If I had the courage of my convictions, Coach Ando would still be coaching." Drops of hot, salty water began scalding his cheeks.

"And instead?" Dad pressed.

"Instead, I ruined him, and committed a crime that's going to hurt you, and Mom, and all of us." He dropped his gaze to the rocks.

"What do you think you should do about it, son?" Dad still stared at the glacier.

"I'm not sure. I've got to make it right somehow, but I don't have the courage. First, I thought I could escape by coming to New Zealand. Then I tried to escape to my own land. If I could live up to my name, and all those quotes you've given me, I'd probably go back to the States with you and stand trial. But I don't think I can do that alone. I would just run away again if I got a chance. Will you help me, Dad? I really don't know what I should do now. I'm afraid I'll have to go to jail, but at least I would get it settled. Then maybe I could start over and be a real man of character. Maybe I could learn how to have manly courage."

Mr. McKean's eyes never wavered from the glistening blue glacier, but tears blinded sight; a lump impeded speech. He had never imagined Andrew's problem to be so immense. No wonder the boy had fled. He threw both arms around his son's shoulders and hugged him fiercely, silently.

When words finally came, it was a husky voice that said, "You are on your way, Andrew." He broke the embrace and reached for a handkerchief. A few minutes later, he was able to speak again. "Do you remember the Winston Churchill quote we gave you?"

Andrew nodded and quietly repeated it:

*Courage is the first of human qualities because it is the quality which guarantees all others.*

"Courage to live up to your convictions," said Dad. "With that kind of courage, you can grow into a great man of character — and I'll help you, son."

They cried unashamedly, then. They cried until the well of troubled tears was dry.

Dad stood first, extended his hand to his eldest, and sealed his commitment with a firm handshake; the kind of handshake Grandfather would have given. Together, they turned to drink in once more the glory and awe of the mighty Franz Josef Glacier. "We'd better go, Andrew. Your mother will think we've gotten lost."

The cool air relieved the puffiness around their eyes as they tramped back to the car, and nobody noticed anything amiss when they arrived.

The McKeans spent the remainder of the day in glacier country, heli-touring both glaciers, and walking right on the surface of the frosty Fox

Glacier. Caleb and the girls laughed and slid on the ice, but Andrew was strangely quiet.

That evening, they visited a glowworm park, a canopy of bushes filled with the tiny lights of the unique New Zealand glowworm. Andrew wrote in his journal:

*Dear Penny (if you still care),*

*New Zealand glowworms are really not worms, but courageous little insects. They start life with their lights on, and use stuff from their mouth glands to build very small tunnel-like hammocks, which they attach to the ceiling of a canopy or a cave. Their lights attract bugs for them to eat, and they let down sticky ropes to catch the bugs. They can turn off the lights for safety, and they do when they are afraid.*

Marveling at the little glowworms, Andrew whispered to himself, "Be strong and courageous. Don't turn off your light. God is with you."

He was at peace now, at least reasonably so — more than he had been. There was a long trek ahead, but he would make it.

# 21

## *Breathing Space*

Contrary to Andrew's initial prediction, the two weeks did not drag. From glacier country, they drove southward to Queenstown. The drive was awesome, despite torrential rain. Regal, arched hills rose through the rain, waterfalls dancing and sparkling down their emerald knobs in a merry crowd. Behind the hills, rugged Mount Aspiring and the magnificent, towering peaks of Mount Cook already wore pristine snowcaps. At their feet, young lambs and deer frolicked.

As the others sampled Kiwi TV that evening, Andrew sat on his motel bed and wrote:

*Dear Penny,*

*The drive to Queenstown was outstanding, The rain stopped just before we got there, and we saw a big peaceful lake that looked like a sheet of clear glass. The wet green hills rolled fluffy white sheep right down to the water's edge. We saw dozens of deer farms, too. The South Island is fifty times more beautiful than the North Island. They named the mountains near Queenstown the Remarkables, which says it all. We went to a gorge near Queenstown to watch bungee-jumpers where the sport started. We didn't have time to try it, but it was hilarious to watch. The guys running it are a bunch of jokers, and they tried to yank off one guy's boxers as he went down. The river was so high that all of the jumpers got dunked.*

*I wonder, if I tried to bungee-jump there, would God snap the cord on me?*

*The other kids have asked for their paua box gifts every day, but I keep telling them to ask at a better time. I don't want to think about the paua box right now. It's nothing but a reminder of what I have to do.*

Dad came in just as Andrew finished, and confided that he really wanted to visit the fjords, but there was still the South Island's east coast, and the North Island, if they had time. "I guess we'll leave Fjordland for another time, when we come back to visit you on your land."

That was all he said, but the next morning, as they reached the turn to Fjordland, he paused, gazed longingly down the road, and sighed before hurrying on toward Invercargill.

Invercargill was the southernmost city of New Zealand: a flat, windswept community whose only reason for existence was to provide shopping for the cattle, sheep, and deer ranches. Beyond Invercargill lay Stewart Island, the last outpost of civilization — "the end of the earth," said a Kiwi at the petrol station. "Nothing beyond that except Antarctica."

"And maybe escape," thought Andrew. "No, I have to go back. I have to confess."

It was in an Invercargill restaurant that Andrew's green jade koru popped from under his shirt. "What's that?" Caleb asked, and four more pairs of eyes fastened on the smooth green swirl.

"This? It's the jade koru Grandfather left me," said Andrew. "It's the shape of a furled fern frond. The koru is supposed to represent a new beginning." He smiled bravely at Dad. "And hope for the future." Andrew finally decided, then, to open the little paua box for them, and hand out the gifts bequeathed by Grandfather.

From Invercargill to Dunedin, the small towns seemed as deserted as the highway, on which they counted twenty minutes without seeing a single vehicle moving in either direction.

Arriving in Dunedin, Dad paid for a family tour of the Albatross Center, then toured the whole peninsula, seeing fur seals, yellow-eyed penguins, and the little blue penguins that had become Andrew's favorite. They picnicked on a grassy knoll overlooking the Pacific Ocean, and drove into the city for dessert.

At 2:30 P.M., Dad gave them one hour to shop for souvenirs before leaving for Christchurch, and the four redheads hurried off together.

Cathryn bought a colorful upside-down map in the first shop they entered. She giggled as she observed, "Now America is down-under and New Zealand is up-over!"

In the next shop, a marvelously soft little sheep made of white lamb's wool coaxed Alicia to take it home, but Andrew had told her about the beautiful paua jewelry, and she wasn't sure what to do. Andrew watched her for a minute, then opened his wallet. "Buy the lamb for my favorite fourteen-year-old sis," he said. "You can save your money for a paua necklace." The gesture should have salved his conscience, but it didn't.

At the Scottish shop, Caleb purchased a scale-model bagpipe, and asked the clerk to wrap it in McKean tartan paper.

They met Dad and Mom at three thirty and, amidst much showing and telling, were off for the city of Christchurch. As it turned out, though, they never got there that day, but that was because of Oamaru's Blue Penguin Colony.

Dad had miscalculated the distance, and their motel reservations at Christchurch had expired by the time they reached Oamaru, so they decided to stop at an Oamaru motel instead.

"Will you be going down to watch the little blue penguins parade?" asked the proprietor. He held open the door to a family unit.

"Where's that?" asked Dad.

"The Blue Penguin Colony. The penguins come up from the ocean after dark every evening. For about an hour, they come up the cliff and cross a wide sort of parade ground to their nests. There's a viewing stand that lets you watch without disturbing them. I'll take you down if you wish."

There was no question about it. They must see the penguins. They ate dinner, and followed their host to the Blue Penguin Colony. He had binoculars for all, and found good seats in front.

"Oh, there's one now," said Mom. "It's so little. Is it a chick?"

"That one's full-grown, so he's about twenty-five centimeters. Weighs about one kilogram. These are the world's smallest penguins."

Andrew whispered, "Ten inches, and about two pounds." At least he had learned something.

The penguins were delightful — eight to ten inches of furry blue-gray feathers waddling across the ground. Two penguins headed toward the viewing stand before turning to follow their playmates into burrows, and Andrew silently named them *toa* and *maia*. He counted fifty-two penguins in all, including the two that made the wrong turn.

Later that night, Andrew himself made a wrong turn on his way to sleep. Two hands stretched toward him from the road — right and left. On the right hand, little blue penguins, so free of worry, swam and dived in the waves. On the left hand, a haggard teen sat huddled over a cold steel table, gorging on worry.

Andrew got up and went to the lounge, turned on the TV set, and sank into a chair. BBC was broadcasting news, as was CNN. Other than that, there was nothing. He snapped it off.

Why had Dad said nothing more about Coach — or the trial? Andrew had been so caught up in his confession that he hadn't asked, but by now, Ed and Bob had been sentenced. To what? Wonder if there's a can of bubbly in the refrigerator. Might as well have caffeine. Sleep's out of the question anyhow. He opened a can of soda, and rummaged for a leftover sandwich.

"Is there enough for two?"

"Dad! Give a guy some warning!" he hissed.

Dad reached for the last soda. "I made as much noise as you did."

Andrew closed the refrigerator and threw Dad an exasperated look. "I couldn't sleep."

"Me either. Anything left from the picnic?"

"One sandwich. Here."

"Just half. You eat the other half." Dad snapped on a light and divided the sandwich. "Might as well sit down," he invited.

Andrew straddled one of the small chairs.

They lapsed back into silence. Dad studied his soda can as he chewed, but he said nothing until the sandwich was gone.

"Um. Almost as good as its predecessor." Dad took a long gulp of soda. "You know, I've been doing a lot of thinking since we left the glaciers."

Tough love coming up.

"I've been thinking that it's a shame to be so near the Fjordlands and put off going there. I know I said we could go later, but I may never get back. I'm going to take off a third week."

"You mean go to the Fjordlands now?"

"Absolutely! I should be spontaneous once in my lifetime. The others won't mind. Will you?" Dad reached for a brochure. "Look. Milford Track. We can go on a guided one-day tramp and see Fjordland on the trail, spend a day fly-fishing, and one more day cruising Milford Sound. Listen:

*Stunning deep blue lakes, opulent ancient forests, hauntingly silent fiords, towering mountain peaks, sheer granite canyons, and imposing waterfalls. Breathtakingly photogenic on a sunny day; magical when it rains, and copious cascades of water adorn every mountainside. That's the Milford Track and Milford Sound.*

He handed the brochure to Andrew. "We can drive back through the Southern Alps to Queenstown and take the guided tramp. Then, Mom and the kids can explore Queenstown while you and I go fishing. The third day, we all cruise the Milford Sound. What do you think?"

Andrew skimmed the colorful pamphlet. "Uh, Dad. Did you look at these prices?"

"It's a bit pricey, but the exchange rate cuts it by more than half."

Andrew looked at Dad's face. Dad looked excited. Dad, the accountant, really wanted to hike the wilds of a foreign land. "Let's do it, Dad."

* * * * *

They were on the road before six the next morning, driving back toward Dunedin.

Mom was sleepy for the first hour, but when she began to see straight, she asked, "William, aren't you going back the way we came? You are, William. We won't see much of New Zealand if you get us lost." Her eyes flashed.

Dad smiled quietly. “You often say I should be spontaneous,” he answered. “I called the office and extended our vacation another week, so we have time to see some of the fjords and still do the North Island. We will skip Christchurch, but I think the fjords will more than make up for that.”

A cheer went up from the back seat. “Are we going to the unexplored wilderness?”

“We’re going to hike the Milford Track,” said Dad. To Mom, he added, “I need more private time with Andrew. He’s pretty confused right now.”

The ensuing chatter about fjords and the trek consumed the miles until they stopped for the night. The next day, the chatter carried them to the gateway of Fjordlands National Park.

Dad hurried to sign up for the hike.

“The tall mate there goes as an adult, so that will be three adults and three children,” the reservations clerk said jovially. “Your total will be $591.00 New Zealand.”

Dad did a quick mental conversion, and produced travelers’ checks. “$273.51, right?”

“Good as gold, mate. Good as gold!” You should check in tomorrow at 8:55 A.M. Your walk departs at 9:15 A.M., cruising to the head of Lake Te Anau, where the Milford Track begins.”

“This walk is easy enough for all of us, isn’t it?” asked Mom. “I’m not really in shape.”

The clerk beamed at her. "Just follow the guide, and Bob's your uncle!"

Mom turned questioning eyes on Andrew, but he shrugged. He didn't know what it meant.

"*Bob's your uncle*," the man repeated. "Means *that's all there is to it*. It's an easy walk — about six leisurely hours — less than seven miles. The whole trip takes only nine hours, including the cruise, walk, and lunch."

"What should we bring?" Mom asked

"Bring your own lunch, drinks, and snacks. You'll also want comfortable walking shoes or boots, a cozy woolen jersey, sun protection, and insect repellent. The sand flies can be nasty."

"But we have no backpacks," Cathryn said.

"She'll be right, mate." The man smiled at her. "We provide each of you with a daypack, a waterproof jacket, and hot drinks on the launch."

Satisfied at last, the McKeans thanked him and went to dinner, then decided on an early bed-time to give energy for the six-hour walk.

Unfortunately for Andrew, sleep refused to come when invited. Far into the night, the teen lay in the darkness, listening to the rantings and naggings of Fear and wishing there were an easier way to gain Courage. If only — if only there was a way out without confession and punishment.

* * * * *

The hike exceeded any promises, read or heard. The balmy morning invited them outdoors to relax on the viewing deck as the launch cruised the lake. The skipper's commentary fascinated them, as did the stunning scenery. Birds called from secluded choir lofts along the shore. Ducks entertained on the glassy water.

At the lake's head, the little party, limited to twelve hikers, shouldered their daypacks, and the hike began. The gently rising path was as easy as advertised, and led to an idyllic spot beside a crystal stream. Here, the guide stopped for lunch.

The view expanded beyond what eyes could hold, lush green forest bathing at the lake's edge before running up across steep mountains.

After lunch, their trail descended through perfect Fjordland rainforest to the emerald green of the Clinton River. The leisurely stroll along the river was peaceful, allowing plenty of time for photographs — and for solemn thoughts — for introspection in the rare solitude.

"Everyone go at your own pace," instructed their guide. "We'll stop now and then to be sure you are doing all right."

"I can imagine fairies dancing among these ferns in the moonlight." Alicia ran light fingers over the green fronds. "It's a magical forest."

Andrew paused on a small rise beside the clear river, and whispered, "Look Dad, there are five trout lying right beside that boulder."

"Tomorrow," whispered Dad. He had not yet told Mom that there would be more days here.

They reached the hut mid-afternoon, and the guide served tea, which the McKeans politely declined, opting for soda from their daypacks. Dad and Mom chatted socially with the guide and the six Kiwi hikers who completed their group, but the four siblings chose to explore outside.

When the guide called to shoulder packs and start the return trek, Dad nudged Andrew and motioned toward the back of the line. "Let's talk," he said. "Mom will keep Caleb and the girls up ahead with her."

This was it — time for Dad to lay down the law — to give Andrew orders — to report what Andrew's sentence would be when he went back.

The teen fell in step with his dad, shrugging his daypack higher on his shoulders. Tall summer grass whispered against their legs and arms. The distant craggy peaks stretched to push their snowcaps into white cumulus clouds. All was right in the world of the fjords — all except him.

Dad began gently. "Did Caleb or the girls tell you about the trial?"

"No." Andrew chewed his bottom lip.

"Ed and Bob stood their ground, and your name never crossed their lips. The case closed with a declaration from the boys that they had used a copy store's printer, and had operated alone."

Case closed? Operated alone? Then — then Andrew was home free! No confession needed. He could stay in New Zealand. Nobody would ever know — only Dad — and Morgan. No FBI check. No reason to leave New Zealand!

The path narrowed, and Dad took the lead. "Coach Ando was vindicated. He was cleared of all suspicion of molestation," Dad continued, "since the guys confessed to fabricating the tale. The school refused to take him back, though. Too many parents still believed he might be guilty, that there might be more than a prank behind the boys' story. Mr. Ando's reputation is tarnished beyond repair, I'm afraid. He may be forced to change careers." Dad's voice floated back across the tall green grass, tainting the pure mountain air.

A sudden stab of anxiety hit Andrew in his stomach. Penny's father might have to change his career because of a prank? That wasn't fair.

Mr. McKean turned and faced Andrew. "The coach was fortunate, son. He could have been sentenced to years behind bars. They sentenced your buddies to five months of community service for making false allegations."

"What does that involve?" He found his voice, but it sounded dusty.

"Four hours a week — wearing orange vests — picking up trash in city parks, painting over graffiti, weeding city gardens, mowing park lawns, and washing the coach's cars." Dad discarded his leisurely gait and moved to rejoin the group.

Andrew hung back. Bob and Ed would be the laughing stock of the school. They deserved a note of appreciation for not implicating him — a gift even — yeah — something from New Zealand. Maybe they should have a jade koru so they could make a new beginning. They deserved that.

But what did he deserve?

No, he couldn't go back and confess. He would make a new beginning, though — in New Zealand — on his own land. It was meant to be. It explained the trip to New Zealand, away from the trial. God meant to give him a second chance. That was it.

Suddenly, he understood. That was it!

*Be strong and courageous, do not be afraid or tremble at them, for the Lord your God is the one who goes with you. He will not fail you or forsake you.*

God had gone with him to New Zealand, had taken him away from the trouble, so he no longer had to be afraid or tremble. Now God would not fail him or forsake him as he settled on his new land — as he started a new life.

He inhaled a deep breath of the Fjordland's pristine air. His had been a passport to freedom after all. Fear had lost. He was free!

He jumped to his feet and raced up the grassy trail on unfettered joy.

# 22

## Kia Toa - Be Courageous

*Penny,*

*I guess this is good-bye. Or, as the Kiwis say, cheerio. It looks as though you never will read these letters. I haven't heard a word from you since I left, so it really doesn't matter — if you ever get to New Zealand, look me up. I'll be living near Masterton.*

Andrew closed a chapter of his life and turned off the light. He sat alone. The family had gone on an evening walk, but he had begged off. Their vacation was almost ended — would end tomorrow at Masterton — and they would return to Wilmington without him — would catch a late flight from Wellington to Auckland, and fly out early the next morning. They would drive down to Wellington right after Mr. Raumati's *hangi.*

*Hangi* — food cooked underground. If it was as good as that at the hakari, he would cook that way most of the time from now on. What would they cook tomorrow — mutton? That ought to be easy to get. Never had so many sheep grazed in so many settings — from Invercargill to Cape Reinga — everywhere.

Well, maybe not everywhere. Not Cape Reinga. Nothing could live there but that crimson blossoming thing called a New Zealand Christmas tree.

Even dead spirits chose Cape Reinga as their point of departure for the underworld — according to Maori beliefs. It was beautiful there — northern tip of the country, windswept point of land wearing nothing but a few shrubs and a lighthouse — sheep probably would not live there.

Andrew stretched, flinging one leg across the chair arm. That last talk with Dad seemed so distant. They had seen so much since then.

He closed his eyes and remembered. They had skimmed the South Island, and flown back to Wellington from Christchurch; had rented a black van in Wellington, and circled the North Island.

Satisfaction wafted from the memories. New Zealand was a good land — a land that was at once child and adult — adventure and responsibility — fear and courage — a land that urged one to play while requiring one to work. It was his land now. In time, he would explore it all.

But when? He opened his eyes.

"What," he asked the barely visible ceiling, "are my choices? I see only two. I can be a martyr and go to Wilmington to stand trial; or I can be sensible and stay here on my land."

The ceiling withheld counsel.

"Really," he argued, "it makes more sense to stay here. Everybody's always saying I should be courageous — even Morgan. Well, does it take more courage to go back and live with my mommy, or to cut the apron strings and become a man? I say it takes far more courage to strike out on your own, but how do I convince Dad?"

The door burst open, and he jumped. "Why are you sitting in the dark?" Cathryn snapped the light switch. "You should have gone with us. We had Hokey Pokey ice cream."

Andrew stood up, stretched, and yawned. "That's good. I'm tired. I guess I'll hit the hay."

"We all will," said Dad. "We need an early start tomorrow so we can enjoy our last day." They divided into the suite's three rooms, and chatter gradually gave way to silence.

* * * * *

The trip back to Masterton was uneventful. Their eyes, satiated, left the scenery more often; their lips hastened toward home more often.

The conversation ebbed and flowed as the miles rippled out behind them, but Andrew ignored it for the most part.

He had reached a decision during the night, that period of darkness when others slept but he did not. He had examined and reexamined his two options, and had decided. His mind was set, and he knew he had chosen the path of courage, but he didn't know how to tell Mom and Dad.

Look at Dad, savoring every mile, every moment of this last day. Mom, too. She radiated peacefulness. How could he tell them? How could he deal such a blow to his innocent family?

Andrew reached into his pocket for his handkerchief, and the paua box came out with it. It now contained only the paper on which Grandfather had written the Maori Bible verse.

Andrew had memorized it in English, but it might be interesting to memorize it in Maori. It would take his mind off the decision he had made.

*Kia maia* — be strong
*Kia toa* — be courageous

By the time Dad drove through Palmerston North, *kia maia* and *kia toa* had become easy to say — *Kee'-uh mah'-ee-uh. Kee'-uh toe'-uh.* Only seventy-one miles to go.

*Toa* was much shorter than *courageous.* Wonder how the Maori would say *manly courage.*

He had learned from a skit in Maori class that *tane* meant male. Maybe it was *tane toa.*

Andrew — *tane toa* — manly courage.

It was mid-afternoon when they reached Masterton, and drove up to the home of Mr. and Mrs. Raumati.

Andrew craned his neck as Dad parked the van, his eyes running across the land to a distant eucalyptus tree — the corner of his own property.

So many questions remained, as Morgan had said: immigration laws to consider; how to secure a green card; Rotary rules that demanded his return to the U.S.; getting a new student visa. The Bartletts were out of the picture now, but he still wanted Dennis and Janette's approval — and Katherine and Anna's. Would Dad advance him some money? Could he find after-school work?

"Are you getting out, Andrew?"

"Huh? Oh. Sure, Dad." He walked through the cloud of thoughts, took his backpack from the van, and accompanied the family to the house.

Mrs. Raumati greeted them warmly, and hurried to serve tea. Mr. Raumati would be home from work before long, she said. They should feel free to rest or walk around. She had preparation yet for the hangi, but her daughters were coming to help, so there was nothing Mom could do.

"Perhaps Andrew will show us the land he inherited from his grandfather," suggested Dad.

That was his cue — exactly what Dad was supposed to say. Andrew gave a nervous smile. "You had better change shoes, Mom. I haven't paved a path for high heels yet."

Promising to return before six o'clock, the McKeans followed Andrew's stumbling feet down the drive and across a meadow to his land. As they entered the cathedral of virgin timber, two bell birds announced their arrival with chorused chimes. They paused and drank in the beauty.

"This is majestic," said Dad. "It tempts me to leave Delaware and homestead with you." He smiled briefly. "Of course, it isn't mine. I have no right to homestead here."

Mom spotted a clump of white heather, and the others fell behind to look at it as Andrew led Dad along the path, pointing out paddocks where his sheep would graze, and sunlit clearings where he would plant a garden. This knoll would be a great place to build his house, using the pines that reached tall to the sky. The river sparkled at the foot of the knoll, so water and fish would be close at hand. The highway lay in that direction, but several acres away. This spot would be peaceful.

Andrew accelerated his chatter when they reached the eucalyptus log. "This is where we sat when Mr. Raumati gave me the deed. Sit down,

Dad. I'll show you." He straddled the log, and spread the creased paper across his knee. "The Raumatis are my neighbors on this side; the road is out here; the stream runs all the way through it from here to here; and I've decided to not go back to the United States with you now, but stay on my land and develop it." He finished defiantly.

The ensuing hush deafened him.

Dad took the deed, and studied it intently, turning it to get his bearings. One hand crept toward the upper lip and began moving among the short red hairs of the pencil moustache. Each hair received deliberate, detailed attention. "Have you considered the ramifications, son? Do you know whether New Zealand will let you stay, and whether Mr. Raumati will help you?"

"I'll work it out, Dad. As the Kiwis say, 'She'll be right, mate.'"

"And are you willing to be a coward, to live your life with the knowledge that you committed a crime and never took the consequences? Are you willing to give up so easily on developing courage and character? Or will you go back — go back and accept your sentence with courage — go back and do your community service with character?"

Dad stood with dignity and deliberation. He folded the deed with precision, and handed it to Andrew. "A privilege of adulthood is the right to make your own decisions," he said. "You are not an adult, Andrew." Dad coughed. "You are not yet an adult, but I am going to grant you that one privilege of adulthood."

"You mean I may stay?"

"I mean that you may make the decision. I hope you will consider fully the responsibility that accompanies it, whichever path you choose, but that will be up to you. The family and I will be leaving for Wellington right after the hangi, so you have a few hours to decide. Stay here and think about it, son. I will take the family back to the house."

Andrew's mouth refused to close. His eyes had the decency to lower, but they leapt up again as his deepest voice said, "Thanks, Dad."

Dad nodded as he clapped his eldest on the shoulder. He cleared his throat, and walked firmly out of the forest.

Permission to stay!

Andrew waited until Dad was out of sight. Then, running deep into his forest, he leapt to a tree stump and warbled the four notes of the bell bird. "I'm staying," he whispered to the ferns at his feet. "I'm staying," he said more loudly to the gnarled New Zealand Christmas trees with their crimson beauty. Then, flinging his arms into the air above his head, he shouted, "I'm staying!"

He threw himself to the ground, noticing another clump of white heather, and closed his eyes. Someday Dad would see that it actually took courage for him to stay here — manly courage. It would take courage to build his house, but he would build it, and he would be the master of it. No one would tell him what to do. No one would infringe on his rights. It would be his castle.

Two ghosts floated into his castle. Thomas McKean came first, murmuring, "Courage? I had courage, Andrew. I feared the British, but I acted on what was right, and accepted the consequences of my actions. Are you truly my descendent?"

The second said, "Listen to Grandfather, Andrew. I was courageous, too. I risked my life to witness to truth. A soldier's courage is proven only where the battle rages — to fight anywhere else is flight, not courage. Andrew, did I give you a passport to fear — or a passport to courage?"

Andrew opened his eyes and stared into the blue evening sky. Courage was a very dangerous trait to have, he decided, and difficult to capture.

He stood up and hurried back to the house, arriving breathless just as the hangi pit was opened, and slipped into his seat.

The meat was pork, not mutton — and cooking underground was definitely worth learning. He ate as though preparing for famine.

When Dad looked at him once, and asked the big question with both eyes, Andrew shifted and re-shifted his feet, but he gave Dad his most mature look, and nodded his affirmative.

Dinner over, the family prepared to leave, and Dad took Andrew aside. He pressed a check into his hand, and said, "Use this to get started, and write to us often, son."

Andrew thanked him, and pocketed the check. He watched Alicia, Caleb, and Cathryn get into the van, opening windows to call good-byes. They thought Andrew would be returning to the Bartlett home, and to school, now that vacation had ended.

Mom hugged and kissed him, and slid into the front beside Dad. He said nothing to her. She didn't seem to know either.

"Everyone ready?" called Dad.

Andrew began to wave, but stopped. "Just a minute, Dad," he said. "I forgot something." He dashed inside and stumbled up the stairs. Three minutes later, he stumbled back down. He slid open the back of the van, stowed two big suitcases and a backpack, and crawled over the seat to settle, breathless, beside Alicia.

"Ready, Dad," said Andrew.

* * *

# New Zealand

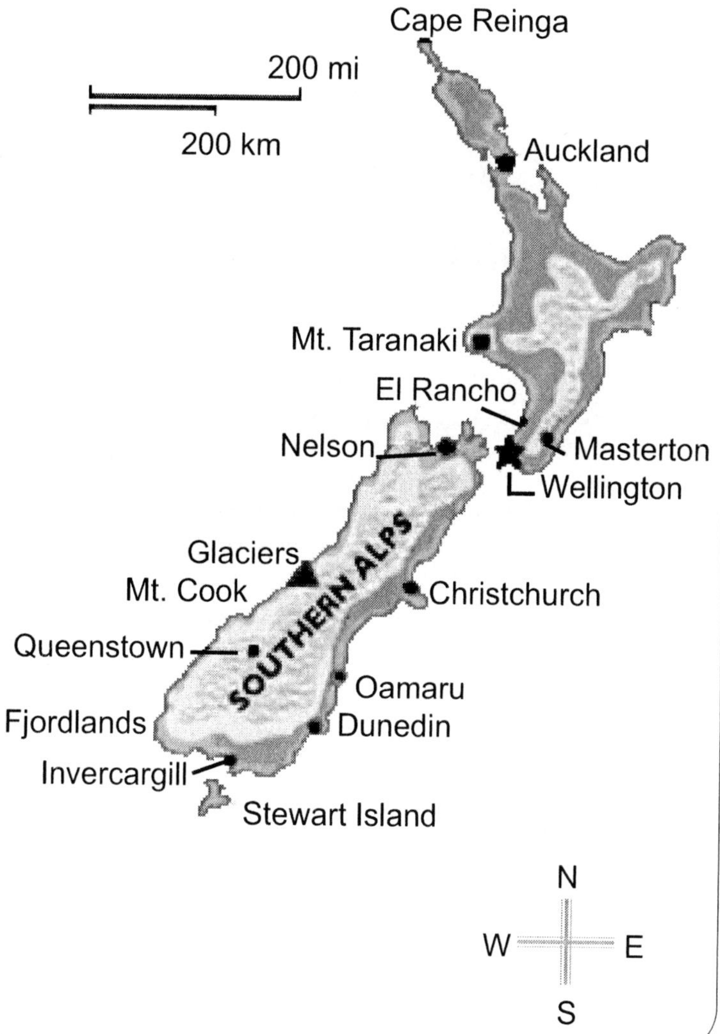

Cape Reinga
200 mi
200 km
Auckland
Mt. Taranaki
El Rancho
Nelson
Masterton
Wellington
Glaciers
Mt. Cook
SOUTHERN ALPS
Christchurch
Queenstown
Oamaru
Fjordlands
Dunedin
Invercargill
Stewart Island
N
W
E
S

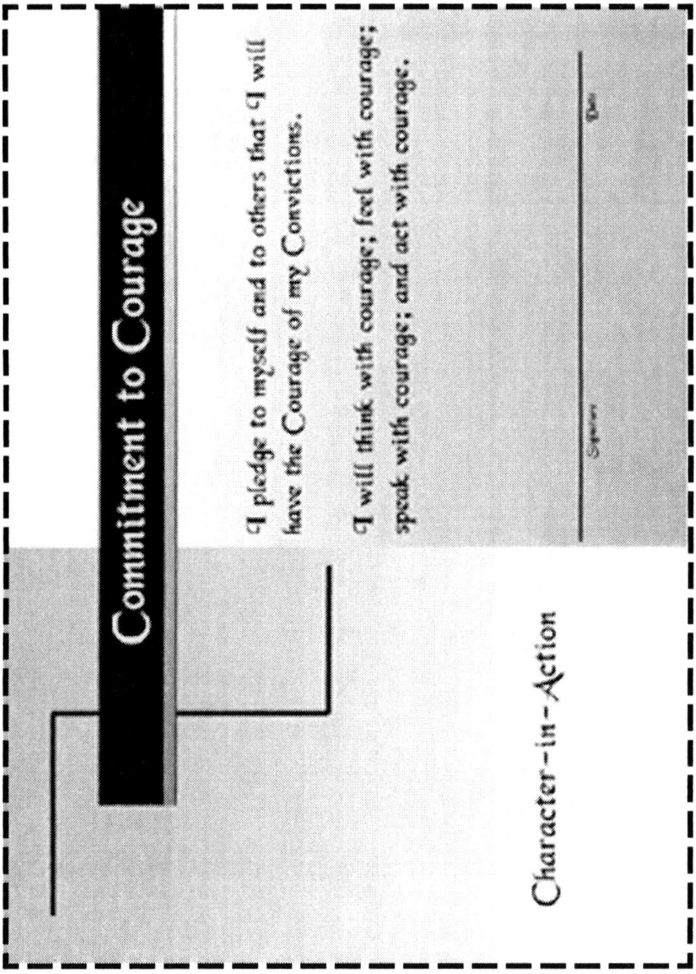
Commitment to Courage
I pledge to myself and to others that I will have the Courage of my Convictions.
I will think with courage; feel with courage; speak with courage; and act with courage.
Character-in-Action

Would you have done as Andrew did? Do you have the courage of your convictions? Put your courage into action. Sign the Commitment to Courage pledge above, cut it out, paste it on a card, and begin acting on your convictions.